When the scent of Jas⸻ stopped dead.

I should go now, I thought, ⸻ the bed anyway.

No sound accompanied my scream.

In a blink I took in the sight: Jasmine, lying on the hardwood floor like a white Madonna, hair perfect, skirt modestly pulled down, legs bent to the side, ankles crossed as if to display her strappy spikes to best advantage, pearls scattered around her.

She might have fallen into a graceful faint, except for one thing.

Had I thought earlier that she needed only a veil?

She had one now . . . tied tight around her throat.

PRAISE FOR

The Scot, The Witch and The Wardrobe

"Sassy dialogue, rich sexual tension, and plenty of laughs make this an immensely satisfying return to Blair's world of witchcraft." —*Publishers Weekly*

PRAISE FOR

The Kitchen Witch

"Blair has crafted a fun and sexy romp." —*Booklist*

"Magic. *The Kitchen Witch* sizzles. Ms. Blair's writing is smooth as a fine Kentucky bourbon. Sexy, fun, top-notch entertainment." —*Romance Reader*

A Veiled
DECEPTION

ANNETTE BLAIR

BERKLEY PRIME CRIME, NEW YORK

THE BERKLEY PUBLISHING GROUP
Published by the Penguin Group
Penguin Group (USA) Inc.
375 Hudson Street, New York, New York 10014, USA
Penguin Group (Canada), 90 Eglinton Avenue East, Suite 700, Toronto, Ontario M4P 2Y3, Canada
(a division of Pearson Penguin Canada Inc.)
Penguin Books Ltd., 80 Strand, London WC2R 0RL, England
Penguin Group Ireland, 25 St. Stephen's Green, Dublin 2, Ireland (a division of Penguin Books Ltd.)
Penguin Group (Australia), 250 Camberwell Road, Camberwell, Victoria 3124, Australia
(a division of Pearson Australia Group Pty. Ltd.)
Penguin Books India Pvt. Ltd., 11 Community Centre, Panchsheel Park, New Delhi—110 017, India
Penguin Group (NZ), 67 Apollo Drive, Rosedale, North Shore 0632, New Zealand
(a division of Pearson New Zealand Ltd.)
Penguin Books (South Africa) (Pty.) Ltd., 24 Sturdee Avenue, Rosebank, Johannesburg 2196,
South Africa

Penguin Books Ltd., Registered Offices: 80 Strand, London WC2R 0RL, England

This is a work of fiction. Names, characters, places, and incidents either are the product of the author's imagination or are used fictitiously, and any resemblance to actual persons, living or dead, business establishments, events, or locales is entirely coincidental. The publisher does not have any control over and does not assume any responsibility for author or third-party websites or their content.

A VEILED DECEPTION

A Berkley Prime Crime Book / published by arrangement with the author

PRINTING HISTORY
Berkley Prime Crime mass-market edition / January 2009

Copyright © 2009 by Annette Blair.
Cover illustration by Kimberly Schamber.
Cover design by Rita Frangie.
Interior text design by Laura K. Corless.

ISBN: 978-0-425-22640-7

BERKLEY® PRIME CRIME
Berkely Prime Crime Books are published by The Berkley Publishing Group,
a division of Penguin Group (USA) Inc.,
375 Hudson Street, New York, New York 10014.
BERKLEY® PRIME CRIME and the PRIME CRIME logo are trademarks of Penguin Group
(USA) Inc.

PRINTED IN THE UNITED STATES OF AMERICA

10 9 8 7 6 5 4 3 2 1

With love to my girls:

Robbie-Lynn Blair:
Your vintage handbag collection now inspires
my muse, rather than my amusement.
Thank you for sharing.

Theresa Blair Mullens:
Here it is, a mystery especially for you.

Briana Mullens:
This one you can read, sweetie.

Tricia Blair and Kelsey Mullens:
I named a character for each of you.

Author's Note

Mystick Falls, its police department, the Phantom Coach Road, and the carriage house on Bank Street are figments of my imagination. I also took the liberty of eliminating River Road. I located Mystick Falls where Connecticut's Peace Nature Sanctuary sits across the Mystic River from Mystic Seaport. The river, the seaport and its ships, historic downtown Mystic, and Mystic Pizza—of movie fame—are real and well worth a visit.

One

My father would never have asked me to take a leave of absence from my job in New York City if he could have handled my sister's wedding and the "Jezebel" plotting to preempt it without me.

By default, I can fix anything. My name is Maddie, well, Madeira—not that my mother had to get drunk to conceive, she just had to learn to relax. I'm the polar opposite of my mother. I'm so relaxed that I act, then I think. Mom and I came from different planets—neither of which is inhabited by my father. Dad lives on the planet Academia, a world best appreciated by other English lit professors who still use words like "Jezebel" without cracking a smile.

I'm the oldest of four and I'm about to face the ultimate wake-up call. My youngest sister is getting married before me. Her name is Sherry. Don't get me wrong. I love the brat. She's the baby of the family who's enjoyed every privilege attached to the title, which is partly my fault. For all intents and purposes, I became her mother when she was two and I was ten, but who's counting?

Yes, Sherry and my father need me, but I have a problem of my own. Sherry's engagement has somehow embedded a prompt, like a pesky splinter, beneath the tender skin of my ticking body clock, hourly reminding me that I don't have a life. Not that I need a man, mind you, just a life. A little forward momentum wouldn't hurt, either.

Speaking of which, the big-ass orange pimpmobile I rented sat in bumper-to-bumper traffic, me steaming with it.

The rising tide of my frustration calmed when the masts of Mystic Seaport's *Charles W. Morgan*—the last American wooden whale ship—came into view, an icon calling me back to my roots.

I turned to my passenger. "I'll save you!" we said together.

Eve Meyers and I have been friends since we toured the *Charles Morgan* in kindergarten. That day, I accidentally dropped my beautiful new red-velvet purse into the water and dove in after it. Hey, it matched my jumper, and even at five, I was an impetuous fashionista.

On that tour, Eve had shouted, "I'll save you!" and followed me into the briny deep.

Twenty-three years later, she's still saving me . . . mostly from myself.

Inching the pimpmobile forward as summer tourists crossed Route 27 to tour Mystic Seaport, I turned off the AC, powered down the windows, and let a bold sea breeze scramble my hair. "I love feeling free and alive behind the wheel of a moving—well, crawling—vehicle."

New Yorkers don't own cars. Everything we need is a short walk away.

"I want a car," I said.

Eve's wild copper curls danced in the wind. "Big surprise.

You've been threatening to leave Bulimics 'R' Us for months." She understood my dissatisfaction with designing cutting-edge outfits for praying mantis models. She'd been sharing my Manhattan apartment since she started her grad work in computer science at Columbia—a comfortable cohabitation soon to reach its inevitable end.

I sighed. "I'm not cut out to be a fashion designer, pun intended."

"You're a great designer," Eve said, "but you suck at kissing up to the feral feline puppet master pulling your strings."

I did a double take. "I'm taking that as a compliment."

"You should, and while you're home planning your sister's wedding, you should think about what you want to be when you grow up, and whatever it is, consider putting yourself in the driver's seat for a change. You know what Fiona says: 'We make our own magic.' "

Eve's acuity called for another hundred-calorie cheesy fry from the box on the storage console between us. We each took one and raised them in a toast to her wisdom. In sync, we made the obscenely enthusiastic noises we'd created for great food or great sex—the former being the usual substitute for the latter.

"You're right. It's time," I admitted. "I knew that."

"Past time," Eve said. "Indecision is not your style. Your twenty-ninth is looming and I'm moving back here to teach at UConn thanks to your dad."

"My dad . . . the real problem."

"Your dad is a problem? Since when? Harry Cutler is a mature, mild-mannered professor who makes coeds drool. If he raised his voice, I'd faint from shock."

"Yeah, well, quiet disapproval is a heavy burden." I sighed. "He paid big bucks for my degree in fashion design, and he's proud of me. I don't want to disappoint him."

"Maddie Cutler, you could never disappoint your father.

3

He'd be the first to tell you that life is too short not to be happy." A lesson Dad learned the hard way. ·

After I crossed the historic Mystic drawbridge, I turned right, after Mystic Pizza, and drove into the weedy parking lot of the huge, weather-worn building at the opposite corner of West Main and Bank. Doors and windows now cross-boarded, the building once housed the county morgue and finished life as a carriage house for the long-defunct Underhill Funeral Chapel.

"I love this place," I said. "It has so much potential."

"So you've often said, but stop salivating. It's a shack, not a vintage Versace."

"I wonder what I could do with it."

Eve gave me one of her horrified "I'll save you" looks. "You can do nothing with it," she said. "It's not a family problem you can fix with logic and love, nor a vintage outfit that you can bring to life with your own brand of magic."

"You think I can work magic?"

Eve rolled her eyes. "On vintage clothes, yes. On shacks, no."

Nevertheless, I couldn't take my eyes off the place. Neither could I forget the recurring dream I'd had last night, because it always seemed to presage a significant change in my life. In it, I'm a toddler bouncing in my mother's arms and loving it. Mom and Aunt Fiona are laughing and dancing by the river at night and singing nonsensical songs about the moon.

A significant life change. "Eve . . . what would I do if I wasn't a fashion designer?"

"Leave New York?"

"In a New York minute, which is all your fault." I wagged a finger her way. "You spoiled me. I won't like the Big Apple without you. Who'll protect me from the worms?"

I started the pimpmobile and headed down West Main to the Phantom Coach Road and Mystick Falls, the close-knit community of my birth. The houses stood grander and farther apart than in Mystic's historic district. Here, mature Victorian Ladies dressed in bright paint with wrap-around porches, seasonally vibrant flower beds, and lush sprawling lawns.

"You're coming over to say 'hi' to my dad before you go home, right?" I asked as I passed Eve's parents' house.

"I *guess*," Eve said looking back.

Pulling into our long circular drive, I could barely find a place to park with so many cars out front. "Looks like Dad's got a houseful. I hope everything's okay."

"No worries," Eve said, searching for the black bag she used to accessorize her Hells Angels jacket and combat boots. She pulled her head out of the car and slung the clunky canvas backpack over a shoulder. "It's probably a get-together that your dad forgot to tell you about, *again*. There must be free food in the offing, too, because Nick's here." Eve winked. "Your Nick. Are you wearing your lucky panties?"

"Nick's not mine," I said, leaning over to grab my "Diamond in Bondage" eighties disco bag by Mugler. "Nick's a gift to womankind. If you don't believe me, ask him."

My on-again/off-again, Nick Jaconetti, and I have been toying with our charged relationship, like kids and fire, since junior high. Though we've both matured, our relationship has not, unless you count the way in which we now express ourselves, which can only be compared to rare flashes of spontaneous combustion.

A fixture at our house since the day I first brought him home, Nick is now my brother Alex's FBI partner and might as well be a member of the family.

A rush of anticipation shot through me, and my face warmed at the thought of seeing him after so long. Annoyed with myself, I slammed the car door on my own insanity.

The next move should have been his, the toad, yet he'd been silent as a pond stump for months.

I decided to keep it cool. Give Nick the cucumber. Focus on coming home, I told myself.

I looked up at our renovated old coach stop and tavern, a stoic 250-plus-year-old Connecticut Yankee—depending on which section of the tri-structure you stood in—that had spent the better part of its life on the old Boston Post Road. Contrary to so many claims, George Washington did, indeed, sleep here. So did Benjamin Franklin. At different times, and early in their separate careers as land surveyors.

Amazingly, this is where I grew up, across the river from Mystic Seaport, where the old *Yankee* had been deposited early in the last century. I loved to look across the river at the historic village within the seaport, its lighthouse and array of ships, including the *Charles Morgan* and a riverboat whose passengers never failed to wave.

The house welcomed me with a sunny windowpane wink—or a ghost walked by—hard to tell which. I'd been able to see our otherworldly inhabitants from the cradle, but the day my brother called me a liar for pointing one out, my mother took me aside.

She could see them, too, she said, but most people couldn't and wouldn't believe me if I mentioned them, so they'd have to be our little secret, a bond I cherish to this day.

No, we had never lived here alone, but we did live in peace . . . more or less.

Two

A fallen blossom returning to the bough, I thought—but
no, a butterfly.
                                    —ARAKIDA MORITAKE

"Come into my bosom," the house all but whispered. But
when I opened the front door, it seemed to groan and shiver,
vibrating the air with a sinister hum. "Run for your life," it
rasped.

I took the warning to heart, but stood my ground.
"Merriment or mayhem?" I asked Eve as we stood in the
doorway. "Are they having a party or trying to kill each
other?"

Eve scanned the combat zone, originally known as the
keeping room. "The aromas of baked ham and roast turkey
should give you a clue," she said, fearlessly entering the
fray and heading for her parents.

My brother, Alex, and Ted Macri, one of his high school
buddies, were facing off, deep into a hockey debate, while
my sister Sherry and her fiancé, Justin, stared silent daggers at each other. A lover's quarrel, in public no less.

Oblivious, my father chatted with his cronies in the quiet
corner near the buttery, wearing his academic blinders.

My chest tight, I couldn't seem to pry my hand from the ancient latch. Family is a powerful form of birth control. In counterpoint to my speeding heart, my body clock seemed to stop dead.

The chaos before me indicated that the world might survive, probably even thrive, if I failed to stuff another Cutler Clown into the Volkswagen of life.

Sherry swooped in for a hug, as if her sutured Frankenbunny had gone missing and only I could find him. My very real baby doll, Sherry seemed to have left fun-loving and whimsical behind for today, trading it for plucky and stoic. I might blame the figure-hugging cornflower halter gown I'd designed for her birthday, and call her classy and sophisticated, if not for the icy hand beneath my own. With the temp in the room at a hundred people-watts and climbing, this did not compute.

I stepped back to read her. "Hey, Cherry Pie, you okay?"

"Mad, I'm so glad you're home."

"Need a rescue, sweetie?"

Sherry stepped closer. "*She's* ruining everything."

"Who is?" I asked, finding the preemptive Jezebel guilty without a sighting.

"Jasmine Updike, Justin's old college study partner, or so *he* says. She acts like she's his hot ex, hanging all over him and playing 'remember when, pookie pie?'" Sherry used the international hand signal for "barf," particularly effective with a rhinestone-studded French manicure.

I turned her toward the wall so no one else could read her agitation, smoothed the back T-strap that buttoned at her nape, and then I went around to face her, finger-combing the blonde waves away from her temples.

"Dynamite," I said, returning her self-confidence while keeping an eye on the players behind her. "What's Justin's ex . . . anything . . . doing here?"

"The million-dollar question." Sherry's sapphire eyes

narrowed and darkened. "She showed up a few weeks ago, not long after Justin and I got officially engaged, and Deborah welcomed her with open arms."

Deborah—never Debbie—the wannabe society queen of the country-club set, happened to be Sherry's future mother-in-law. "And that's bad?" I asked, "because . . ."

"Deborah acts like Jasmine's her long-lost daughter," Sherry whispered furiously, "and I'm dog poop beneath her Vivier's."

"Ah yes." Deborah had made it clear when Justin and Sherry dated in high school that she'd like her son to marry a woman with a pedigree rather than a PhD.

Lucky for Sherry, Justin had a mind of his own.

How his easygoing father, Vancortland Four—or Cort, as he'd been dubbed early in life so as not to be confused with his father, Vancortland Three—could have chosen the social-climbing Deborah to marry stumped more than this Mystick Falls native.

Just then, a woman dressed like a maid, except for her earrings, approached us with a tray of mini wedding cakes. With a napkin, she handed one to each of us. The white dots on white reminded me of dotted Swiss, and patterns of brocade and lace.

"Dad hired a maid?" I asked after the woman left. "Is he running a fever?"

I bit into the most delicious cake I'd ever tasted. Hazelnut heaven. "This is unbelievably scrumptious."

The maid served Justin's father a cake, the two of them examining each other inquisitively, circling almost, but at a distance as if they'd caught some kind of shared radar. Did the unpretentious Cort have a wandering eye? I hadn't thought it possible.

Sherry watched them as well, but with less suspicion. "The server's name is Amber, and she's not a maid; she owns a shop called the Cake Lady," my sister explained.

"She offered us complimentary cakes in every flavor for the dinner party."

"*Dad* and *dinner party* do not belong in the same sentence," I said, "which is why he asked me to come home and help plan your wedding in the first place."

Sherry shrugged. "The cake lady herself suggested this informal engagement party as a venue for us to try her cakes, and Jasmine or Deborah—not sure which, since they're connected at the hip—ran with the suggestion."

"Why didn't you speak up?"

"I wasn't there."

"How dare they accept without you."

"Why wouldn't they? They went cake shopping without me."

"Okay, so now I'm on board with my own case of battitude. Why did Dad buy into it and host the pretentious party?"

"I think he wanted to prove that we can use utensils . . . and not with our toes." Sherry gave me another bruising hug. "I'm so glad you're home. Just talking to you makes me feel sane. It *was* pretentious of them, wasn't it?"

"And plain old ballsy. Hey, I like that smile."

Sherry let it blossom into a giggle.

"Let the wedding plans begin," I said, my heart lighter. "The real plans. *Yours.*"

"Mine," Sherry said with a sigh, her expression softening to reveal her quirky exuberance. "That reminds me. I bought a great vintage veil that I'm dying for you to see. I just *know* you can fix it."

Naturally effervescent, it had still taken Sherry way more than the usual beat to bounce from distress to animation.

I fluffed her wavy blonde hair. "Which one's the Jezebel?"

"Jasmine? She's the gorgeous blonde vamp clutching

Justin's sleeve and hanging on Deborah's every word, of course."

I tilted my head and squinted to fuzz up the picture. "Nope, can't shake it. She still reminds me of you."

Sherry gasped. "Bite your tongue!"

"Not in personality. I mean her skin tone, hair color, height. They met in college, right? After you and Justin broke up? Hah. Be flattered. He wanted you and settled for a pale imitation. Look, Jezebel's got him in her talons, and Justin looks like he wants out. "Why don't you go and rescue him?"

"He doesn't deserve it, Maddie. He thinks this whole power play between me and Jasmine is amusing. Look at Deborah discussing cakes with her as if it's *her* wedding, not mine, like Jasmine's the second coming or something." Sherry's voice rose with her ire and not even my hand on her arm or my quiet "shh" reached her. "Well, she'd better not be coming . . . or I'll kill the bitch!"

That final clichéd declaration fell loudly into one of those unexpected wells of silence.

The cake lady raised her brows. Other looks were not as kind.

"Madeira! You're home!" My father rushed over and gave me a bone-crushing hug. "Thank God," he whispered, his effusive welcome having the desired effect of shattering the awkward moment.

Everyone started talking at once.

Jasmine nibbled a chintz-style wedding cake and coyly whispered something in Justin's ear.

He smiled, and she checked, from the corner of an eye, to make sure she had his full attention. For his benefit, she swung her hips as she left him to sashay our way, her grin as bogus as her "Klein."

Her flirty dress in white knee-length cotton voile was so evocative of a wedding dress, it came off as a bad joke.

Seriously, only the veil was missing.

And Jasmine's perfume? Let's just say my expertise was coming into play, and I smelled a skunk. The faux fashionista couldn't know that I was head assistant to Faline, the world-famous designer, or she'd shrink in embarrassment and slither away. "So you're the Jezeb—ouch!"

I stepped away from my father and rubbed the back of my arm.

He'd pinched me!

"Excuse me?" Jasmine asked, nose in the air, as if she smelled something bad . . . like her counterfeit Opium.

"Leg cramp," I said, bending my knee back and forth. "I've been driving all day."

Jasmine the Jezebel looked me up and down with unveiled surprise, failing to conceal a greedy dislike. "Nice outfit," she said, revealing the reason why.

"Nice earrings," I said. Costume jewelry, but a great design.

She preened. She knew couture when she saw it, though my circuitous route around a return compliment missed her pea brain by a mile. I faked a smile. "Smart, as well as pretty."

The fraud raised a condescending brow, ignored me, and hooked an arm through Sherry's, as if they were best buds. "Come along, darling. Mom's got a surprise for you, and I get to keep you distracted so as not to spoil it."

"Oh, I'm distracted, all right," Sherry said, rolling her eyes my way as Jasmine led her through our rabbit warren of a house, heading for the ladies' or gentlemen's parlors, dining room, taproom, or any of several stairways and outside doors at the back of the house.

I shivered, as if someone had walked on my grave, I thought, quoting my mother, and nearly called Sherry back. But my dad was steering—well, propelling—me away from the keeping room, through the parlors, and into the blessedly empty taproom, his personal den, a rough-hewn tribute to leather, tweed, and cherry-blend pipe tobacco.

I sat on the sofa and crossed my feet on the scarred cobbler's bench he called a coffee table. "Jasmine thinks of Deborah as Mom?" I asked. "And she assumes that Sherry does, too?" I chuckled. "Deborah as a mother figure strikes me as something like the Tin Man trying to nurse a kitten."

"You're being kind," my father said, lowering himself into his voting-age easy chair and loosening his tie with a tired sigh. "Sherry's just lucky Justin grew up unscathed," he added. "What time is it?"

"Sherry will be lucky if she *gets* Justin. It's eight o'clock. Why?"

"I'm wondering how long till this is over."

"Dad, why didn't you tell me you were having a party?"

"You were driving in from the city. I didn't want you to get into an accident hurrying to make a party." He took my hand and squeezed. "Madeira, do you know how happy I am to have you home?"

"You're not cut out to be the mother of the bride, are you, Dad?"

"I've missed your mom every day for eighteen years, Madeira, but never more so than since Sherry got engaged."

I raised a brow. "Speaking of the engagement, what do you make of Jasmine?"

He steepled his hands, his thoughts reflective and darker than I'd seen in ages. "Premeditation and desperation are driving the girl," he said. "She's out to prove she's better than Sherry. Makes me think of a quote by Churchill: 'I am easily satisfied with the very best.'" My father sat forward. "Madeira, I'm hoping you can help me become the anti-quote."

I raised the back of his hand and kissed it. "You're a good dad . . . and a hell of an English prof."

"It'll be great having you around for the next few weeks, sweetheart."

"It'll be a busy month. When they finally set a date, they don't kid around."

Feminine sighs of appreciation caught my attention as the taproom shrunk in proportion to Nick Jaconetti's entrance. I wondered where he'd been, but I would never let him know I cared.

Tall, dark, wide-shouldered, and classically handsome, a roman sculpture come to life, Nick left three young neighbors drooling in the doorway as he shook my father's hand. "Let's join forces, Mr. Cutler, to keep Maddie around for a good long while."

I schooled my expression as Nick bent to kiss my cheek—I thought—but he caught my lips with a finely honed skill that had nothing to do with his FBI training. My frustration melted and the years fell away. Winter Ball post-party, eleventh grade, my bedroom. The world slept while we lost our virginity to each other. What Nick had lacked in expertise that first time, he'd made up for in gentleness, gratitude, and enthusiasm.

My father's mumbled retreat from the den brought me back to my surroundings with a jolt, and though it had only been a short kiss, Nick packed a wallop.

"Aren't you married or accounted for, yet?" I asked in self-defense.

His wide eyes and deep breathing matched mine, which I appreciated. Inwardly, I grinned and stretched like a satisfied cat, seeing exactly when his man brain stopped doing his thinking and his real brain caught up with my question.

"I wasn't accounted for when we hooked up in New York a few months ago," he answered, still somewhat dazed; yay me. He gave my hair a half stroke, his expression inscrutable.

I leaned against the cushions, kicked off my Versaces,

curled my legs beneath me, and crossed my arms to keep from pulling him down, because we were both much too willing. "Oh, that's right," I said. "You did come to New York . . . once. About seven, eight months ago? I figured either you'd been on a secret mission since . . . or the FBI didn't budget for cell phone batteries."

I damned myself for the slip. We never explained ourselves, Nick and I. That was the beauty of our nonrelationship. Spontaneous combustion was just that, and any attempt to control "spontaneous" was to destroy it.

With a wry, understanding grin, Nick sat beside me, invaded my space, shivered my insides, and put an arm around my shoulders to reel me in, with successful expertise. Scrap. He read me as well as I did him.

He knuckled my cheek, and I embraced the sweet warmth that radiated through me like sunshine after a rainstorm.

Lost, I fell into the depths of his dreamscape eyes. He moved closer and his warm breath at my ear washed over me in stroking waves. "Welcome home, Maddie girl," he whispered.

"I'm a woman, now."

"Don't I know it?"

The flirty feline inside me stretched again, this time in invitation, though I'd tried to keep the minx in check.

Nick probed my expression with his gaze—hot, knowing, and suggestive—until Eve came in and fell into my dad's chair with a huff of disgust. "Cut it out, you two. You're making me nauseous."

Almost grateful, I ignored Nick's sigh of regret while swallowing my own. "Saved by the lady in black."

"Damn straight." Eve gave Nick a satisfied smirk.

It wasn't that she didn't like him. She just didn't like the way he treated me, as if I'd always be there. I never could convince her that I liked playing with fire.

"That Jasmine is such a snob," Eve said. "She's oozing

sugar while pissin' everybody off, except for Deborah. Even your father looks like he's gonna blow. Tunney the butcher said that Jasmine's such a pain, the historic district shop owners are talking about a lynching. And, get this, Mrs. Sweet, the younger, said, 'Speaking for the neighborhood, they can have the sturdiest tree in Mystick Falls.' Mrs. Sweet, who feeds the mice she catches before she puts them out."

I shook my head. "She only puts them out because she keeps mouse motels out there."

Eve hooted. "Fiona's here, by the way. She called Jasmine a toad."

I sat forward. "And? Did Jasmine grow a wart, say 'ribbit,' anything?"

Eve and I laughed. The Halloween we were twelve, after midnight, we'd set out to scare my unflappable godmother.

Fiona's house stood down the road and across the street from ours, so it backed up to the woods, rather than the river.

Several side-window peeks into our search, all the rooms dim and eerie, and too many nighttime noises for our comfort, we heard an animal coming through the woods, several maybe.

An owl hooted and we jumped into each other's arms, the hair at my nape rising. Then someone, or something, emerged from the woods wearing a long black cloak, hood up.

It looked a lot like death.

We squeaked and huddled close beneath the window.

It was coming straight for us, except that he/she/it climbed Fiona's porch steps and went into her house.

Uh-oh.

A dim light suddenly spilled from the window above us and after a minute, we peeked in. Fiona, still cloaked and hooded, her face starkly etched in candlelight, looked right at us.

We screamed and ran.

Dear, sweet Aunt Fiona, who'd soothed my every hurt over the years, inside and out, a witch? A lot of the kids whispered it, but this was our first sighting, and it scared the bejeebers out of us.

Sure, Fiona saw ghosts, too, I'd learned years after making that pact with my mother, but that didn't make her a witch, or I'd be one. Neither did wearing a cape or a cloak. Cloaks were back in style. Posh Spice had worn one last winter. I wore one.

Anyway, Aunt Fiona recognized us because my father met us halfway home and read us our rights. We had none. He grounded us both. The next day, Eve's parents gave him their blessing.

"Remember that night?" Eve said.

"Shut up." Okay, so I'd wet myself, I was so scared, which Eve had used to torment and blackmail me until I had enough dirt to reciprocate. BFF/best friends forever, I thought, the two of us grinning.

Nick cleared his throat. "Eve, Mad and I were having a moment, here."

"You could've had hours, days, if you'd come to New York more often. Chill. Maddie's in demand. Why don't you go out and get her suitcases from the rental, boy toy, and bring them up to her room?"

Nick stood and grinned. "Thanks, Eve. I didn't think you were on my side."

Eve snorted. "I didn't say to camp out up there. Just drop off the suitcases and go home."

Nick squeezed my shoulder and rose reluctantly. "You're all heart, Meyers."

Eve smirked. "You're all testosterone, Jaconetti."

"You got that right." Nick gave me a bawdy wink as he left.

Eve joined me on the sofa. "He's a heartbreaker," she warned.

"But lower in calories and way tastier than cheesy fries." I licked my lips.

Eve twirled a finger in the air, an acerbic whoop-de-do, her favorite hand signal, right after the L for loser.

"As a matter of fact, I could get him to help me work off a few of those calories, if—"

Eve choked. "Do not finish that sentence!"

I wrote in the air, "Maddie one, Eve zero," and chuckled at her disgust. "I shouldn't be enjoying myself," I said. "It's time to rescue the bride."

Eve checked her watch. "Right, and I have a date with your brother's hockey buddy."

"Oh, is Ted a member of your stud-of-the-month club?"

"Dahling, when you've got it, you've got it. I like hockey players."

"He's the coach now."

She wiggled her brows. "He'll always be a player to me."

"Are you notching your bedpost, Meyers? Or are you looking for a man with feet bigger than yours?"

"Maddie wet her panties," Eve sang in payback, beneath her breath, as we returned to the keeping room.

She claimed Ted; they said their good-byes and left.

I hugged Fiona Sullivan, lawyer, possible witch, confidant, and aunt to the Cutler brood, by virtue of her friendship with our mother.

After that, I had fielded questions from our neighbors about my career and love life. Not my favorite sport, but everybody cared about everybody else in Mystick Falls, and to be fair, most of them had taken a hand in raising the four of us.

I hugged my brother, Alex, gushed over the pictures of his pride and joy, two-week-old Kelsey, a little blonde doll, at home with her mom, and made him promise to let me play auntie soon.

Eventually, I had no choice but to greet Deborah, the society-queen wannabe, who made me feel dowdy, despite my Faline halter dress and Versace platform mules. Somehow, Deborah *knew* that my outfit came with the job and I'd rather be wearing vintage.

Still conspicuously absent from the gathering, however, were Jasmine and the bride.

No good could come of that!

As I climbed the keeping room stairs, foreboding crept up my spine until I shivered. I was ten again, on my way up to visit my mother, who was recovering slowly from a car accident. The same sinking sensation had churned in my stomach then . . . right before I stood at Mom's open bedroom door to find my father crying with his head on her chest, Mom still and silent in the bed.

Even now, I avoided looking toward the master bedroom and headed straight for Sherry's room, but the lavender-scented chintz exhibit stood empty.

Three sets of stairs beckoned: front, back, keeping room. The smart thing to do would be to take one of them down.

I wish I could say that I always did the smart thing.

Closed, latched, oak-planked doors wearing their age-old patinas surrounded me, but only one door interested me, and I wasn't sure why. Brandy's.

Yes, Brandy, who detests her name more than she detests designer clothes. Brandy—middle sister but third child—works for the Peace Corps somewhere . . . anywhere in the world, except here. On the off chance the bride was hiding, which I might be inclined to do in her place, I should check Brandy's room.

My hand hovered over the matte black latch while I questioned my nebulous inclination to go inside.

Why Brandy's room? I turned away and turned back, then finally clutched the latch handle almost as if I expected it to burn.

I found it cool to the touch, smooth, and easy to open.

Too easy?

I had to push on the door and it wailed in protest. In this place, doors occasionally opened and shut on their own, which I attributed to our otherworldly inhabitants, but this, this *resistance* was odd.

Should I heed the warning and leave?

No sooner did I stop pushing than the door opened before me.

For the second time in five minutes, I succumbed to a shiver of alarm as I stood rooted. If not for the gorgeous antique wedding gown hanging from the mahogany wardrobe door, I might have backed out, never to return. But the gown pulled me in, infusing me with a surprising sense of reassurance, as if everything would be all right, which—

Of course, it would.

Brandy's curtains flapping out the window startled me and returned my dread in spades. Who in the family would leave a window open in August without pulling down the screen?

Though birds chirped in the getaway tree outside the window and gulls cried in the distance, the room's dense and heavy silence seemed so far beyond normal as to steal my breath.

A strong wind grasped the curtains and fluttered them in a quick whirr of sound. Get out, get out, get out, get out.

I hesitated, called myself an idiot, and approached the gown hanging near the foot of the bed on the opposite side of the room.

When the scent of Jasmine's fake Opium hit me, I stopped dead.

I should go now, I thought, and hesitated . . . but I rounded the bed anyway.

No sound accompanied my scream.

In a blink I took in the sight: Jasmine, lying on the hardwood floor like a white Madonna, hair perfect, skirt modestly pulled down, legs bent to the side, ankles crossed as if to display her strappy spikes to best advantage, pearls scattered around her.

She might have fallen into a graceful faint, except for one thing.

Had I thought earlier that she needed only a veil?

She had one now . . . tied tight around her throat.

Three

Black and white signs are like familiar antipathies of the past—day and night, angel and devil, good and evil . . .
—VICTOR VASARELY

I fell to my knees, ignoring the pearls digging into them, and struggled to unknot the veil with trembling hands. Up close, I could see the hint of blue smudging Jasmine's firm lips. "Wake up," I said. "Wake up."

I tried to breathe for her as I released the netting, wincing at the angry welts beneath it, and then I lifted her into my arms so she could breathe easier. "Jasmine?" I called, patting her cheek. "Jasmine!"

I don't know how long I held her and called her name but suddenly Nick rushed in. "Mad, you sound hysterical. I came because Fiona led me to the front stairs and whispered that you needed me, then I heard you calling—"

His gaze fell on Jasmine. He squared his shoulders, his FBI persona falling into place like a hard-edged mask devoid of emotion. He knelt beside me, taking in every detail of the scene. "What happened?"

"I found her like this, but the veil, Nick. It was so tight; I had to loosen it so she could breathe."

The pearl-tipped veil now hung like a scarf knotted loosely between Jasmine's breasts.

Nick frowned and checked her pulse while my heartbeat tripled at the implication, then he took her from my arms and lay her back on the floor. With his cell phone, he dialed 911 and asked for an ambulance then he hit speed dial. "Alex, come discreetly up to Brandy's room, alone. Don't rush, but don't let anybody slow you down."

No explanation necessary, I thought. Partners. They understood and trusted each other.

I looked closely for the rise and fall of Jasmine's chest, but the longer I did, the more my vision blurred, until I had to wipe my cheeks with my fingertips. Breathing for her wasn't working, either. I went limp when I stopped trying.

Efficient and official, Nick turned as if to shield me from the sight and handed me his handkerchief.

I tried to push him aside. "No, Nick, we have to help her."

He brought my head to his fast-beating heart, kissed my hair, and stroked my cheek with the back of a hand, offering shelter from the storm, a place to hide . . . literal and emotional warmth, a rare moment in which I didn't have to be "the strong one," except that I did. "Nick," I whispered, looking up at him. "I have to fix this."

"There are some things, Maddie girl, that even you can't fix."

We turned to the sound of Alex sprinting up the last few stairs. Nick took me up with him as he stood to give his partner room to assess the situation.

"You okay, Sis?" Alex asked.

"What do you think?" I snapped at my brother with an absurd urge to add, "You dumb puck," like the old days, but I held my tongue. Very rare. I must have been in shock.

Alex turned to Nick. "Did you call the coroner?" he asked, and I gasped, though a part of me had suspected the worst. Still, I'd known my mother was dead that morning, too, but I didn't cry until my father sat me down hours later and told me so.

Denial weaves such a sturdy suit of armor.

"I called the paramedics," Nick said. "Let *them* call the coroner, who will in turn call the police." Nick eyed me. "If necessary," he added, for my sake.

Alex nodded. "Better we shouldn't take over and tick off the local PD. As it is, whoever gets the case will beat his chest when he sees FBI on the scene before him."

I raised my chin and looked from my brother to my sometimes significant other. "They're gonna think Sherry did this, you know, because of what she said during the party."

Alex chucked me under the chin. "Mad, you're in mother-chick panic mode."

I appreciated his brotherly try at easing my worries.

He nodded. "Sherry will have an alibi like we all do."

Nick cleared his throat. "Except that one of us doesn't."

I shivered and went to shut the window.

"No!" Nick and Alex shouted loud enough to startle me.

I turned on my heel.

My brother made a cross with two of his fingers, as if to ward me off, a reminder of our teenage years when crossed tampons had that effect on him.

His suddenly ruddy complexion told me that he remembered his goofy reaction, as well.

Nick came for me, his hand at my back. "We can't disturb a crime scene, Mad."

That was the difference between a brother and a sometimes lover. One treated you like—well—a brat, and the other gently conveyed a message.

Alex nodded. "Bad enough you tampered with the murder weapon."

"He's right, ladybug. You might have to answer for that. I'm sorry." Nick frowned at my brother.

I huffed at them both. "I didn't tamper with anything!"

"You did," Alex said. "You untied the veil."

"Have mercy," I snapped. "I was trying to help the woman breathe!"

Alex rubbed the back of his neck. "I can't believe this. Our home, a crime scene."

Sounds of parting guests and their relieved host floated up the stairs, telling us that Dad, and everyone else, remained blissfully unaware of the horrific drama unfolding on the floor above.

"Alex, I'm worried about how Dad will take this. What will you tell him?"

"*I'm* not telling him. You tell him." With barely a move between them, Nick and my brother suddenly closed ranks—big, bad, macho FBI ranks.

Nick's expression softened. "Mad, you do deal with your father better than anyone. You really should be the one to tell him." He checked his watch. "Ambulance could be here any minute. Better do it now."

I planted my hands on my hips. "The two of you could take down a terrorist in a snake-infested swamp, but hurting an old man you love, *that* scares the bejeebers out of you."

They firmed their stances and puffed out their chests. Alex tugged on his cuffs. Nick jiggled the change in his pocket and rocked on his heels.

I sighed. "I'll do it!"

After I checked the second-floor rooms for Sherry, without luck, I made my way downstairs, in no rush to shatter Dad's bubble of relief at the party's end.

Aunt Fiona met me at the bottom and hugged me.

I held on for a minute. "How did you know?" I asked.

We stepped out a side door, and Aunt Fiona shut it behind us. "I felt a gut-wrenching wash of emotional pain," she said, "and knew it belonged to you." She cupped my cheek. "By the looks of you, I'm guessing I was right."

"You were. Thanks for sending Nick." I wasn't ready to talk about Jasmine, especially to my father. I saw a reprieve as I noticed the full moon coming into its own. "You know what that moon reminds me of?"

I told her about my recurring dream.

She listened, giving away nothing.

"I usually wake up after and expect Mom to be in the room with me. When I saw you at the bottom of the stairs just now, it came to me."

"What did, sweetie?"

"It's not a dream, is it? It's a memory."

Aunt Fiona took my hands. "One of my favorite memories," she said, squeezing, asking for . . . approval or acceptance, perhaps.

Me, Fiona, and my mother, dancing to a full moon. This *so* wasn't the time for witchy questions or revelations, not spoken ones, anyway. The best support I could offer was to squeeze her hands back.

It was enough; I could tell from the way her features relaxed.

Still, in a bid for self-preservation, I took the conversation in a different direction. "Who else's emotions can you—"

"Strong, life-altering emotions," she clarified.

"Ah. Who else's strong, life-altering emotions can you sense, besides mine?"

She shrugged. "I sense emotions in the people who need me to."

In other words, she'd help anyone who needed her, whether it fueled her rep as a witch or not. I'd never known for sure whether Fiona practiced witchcraft. Despite our close relationship, it wasn't a question I'd ever felt comfortable asking her.

After my mother passed I'd never talked about my ghost sightings with anyone. In an odd way I'd felt a reluctance on Fiona's part to discuss the subject. Not sure how I felt myself, I'd kept quiet. I'd heard rumors in town about Fiona being a witch, but in general it wasn't something people discussed, especially if she had helped them. Aunt Fiona was known as the town lawyer, not the town witch.

"Some people's emotions are harder to sense than others'," Aunt Fiona said. "Reading you and your mother always came easily and naturally."

"Which is why you got here before Dad had a chance to call you the morning Mom died."

She nodded and a tear slid down her cheek.

The sound of wailing sirens in the distance brought me back to my purpose.

Sound carried over water, which meant that the ambulance and or police could be farther away than they seemed. Maybe.

I hugged Aunt Fiona once more, and we went inside.

At least with her there, Dad wouldn't be alone when he got the news, though they'd rarely spoken more than two words at a family gathering since my mother passed.

Dad saw us come in. "Blasted night's finally over." He lifted the curtain as the sound of sirens came closer. Much closer. Scrap!

"Not by a long shot, Dad."

He did a double take. "Mad, that ambulance is pulling in here." He, of course, expected me to explain why.

What else was new?

I squeezed his arm as I passed him on my way to the

27

door. "I'm afraid that we need them," I said and opened it. "Up the stairs, fourth door on the right," I told the paramedics as I led them to the front stairs.

Dad lowered himself to a keeping-room chair as I returned. "Madeira, tell me that my children are all right."

Aunt Fiona tilted her head. "Maddie, love, what exactly *is* going on?"

"Let's go into the taproom," I suggested, "where we can be more comfortable." Eventually the coroner would arrive, and Jasmine's body would be taken down the front stairs and out the door . . . the way my mother's had been. And you couldn't see the front stairs from the taproom.

Bad enough Dad would have to face the police later; he didn't need to see a replay of the worst day of his life. "Dad, would you like Aunt Fiona to make you a cup of tea?"

Fiona stopped and waited for his answer.

My father narrowed his eyes. "Must be bad, if you think I'd drink one of her twitchy brews."

Aunt Fiona bit her lip against one of her signature cutting remarks, and I appreciated it.

Twitchy? Hmm. Did he mean witchy?

I believed that our childhood suspicions about Aunt Fiona being a witch had been founded in truth. Did Dad believe it, too?

Good grief, did he know that my mother had actually moon danced with her best friend . . . and taken me along for the ride?

"Fiona," he said, brows furrowed, his defenses weakening before my eyes, as he took his comfortable chair. "I'd appreciate a cup of tea. Thank you." He gave me one of those parental looks. " 'Ignorance is the parent of fear.' "

A literary quote for every occasion, I thought. "Who's the author of that one, Dad?"

"Herman Melville and I never knew how right he was." Dad then tried to drill the information out of me with his

"Dad does the guilts" look, the one he'd given me the morning after that fateful Winter Ball when Nick and I had lost our virginity to each other.

I didn't break then, either. Nick had successfully escaped at dawn via the tree outside Brandy's window with no one the wiser.

"Give it to me straight," my father snapped. "'I am never afraid of what I know,' Shakespeare. And, Madeira, I'm smarter than you think."

Uh-oh. What did that mean? "Where's Sherry?" I asked, too worried about my sister to consider my unending list of past transgressions.

My father picked up his pipe out of nervous habit and put it down again. "I haven't seen Sherry since she and the Jezebel disappeared so as not to spoil 'the surprise.'" Dad gave a strained half smile. "When Deborah left, she was fit to be tied that it hadn't come off."

Whatever *it* was. "Mary Quant, mother of the miniskirt, where the Hermès could Sherry be?" I looked out every one of the taproom windows. I even lifted the board covering the coach-stop drive-through window. Normally dim, because of the raw boards and corner logs it was made of, the room darkened and grew chill as if with our spirits.

My father huffed. "Madeira, you will explain the ambulance this minute."

Aunt Fiona brought his tea before I could answer. Not that I was putting off telling him, but I'd rather eat dirt.

Alex owed me big time for this one.

Dad acknowledged his tea with a grudging thanks, raising his mug in approval. She'd not been so foolish as to give him a teacup. "Fiona," he griped. "Mad still hasn't told me."

I sat, hemmed and hawed, sighed and swallowed, and finally revealed what I knew, and until I'd come down, I pretty much knew more than anybody.

As a child I thought my father never left his stately

academic demeanor behind, but for the second time in my memory, life shocked him speechless.

By the time Aunt Fiona and Dad recovered, and I'd fielded a thousand or so questions, most of which only Jasmine could know, Nick and Alex ushered in Detective Sergeant Lytton Werner—or Little Wiener, as I'd dubbed him in third grade.

Of all the detectives in all the world . . .

I'd only called him Little Wiener once. Okay, so we were in the cafeteria at the time . . . and the nickname stuck like burrs in his underpants.

That's all I needed today, a detective in a $200 rack suit who owed me for upgrading his geek score. Not that I judged people by their clothes . . . well, yeah, I guess I did. That was my job. But seriously, a bad suit didn't mean he was a bad detective, I hoped.

By high school, everybody had dropped the word "little," because Wiener the Quarterback had turned into six feet of toned muscle. The nickname had still popped up once in a while on the football field, but by then, he could beat the scrap out of anybody who said it.

Still, I'd stayed the Hermès out of his way for the better part of my life.

Werner eyed me. "Still a glamazon, I see," he noted with scrutiny, resurrecting the 'hot button' that had caused his downfall. But from the near side of thirty, having been a grammar school glamazon sounded pretty damned, well, glamorous.

"I hear you make your living taking in sewing," he said, pen and notebook in hand.

From glam to glum in twelve seconds. "I'm a designer, Lytton. In New York. With Faline."

"Who's that? Your cat?"

Four

Disgraceful I know but I can't help choosing my underwear
with a view to it being seen.   —BARBARA PYM, 1934

In the midst of my scissor dance with the Wiener, Nick
rubbed the side of his nose and cleared his throat.

"Right, the investigation," I said, understanding his
amused reminder. But I still felt as if I was about to be
strip-searched. Thank God for the designer label on my
padded underwire and lucky panties.

Lucky? Hah. I had now officially lost faith in pots of
gold and "the pluck of the Irish." "Sergeant Werner, you
remember my father?"

He nodded and shook my father's hand. "I took one of
your English classes. You failed me."

Wooly knobby knits! We wouldn't catch a break if we
kissed the Wiener on his toasted buns and welcomed him
to the family. "And this is Fiona Sullivan," I added, revealing none of my angst.

Werner raised a brow, his expression filled with speculation. "Already decided you need a lawyer, did you?" He
added to his notes. "One of the best . . . they say."

"No. No!" I said. "Aunt Fiona's a family friend. She's here because she hadn't left the party, yet."

"She's a friend but you call her 'aunt'?"

I sighed at the non-relevance but knew that my impatience would only make matters worse. "She was my mother's best friend. We've always called her 'aunt', because she was there for us after Mom died."

"So the murder took place during a party," Werner said, ignoring my explanation as if *I'd* asked the dumb question, "and nobody heard a scream? A scuffle? Anything?"

All I could think about was the fact that we'd all heard Sherry's threat.

Everyone shook their heads, except for Nick. "Well," he said, "I heard Maddie scream Jasmine's name when she was trying to rouse her, but only because I was on my way up to find her."

"To find Jasmine, or Maddie?" Werner asked.

"Maddie, of course."

"Of course." Werner looked me in the eye. "So *you* found the body?"

Why did he seem almost . . . entertained . . . by that? Payback?

"Unfortunately," I said.

He hadn't blinked since his gaze caught mine and held it captive. "I got the official FBI version," he said, "now give me yours."

I told him everything that happened from the time I went into Brandy's room.

He asked who'd attended the party and we all answered at once with different names. He held up a hand. "Just give me the guest list."

We all looked at each other.

"No guest list?" Werner said. "That's convenient."

"It's not convenient," I snapped. "It's small-town, last-minute, word-of-mouth informal: 'Come and bring your brother's girlfriend's sister.' "

"Funny," Werner said to himself, head down, scribbling. "I didn't get an invite, directly or indirectly."

I rolled my eyes.

Werner raised his head in time to catch me. "Attorney Sullivan," he said, not taking his gaze from me, "start a guest list. Put down everybody you remember, then pass it around so you can each add names that might have been missed. Bring it to the station in the morning when you come to give your official statements."

"Then what?" I asked.

"Then I'll bring in your party guests for questioning."

Scare tactics. He couldn't question them in their own homes.

A uniformed team came downstairs and spread through the house like fire ants at a picnic. I felt a hot sting at every door, drawer, or box they opened. They snooped into every corner, one going so far as to open my father's humidor and smell his pipe tobacco.

"She wasn't smoked to death," I snapped. "You knew that was tobacco. Smelling it was just rude."

My father wanted me to shut up, but Werner gave the officer a look that said the man would hear more about it later.

Hmm. Maybe Werner did have some redeeming qualities. Well, one.

Aunt Fiona, Nick, Alex, and my father stood back, while I kept track of the officers, and Werner kept track of me. In the kitchen, they checked the leftovers and took samples, spooning a bit from each dish into small clear-plastic zip bags. They also dusted the kitchen for fingerprints.

"Good grief, she wasn't poisoned," I said. "She was strangled."

"With a bridal veil bearing your fingerprints." Werner spoke so close to me, he startled me and nearly smiled when I jumped. "Another statement like that and I'll assume you know what you're talking about." He made a few more notes. "Tell me again why your fingerprints are all over the possible murder weapon."

"Jasmine couldn't *breathe*!" I snapped.

"So she was struggling?"

"No."

"Twitching?"

I released a breath and shivered. "No."

"Not even a little finger?"

"Wait a minute, people pass out cold all the time and they're roused."

"So you gave her mouth-to-mouth?"

"No, damn it. I panicked, untied the veil to allow air into her lungs, and sat her up so she could breathe easier. I wish I had thought to give her mouth-to-mouth."

"Panic," Werner repeated. "Do you always panic, as if you're personally responsible, when somebody's hurt? Did you panic at every body you saw on the New York streets?"

I tamped down the precise fury that had driven me to mock this man when he was a boy.

I'd panicked because my sister would likely be blamed, damn him. "This is our home," I said. "Jasmine Updike was a guest here. Of course I felt responsible."

"Good enough." Werner removed his sharp, assessing gaze from my expression, and walked around the main floor, poking into the buttery, chimney cupboards, kitchen cabinets, fireplaces, hutches, jars, and canisters, before making his way back to the den.

"Stairs," he said. "How many sets of stairs in this house?"

My father cleared his throat. "Five."

"Five?" Werner frowned and looked at me for an explanation.

I ticked them off on one hand. "Front stairs, back stairs, keeping-room stairs, cellar stairs, and attic stairs."

"Well, that explains how a killer could slip away so easily in a house full of people. The wedding dress upstairs," he said, changing tack. "Who does that belong to?"

I shook my head. "I've never seen it before."

His gaze slid from me to Nick and back. "I would have expected it to belong to you."

"Me and Nick? No way."

Nick winced.

My father sighed. "It's the Vancortland family wedding gown, the surprise Deborah was going to give Sherry."

"Dad, how could you let Deborah do that?"

Clueless, my father furrowed his brows. "What? Why not?"

"You should have told Deborah that I planned to design Sherry's wedding gown. We've only talked about it all our lives."

My father cupped his neck and stood to stare out the window, probably wishing again that my mother were here.

Nick cleared his throat. "Mad, I moved the gown as soon as Sergeant Werner gave me the okay. It's in your closet like you asked, so Sherry wouldn't connect it to the murder, in the event she ended up wearing it."

I questioned Werner with my look. "So you knew from Nick that it was probably Sherry's?"

Werner shrugged as if he could care less what I thought.

My father straightened and tilted his head my way. "*You* knew it was likely Sherry's, as well."

"It's a wedding gown, Dad, and Sherry's about to get married. It doesn't take a rocket scientist to make the leap. Sure, *I'd* like a vintage wedding dress, if the time ever comes, a gown I'd prefer to choose myself—but Sherry isn't me. And Deborah isn't Sherry's favorite person."

My father shook his head. "And you expected me to think like you and make sense of all that emotional and preferential information?"

"Dad, it's okay. Now that I think about it, Deborah probably wanted to make a scene of presenting the gown, so she'd look gracious and generous. In company, Sherry wouldn't have been able to say no without looking like an ungrateful brat. Then again, maybe that's what Deborah wanted, a public rift, so Justin would have to choose between them."

Werner raised a brow. "Suspicious, aren't you?"

"And you aren't?"

"Suspicion is my job."

"I'm the closest to a mother Sherry has, so it's my job to protect her."

"Why do you think she needs protecting?"

"Have you ever met Deborah Vancortland, her soon-to-be mother-in-law?"

Werner coughed. "Enough said, but it's only your job to protect your sister to a point. Wait, isn't she your *baby* sister? And *she's* the bride?"

Score one for the Wiener.

Sherry came rushing in, breathing hard, as if she'd been running. "Mrs. Sweet said there'd been an ambulance here. And what's with the cop cars? Did somebody get sick? Was it the cake? I'll bet it was the cake."

"Why would you think it was the cake?" Werner asked without introducing himself.

"Because the cake lady gave it away. Who gives away free cake? Hey, aren't you—"

"Detective Sergeant Werner," I said, giving her a heads-up, trying to cut off the word "Wiener" at the pass.

"Oh, right. What's up?"

·"How well did you know Jasmine Updike?"

"Not very. She hasn't been in Mystic for long. All I know is that she was once my fiancé's study partner."

Werner looked up at her. "And your fiancé is?"

"Justin Vancortland."

"Right. Maddie told me that. Son of Justin Vancortland the Fourth." Werner whistled. "Your future mother-in-law isn't going to like the publicity this is going to cause. She'll be the talk of the country club and not in a good way."

No kidding, I thought, seeing Sherry's confusion. "What publicity?" she asked. "Why? What did Jasmine do, steal the silver?"

Werner regarded Sherry with a cryptic expression. "I take it you don't think much of Jasmine Updike."

"I think she's a conniving bitch, and I wish she'd stop trying to steal my fiancé, if you wanna know the truth."

Werner nodded. "The truth would be helpful in this situation."

Sherry folded her arms and huffed. "What situation?"

Though I'd been trying not to beat my head against the wall as my sister dug herself deeper, I stepped her way and took her hands. "Sweetie, Jasmine was . . . is . . . she's—"

"Dead," Werner said. "Someone strangled her upstairs with a bridal veil during your party."

Sherry paled as only a blonde could. "I don't believe it."

"Do you own a bridal veil, Miss Cutler?"

Five

I am blessed or cursed, depending on how you look at it, with an incurably restless spirit and the ability to work hard. —SALVATORE FERRAGAMO

"Don't try to pin this on Sherry," I snapped. "I'll prove she didn't do it."

Werner accepted the challenge with the light of victory in his eyes. "I'll pin it on her," he said, "to borrow your cop-show cliché, *if* after the autopsy, and my investigation, your sister is *still* my prime suspect." He dismissed me with a hand flick and turned to Aunt Fiona. "Who should I notify of Ms. Updike's untimely end?"

"Why would Aunt Fiona know?" I asked.

"I apologize," Werner said. "Attorney Sullivan seems always to have such an . . . eclectic . . . store of information."

To give Sherry credit, she had remained stoic at being told she was a suspect, but now, at the mention of notifying Jasmine's family, her eyes welled up and she began to tremble. Touching a finger to her lips, she composed herself. "Jasmine was staying with the Vancortlands," she said. "Deborah would most likely have her home address."

Werner closed his notebook. "I think we're done here

for now. I want you all down at the station around ten tomorrow, to give your formal statements. Agents Jaconetti and Cutler, no need to come down. Access the paperwork and fax it over."

He eyed them cryptically. "Which doesn't rule you out for questioning at a later date, you understand? And, by the way, this is *my* case." He eyed Nick and Alex like a poker player watching for their "tells."

The FBI versus the Podunk PD.

Taller than Nick and damned good-looking for a Wiener, the detective still had a Napoleon complex where the Feds were concerned. I'd have to keep that in mind.

"We understand," Alex said.

"Of course you do." Werner dismissed them. "Attorney Sullivan, please bring the guest list with you when you accompany the Cutlers to the station in the morning." He placed his notebook in his breast pocket. "List caterers, rental company employees, and whoever else worked the party," he added, as if she were his secretary.

From Aunt Fiona's expression, and in light of our earlier conversation, I half expected her to turn him into a slug. I wished I could. Not sure she could, either. Guess I had a few questions about the whole witch thing. As soon as I got up the nerve to bring up the subject again, I just might ask them.

Werner turned to leave and, with his back to us, raised an arm in a half wave.

Hail to the poker player who held all the cards . . . so far.

When the front door clicked shut, Sherry fell into Dad's chair. "Aunt Fiona," she said, her voice faint. "I think I need a lawyer."

"You have one, dear," Fiona said, coming over to stroke Sherry's hair.

"This is preposterous," my father snapped, about as angry as he ever got.

Fiona squeezed Sherry's shoulder and focused on Dad. "Blustering never got you anywhere, Harry. Action is what we need, and information. Did you mean what you said, Maddie, about proving your sister's innocence?"

"I always mean what I say."

My father scoffed. "How can you tell, Madeira, when you say it before you think it through? You practically pronounced Sherry guilty by vowing to prove she wasn't."

"I did not. She'd already told him how she felt about Jasmine, and he knew she was getting married. Of course the veil was hers. I just skipped ahead a few beats."

"Well . . . see that you don't rush Sherry into a jail sentence."

I didn't know who was more appalled at his words, me or my father.

"I'm sorry," he said. "I'm—"

Fiona touched his arm. "Scared out of your mind for your daughter's safety?"

Dad looked up at her in surprise because she, his nemesis, of all people, understood. "Which doesn't give me the right to attack Madeira," he said.

I sat on the edge of his chair and nudged his shoulder. "It's okay, Dad. I understand. I'm as frustrated as you are."

The kitchen phone rang and I ran to answer it.

When I completed the call, I pulled the phone plug.

As soon as word of Jasmine's murder got out, half of Mystick Falls would be calling. They'd rally around us and smother-hen the lot of us the way they did when Mom died, which was wonderful . . . except that one of them has to be the killer.

"That was Deborah on the phone," I said, rejoining the family in the den. "She wanted to know if Jasmine was still here, and I told her that I didn't know where she was." Surprise registered in their expressions. "Well, I don't," I said, my voice cracking.

"On a slab in the medical examiner's office," Alex said. "I understand why you couldn't have said that, Sis. You did fine."

Nick put a strong supportive arm around my waist, and I appreciated the subtle statement that he'd be there for me, for all of us. "Deborah invited us, well, ordered us, to her place for dinner tomorrow night. I'm supposed to bring the surprise to her beforehand without telling Sherry."

Sherry came out of her fog. "What?"

"You may as well know sooner rather than later and with all of us to support you, sweetie, that Jasmine tried to distract you so that Deborah could prepare her surprise for you—the family wedding gown that generations of Vancortland brides have worn."

Sherry sighed. "Oh, goody."

"Sherry, I—"

"It's okay, Mad. I can't think of anything but Jasmine's death and Werner's determination to prove I'm her killer."

"Listen," Alex said. "I hate to bail in the middle of a storm, but I've gotta get on the road. Tricia's been alone with the baby and her mother all day. She must need a break by now."

I touched my brother's arm. "Will you run Jasmine's name through the system tomorrow? See if you can find out anything about her?"

"I'm on my way to D.C. at dawn, Sis. Nick, can you take care of that?"

Nick squeezed my waist. "Will do."

Alex kissed us all good-bye, but he raised Sherry from her chair and hugged her. "It'll be okay, kitten. We've got your back. If you need distracting, go see Tricia and the baby while I'm gone."

Sherry's chuckle landed low on the laugh-o-meter. "I'm plenty distracted, thanks. But I will give her a call."

"Thanks. Bye, Dad." They shook hands, and Alex left.

The click of the front door snapped me into fix-it mode. "Sherry? Where the Hermès were you? You need an alibi and I hope it's airtight and comes with plenty of witnesses."

Looking from me to my father—who'd stood to pace but stopped to wait for her answer—Sherry covered her face and released a sob. "I need to call Justin," she wailed, and ran. The back door's familiar squeal and bounce announced her departure.

"The suspect has left the building." I sighed. "The good news is that Werner won't know what she said about Jasmine at the party unless somebody tells him."

My father paled and reclaimed the chair Sherry had vacated. "I forgot about that. I don't remember her exact words," he said, imploring each of us in turn, "but please tell me that she didn't publicly threaten to strangle Jasmine."

Aunt Fiona shook her head. "Sherry threatened to kill someone, but she didn't mention names, just feminine pronouns. What can I say, I'm a lawyer; I caught the loophole in the statement on the spot. Some might have suspected who she was talking about, but that doesn't matter. Sherry's words could be construed as a lead, *perhaps*, but not evidence. It's also such an overused cliché, it's lost its bite."

I couldn't sit still, so I got up to pace, wondering how to start proving Sherry's innocence. Learning more about Jasmine seemed like a good start, but then what? I guess I needed a copy of the guest list Fiona was going to compile before she gave it to Werner. Then I'd go house to house, if I had to, and find out what the neighbors knew.

I picked up on the heavy silence that had fallen at the same time as I passed an open window in the ladies' parlor and heard Sherry on her cell phone. "No, Justin," she said. "We can never tell."

Six

What I do is about now. It's about the lives we lead.
—HELMUT LANG

Early the next morning, I dressed in tan slacks with a yellow sleeveless summer sweater and camel leather flats. I disliked the world before dawn, and I couldn't face it in a bathrobe.

I stepped from my bedroom and stopped dead. "Crime-scene tape across Brandy's bedroom door." I looked at Nick. "Can you stand it? How weird can life get?"

Wearing yesterday's clothes, suit jacket over an arm, a sock in each pocket; tie hanging loose, Nick gave me a one-armed hug. "Weird is normal in my line of work. It's just never hit this close to home before."

I sighed and tiptoed down the hall.

With Nick bringing up the rear, I sneaked him down the front stairs, shoes in hand, trying to get him out the front door before anyone else got up.

Unfortunately, my father was working guard duty. The back stairs would have been a better choice, but they're *so* squeaky.

We stood frozen as my father, sitting at the old oak breakfast keeping-room table, glanced at us over his wire-rimmed glasses, set down his coffee mug, and methodically refolded his morning paper, dangling us from his hook like squirming bait.

One of Nick's shoes hit the floor with a thud, startling a squeak out of me.

"What's the matter, Nick?" Dad asked. "You didn't want to cross the crime-scene tape to climb out Brandy's window? Or are you getting too old for that?"

Oy. "Dad, I—"

"Sir—"

"Coffee?" My father raised my mother's daffodil octagon coffeepot, postponing his verdict on Nick's predawn presence and making me want to scream.

Nick released his breath, dropped his second shoe, nodded, and toed them on.

I got us each a mug from the kitchen across the hall from the keeping room, though at one time its huge fireplace had been used for cooking.

So the bait sat down to eat with the shark, where plates and cutlery had been set . . . for five?

Beside a basket of sugared blueberry muffins sat a daffodil butter dish and a porcelain beehive honey pot. I reached for a muffin, losing my appetite, however, when my father cleared his throat and placed his glasses by his plate.

Uh-oh.

"Madeira, you're a big girl," he said. "And, Nick, I like you. I'd simply like to know who's living in my house and who isn't."

"I'm not living here, Mr. Cutler," Nick said. "Last night was an exception."

My father raised a speaking brow.

"*Another* exception," Nick said, backpedaling. "It's just that Maddie was upset, and—"

"Justin, Sherry," my dad called out, obviously foiling another getaway. "Come in, join us for breakfast. I went out early and got enough muffins for everybody."

As usual, Sherry failed to hide her blush. Coming down the back stairs hadn't done them any good at all. My father could apparently see through walls.

"Don't mind if we do." Justin slapped Nick on the back as he went to the kitchen for mugs, very much at home and not at all intimidated by my father. That engagement ring on Sherry's finger must be worth its weight in courage.

"You're a cool one, Mr. Cutler," Justin said, returning.

The pot calling the kettle cavalier, I thought.

My father chuckled, and the circulation returned to my legs.

My father wore pride like a badge. "I've taught highly libidinous college students all my life," he said. "You think I'm not hip?"

Nick hid his amusement by sipping his coffee.

My father snapped his fingers. "Rad! That's what it's called now, right? I'm rad," he said. "Or am I the bomb? Anyway, my girls are all grown up."

"And they grew so well," Justin said, eating Sherry up with his bedroom eyes.

My father's cup stopped halfway to his lips. Even Harry Cutler, the hip, rad bomb, had his limits.

We all breathed again when Dad's cup finished its journey and Dad took a sip. "I don't think any of you could have committed a crime," he said. "You're too noisy when you're sneaking around. 'Take off your shoes on the stairs, Nick. You'll wake my father.' You call that a whisper, Madeira? Besides, even whispers echo in this place. Sorry I never told you that."

He watched us over the rim of his mug, put it down, split his muffin, and buttered it with great attention to every crumb. "Justin, my boy, kindly refrain from making my baby girl giggle until you're behind closed doors. Not that I don't appreciate your efforts . . . last night in particular. Sherry needed cheering up and her laughter's infectious. I liked hearing it, though I would have been happier if it had come from a five-year-old playing with her dolls."

Dad raised his coffee mug our way. "Time marches on, whether we want it to or not."

I stood and kissed his brow. "You're an old softy."

"I hear it's in bad form, Madeira, to call a man a softy these days."

I gasped, Sherry giggled, Nick choked on his muffin, and Justin slapped Nick on the back.

My father checked his watch. "Don't the men in this family—who are not on summer break—have jobs to get to . . . showered and wearing fresh clothes, one presumes?"

Justin and Nick checked the regulator clock on the wall between the front windows.

Justin, a VP in his father's conglomerate, jumped up first and booked it for the door, mug in hand. Sherry kissed him as he opened it. "Nick," Justin called before he left. "Come with the rest of the family to supper at my parents' tonight."

"Will do." Nick slipped into his jacket. Then he stuffed the rest of his buttered muffin into a pocket with a dirty sock.

His attempt to kiss me good-bye coincided with my amusement. He pulled back. "Geez, think you could be serious for a minute?"

"With you? Never. See you at the Vancortlands' to-night."

"Count on it."

Alone with Dad, Sherry and I looked at each other, waiting for the other shoe to drop, and I wasn't thinking about Nick's.

Aware that he held the advantage, my father raised a hand . . . and slammed it on the table.

Sherry and I both jumped. Son of a stitch; even when you're expecting it, you're never really ready. A shock like that can stop your heart.

"We have a wedding to plan!" Dad shouted. "Sherry, try on that wedding gown and don't forget that Deborah's holding the remote. Let your sister show you how beautiful she can make it. Practice loving it for tonight when Deborah makes a high ceremony out of presenting it to you. It'll make that boy happy. He loves you." My father grinned. "Think of your gracious acceptance as removing the batteries from Deborah's remote and pissing the hell out of her just for fun."

"When Dad's right, he's right," I said. "Let's go, Sis. My room. Bridal gown fitting."

Sherry hugged my father before we headed for the front stairs, the most direct route to Sherry's room.

"Sherry," my father called after us. "Before you hate the dress, remember the words of George Bernard Shaw: 'The novelties of one generation are only the resuscitated fashions of the generation before last.'"

Sherry leaned close. "I'll bet he looked that up last night just for me," she whispered, and we smothered our giggles.

"Oh," Dad added. "Don't forget that Fiona will be here at ten to go to the police station with us."

Our amusement came to a halt and so did we. Sherry leaned against the wall. "Hard to be a blushing bride when there's a murder charge hanging over your head."

"You haven't been charged," I said.

She sighed. "Yet."

I pulled her forward and we resumed our climb. "Since you didn't do it, I don't see how the Wiener can prove you did."

"You can say that after all the TV shows we've seen where innocent people go to jail every day? And don't tell me that's fiction."

"I won't," I said. "Real life is stranger than fiction, anyway. Don't worry; I'll talk to the neighbors later to see what I can find out about life since Jasmine arrived. "They had strong opinions about her last night, so they must know something."

Sherry sighed. "For the first time in my life, I'm glad that everyone in Mystick Falls butts into everyone else's business."

I felt the same way. "My first stop will be Aunt Fiona's."

"Good," Sherry said. "Maybe she can whip out her crystal ball and see if I'm gonna fry."

Seven

I see myself as a true modernist. Even when I do a traditional gown, I give it a modern twist. I go to the past for research. I need to know what came before so I can break the rules.

—VERA WANG

There were perks to being the firstborn Cutler. Each of us started life in the small room off our parents' corner suite near the front stairs. When we were old enough, we picked the bedroom we wanted.

I still claimed the best, the corner suite at the back of the second floor. As big as the front-facing master suite, it boasted a view of Mystic River, a dressing room, and its own bathroom. The only thing I lacked was a getaway tree.

In addition to my art deco bedroom set, I had three antique sewing machines, a Singer, a Remington, and a Wheeler and Wilson. Each had unique talents and comforting sounds. Sometimes I moved from one to the other to get an outfit just right.

Unlike Sherry's chintz, my room celebrated the craftsmanship of fine fabrics. Pleats, but no ruffles. Embroidered or woven textiles; no prints. I liked to feel the nap and weave, weft and warp on each piece of my hand-quilted spread. I'd textured my walls and used a jumbo knitting

49

needle to draw hanging wisteria vines into the wet compound, then roller painted the walls mauve, leaving the design outlined in white. My antique button collection, sorted by color and kind, filled clear antique glass containers—swans, cats, ducks, boats, and apothecary jars. They dotted the room; a splash of red buttons here, blue there, yellow, green, brass, bone, and flowered china.

I loved my personal space.

Right now, Sherry didn't love it so much.

With trembling focus, she approached the garment bag hiding Deborah's gown as if it might rise in a coil and strike.

"It won't bite," I promised. "It exudes positive vibes."

She looked at me through the corner of one eye. "Since when do you get vibes?"

I sifted through a carved sewing machine drawer of supplies. "Clothes and I, we've always had an understanding."

She unzipped the gray bag in slow motion as if she couldn't bear more than a peek. The lower the zipper, the more her shoulders relaxed.

"It's a find," I said, "if it's in mint condition." I pulled the bag all the way off the gown and found its cathedral train. "Wow. This could go for two, maybe three grand in New York."

"You're patronizing me."

"I'm not. I'd pay that much for it, if I was getting married."

"You'd buy that gown for yourself?"

"I would. I love it."

"Which proves two things," Sherry said. "You've lived in New York too long, and it isn't *my* style. It's yours."

Good point, but I didn't say so. "It's everybody's style," I said. "Look at this. Custom made with the talent of a Parisian couture, French seams, hand-stitched silk peau-de-soie lining, extraordinary workmanship, and yards of handwork, inside and out."

"You really think it's nice?"

"I think it's awesome. Listen, Cherry Pie; forget that it came from Deborah, or that she probably has an ulterior motive for giving it to you. Just look at these classic lines."

I laid it out on the bed and stuffed tissue in the bodice, but not in the pouf at the shoulders. Hopefully, Sherry would be willing to surrender the pouf. I'd rather pleat it at the shoulders or better still set it smooth into the cap. "Kiddo, this is imported ivory silk satin brocade aged to a papyrus undertone that collectors covet but can't buy. I love the simple barely-there swirls in the weave. It doesn't *need* the matching peau-de-soie slip, so if it's warm, you won't have to wear it. The trim at the neck and wrist is tulle, but the veil is a yellowed wreck." I balled it up and tossed it in my wastebasket. "I'll make you a new one."

Sherry surprised me with a choke hold.

I chuckled. "Wait, where's the vintage veil you said you bought?"

She paled. "I laid it out on Brandy's bed so I could show you."

"Of course. The one trimmed in pearls." Scrap.

Sherry fell against the wall. "Yeah, that one."

"Focus on the gown."

She nodded, eyes full.

Determined to stay upbeat, I denied my instinct to take her in my arms and cry with her. "This is a lot like today's designer gowns," I said, "because we're in a fashion cycle where old is new again. Ready to try it on?"

She nodded, the barest hint of anticipation rising to replace her negative emotions of a moment before.

I grabbed a bolt of dotted Swiss from the top of my closet and unrolled it, inside out, spreading two lengths side by side on the floor for a clean, wide workspace.

Sherry stripped to her bra and panties and stepped out of her shoes to stand facing my three-way mirror in the center of the fabric stage I'd set for her.

For my part, I slipped twenty-six center-front, self-covered buttons from their loops and took the gown carefully in my arms to slip over Sherry's head. The sheer amount of fabric overwhelmed me until I nearly got lost in it. I must look like Mrs. Frosty, I thought, realizing that all this frill was more Sherry's style than my own after all.

"Raise your arms," I said, "but don't move. I'll do all the work so we don't damage the dress."

Leaving my shoes behind, I slipped the incredible gown over Sherry's head, and it covered her like a scattering of fairy dust, each glistening particle draped in all the right places. It would need a bit of work for a perfect couture fit, but not much.

The sight of her wearing it felt magical, or haunting; I couldn't make up my mind which. Either way, an unnamed emotion pressed in on me, making it hard for me to breathe for a minute. "It fits . . . like the sisterhood of the freaking traveling wedding gown."

Backing up, I took in the sight as a whole . . . and burst into tears.

Sherry's eyes filled. "Is it *that* bad?"

Her joke eased the ache of loss in my heart. "Mom would be so proud. You're the most beautiful bride I've ever seen. I can't believe my baby sister is getting married."

"Are you sure you're not crying because I look like Dumpster bait at a meringue factory?"

I touched her chin and turned her gaze away from the mirror and toward me. "Sherry, you don't already have a gown picked out, do you? I never thought to ask."

"Of course not. I was waiting for you to come home to design and make me one."

So was I. "Hon, this gown is classy, austere, and timeless. An hourglass silhouette to the hip is so today. But *gathers* from the hip, not so much."

I touched my chin as my designing mind went into overdrive. "Aha! I can turn the gathers into a flare from the hip, cut higher in the front. I've got plenty of fabric to work with."

While sliding my hands beneath the gathers to gauge the yardage, my chest tightened again and dizziness overtook me, white spots dotting my vision.

When the malaise passed, I saw a different bride wearing the same gown.

In Sherry's place stood a gorgeous woman with porcelain skin, black-magic eyes, and raven hair, whose stance revealed humility . . . And unease? Unable to stand still, the illusory bride glanced about, as if she might get caught.

Doing what? Playing dress up?

Opening and closing her fists, she habitually grasped the fabric and dropped it, unable to stand still, awkward, not only in the dress, but in her own skin . . . or in her role, real or imagined, as the bride.

Apprehension, fear; that was what I read on her face.

Twice, she tried to hide her work-ravaged hands from a seamstress whose body language spoke of grudging servitude and whose clothes belonged in a rag bag from any era, but whose style hailed from the seventies.

The illusory bride wobbled like Cinderella on her high white heels as if she'd never worn a pair before.

Paradoxically, serviceable black donation-bin work shoes waited beside the round, two-tiered, fitting-room platform and a maid's uniform was thrown over the back of a nearby mission-style rocker.

"Mad! Madeira? Talk to us!"

The scene faded and dizziness overtook me again as I focused on Sherry standing before me, appalled, frightened, and still wearing Deborah's wedding gown. My sister's hands were not rough and callused from work but soft as a kindergarten teacher's, her French manicure perfect.

Eve knelt beside me in her usual Goth black, a radical contrast to the wedding gown. She squeezed my shoulder so hard it hurt, and regarded me as if I'd lost my mind.

"Eve? When did you get here?"

Eve glanced at Sherry, tilted her head my way, raised her hands for emphasis, and let them fall to her sides. "I rest my case!"

Eve drilled me with her look. "Better question. When did you leave here?"

I knew only that I'd dizzied my way out and back again, and right now I needed to kneel very still so as not to keel over. What the Hermès *had* happened to me? My heart still pounded and I fisted my hands so that neither of my protectors could see them shaking. Even my insides trembled.

"Mad, what happened to you?" Sherry asked, stooping down to face me. "Are you all right?"

"Nothing happened to me," I snapped, scared shirtless, almost as apprehensive as the bride of my imagination . . . or hallucination.

"I beg to differ," Sherry said, fanning her face while Eve went to dial up, or down, the air conditioner. "You zoned, Sis. You stared so far beyond me, you might have spotted a pinhole in the ceiling."

So far beyond her that I might have spotted a pinhole in time?

Wooly knobby knits; was I losing it? Had I truly stumbled on a scene from the past?

The illusory bride's gown, the same gown Sherry wore, had been a brighter white, newer, though not brand-new by any means, and her fitting room belonged in a castle.

As soon as I got a minute alone, I'd make a note of what I saw, in my . . . vision? Was it? Or a dream? Or a trip to the dark side?

I either needed a shrink or Aunt Fiona. Since she sensed my emotions, she'd probably expect my call after this.

Nevertheless, I'd record every detail of the mystery bride and her surroundings, in case.

"Well," Eve said. "Are you gonna tell us, or what?"

"What?"

Eve crossed her arms, one of her Doc Martens tapping her gentle impatience, an oxymoron of double proportions.

I shrugged. "You know that clothes speak to me. This one apparently speaks louder than most."

Sherry tilted her head. "Really? And what did it have to say? Any juicy tidbits about Deborah?"

"No, it spoke in tongues. I'll get back to you when I translate. Change of subject. Eve, this is the gown Deborah wore to marry Cort, like her mother-in-law, and her mother-in-law . . . You get my drift. She wants Sherry to wear it to marry Justin."

I gave Eve "the look" we'd practiced for unexpected and unwanted pickups at bars or parties, one that said, "follow my lead." In this case, "say something nice."

"Well, it's no bomber jacket," Eve said, "but you look a hell of a lot better in it than Deborah could possibly have. It's so . . . you."

"Sold!" Sherry said, laughing.

I hugged them both. "Eve, you always know the right thing to say." In this case, she hadn't even said it with her own vocabulary, but I forgave her for borrowing mine, under the circumstances.

Sherry shrugged. "I'm perverse and Eve knows it. Honestly, though, it has some good points. I like the V at the neck and wrist points, and the row of covered buttons have a certain charm, but, Mad, I *hate* the pouf sleeves."

"Good call. That's my girl. Worry not. I'm a brilliant, bodacious de-poufer."

Despite Sherry being paler than pale, hearing me toot my own horn had put some pink into her cheeks.

"I love the idea of turning the gathered skirt into a flare cut high in the front," she said. "I can just picture it."

"Not cut too high." I winked. "Just up to fashion-week runway standards, and since it's an early September wedding, I can make you a coat from a fine Brussels lace."

"What?" Eve asked from my bed, shoes off, head in hand. "Lace made by blind Belgian nuns?"

Sherry chuckled, so I forgave my erstwhile friend for being flip about fashion, which she knew ticked me off. "To marry the fabrics, I'll use strips of the same lace to replace the tulle ruffles at the neck and wrists. That's yellowed, too. It has to go."

"You rule, Sis. You should open your own shop."

Eve snapped her fingers. "Where *have* we heard that suggestion before, Mad?"

"I know, I know; that's what you keep telling me. I'll design the lace coat to flow from a high-standing, scalloped collar and make you look like a queen. It'll V down to three self-buttons beginning at your cleavage and ending at an inverted V that flows to the floor."

I bit my lip. The back hem would be tricky. In fact I didn't want to hem it; I wanted self-scalloped edges all around. "The design will have to give way to the gown's train, somehow," I said. "Don't worry; I'll know how to do it when I see the lace."

"Maddie, this'll be a dream gown when you're done with it. Thank you *so* much." Sherry's eyes filled again. "Justin will be happy because his mother is, and on my wedding day, I'll feel like a queen."

"Madeira, Sherry, Eve," my father called from the bottom of the stairs. "Fiona's here. Time to go to the police station."

Sherry's expression froze, the light leaving her eyes. "Do they let prisoners attend their own weddings?"

I raised the gown over her head. What could I say to that?

"A bit melodramatic, aren't you, Sherry?" Eve asked, helping me lift the gown off her.

I glared at my former best friend, but she gave me a look that said she was standing her ground. Maybe she was right.

I sighed, unsure of anything anymore. "Cherry Pie, you're not a murderer."

"No." She sighed. "I'm only the prime suspect."

Eight

Women are now more comfortable with themselves and their bodies—they no longer feel the need to hide behind their clothes.
                             —DONNA KARAN

I changed quickly into a sage green, scoop-neck pocket tank mini that I designed and made myself, leopard flats from Blahnik, and my camel Fendi hobo bag. Okay, so I changed handbags the way most people changed their underwear. So sue me. I had a thing for purses.

Shoes, almost as much, hats, too, but as my mother once said, I'd turned in my rattle for a handbag and never looked back.

Because of my job, many of my clothes were gorgeous and pricey, but didn't cost a thing, yet I wanted something different. I wanted the classic lines I grew up loving, and I knew exactly where to find them. At Aunt Fiona's.

After we finished at the police station, I'd follow her home, tell her about my "vision," and grab some of my secret, vintage stash.

Sherry came down to leave for the station wearing a black suit and white blouse, her hair pulled back in a twist, as if she were going to a funeral or her own execution.

I wanted to suggest she change into something livelier, but we didn't have time. Instead, I ran upstairs for a Gucci scarf splashed with summer flowers, a pair of multicolor pumps, and a red Dior bag that Mimi Spencer had once called "the equivalent of a yapping Chihuahua."

"There," I said, after I'd accessorized her. "Proclaim your confidence, instead of your fear."

She looked down at herself. "You know, I do feel more confident."

"Go get 'em," I said. "Eve, ride with me to the station, will you? Sherry, you go with Dad and Aunt Fiona, because she might have some last-minute instructions for you. Right, Aunt Fee?"

Aunt Fiona nodded in agreement, gracefully accepting my suggestion. At least now I knew why I'd always gotten the impression that the woman could read my mind.

Sitting in the pimpmobile, motor running, Eve and I watched my dad's Volvo leave the drive.

Eve poked me in the arm. "What happened when you zoned out up there?"

"Ouch. What'd you poke me for?"

"For holding out on me. How can I save you, if I don't know what you need saving from?"

"I know what you need saving from . . . the color black. You keeping a Harley I don't know about?"

"Stop changing the subject. You checked out. Why?"

I eased the pimpmobile out of the driveway. "You won't believe it," I said. "You're a scientist."

"I'm a computer geek. Get your labels straight. Now give."

"I can't even put a name to it."

"Try, dammit!"

"You asked for it. I experienced some kind of . . . vision. I saw a strange woman wearing Deborah's wedding gown."

"How strange?"

"So strange that she lived about thirty years ago, give or take a few years."

Eve whistled. "How much sleep did you get last night? How long since you've seen a doctor? Have you hit your head lately? Is Nick good in the sack?"

I gave her a double take. "What does that have to do with the price of Jimmy Choos?"

"Hey, watch the road." Eve sighed. "I'm skeeved and I'm overcompensating with inane frivolity. So sue me."

"You're taking advantage of my possibly dull mental state to Google me about my sex life."

"Cut me some slack. You scared me."

"You think I'm not freaked?" I snapped. "I scared the wigan out of myself."

Eve tilted her head. "What's wigan again? I keep forgetting."

"It's a bias-cut interfacing. Makes me think of wigging out; ergo scaring the wigan out of myself makes perfect sense."

"To you, Mad. Only to you."

"My coworkers at Faline's understood."

"I rest my case. Something tells me that I'm *not* the one to save you this time."

"I'm gonna tell Aunt Fiona, because zoning out today was the closest I ever came to doing something witchy."

Eve turned in her seat to face me. "Sounds more psychic than witchy."

"You believe in psychics?"

"No, but I took a course in parapsychology. Some academics call it a pseudoscience, though a lot of people believe in it. Because I know you, and you tell it like it is—no matter which of us you get into trouble—let's say that I'm temporarily suspending disbelief."

"Don't bother. We agree. I'm not psychic."

"Maybe not, but . . . you do know what people should wear, what they'll look good in, and what they'll like."

"That's a learned skill."

"Judging their style may be, but knowing what they'll like? Besides, you knew what the other kids should be wearing in kindergarten."

"That's called instinct."

"Okay, but talking both of us out of believing in psychics means that you must be a nutcase."

"Gee, thanks."

Eve snapped her fingers. "What about the time Sherry fell in the river?"

"It's true that I ran to the water for no reason, and there was Sherry too full of river water to call for help. But that's different. That was a mother's instinct." My heart raced with the memory, enough to make me question my own denial.

Eve looked out the window. "Isn't 'mother's instinct' a rather psychic phenomenon? It comes into play when it's needed."

I tried to hide my confusion. "Your point?"

"What's different about today that made you open your instincts to a vision?" Eve asked.

"Different? Everything. I found a dead body last night. Sherry's the prime suspect in the murder. I worked on my first vintage wedding gown today. Sherry's wedding gown."

"Also Deborah's wedding gown," Eve added, absently, focusing as if she were doing math in her head, a party trick of hers.

I thought about that. "And the gown of several dead Vancortland brides, as well, if we're being picky."

Eve focused on me. "We have to be picky. Okay, so let's say that the murder, your first vintage bridal gown, riddled with history, for a murder suspect who happens to be your sister, and your need to fix *everything* . . . freed your imagination."

"It was not my imagination!" I hoped, I think.

"Okay, wrong word. The series of events, and historic conditions, freed, perhaps even cultivated, a sixth sense you've always had, a long-dormant gift . . . that flowers in this kind of life-or-death situation . . . a situation equal to a near drowning."

Why did my dream, er, memory of moon dancing with my mother and Aunt Fiona come to mind when Eve said that? "Say again?"

Eve sighed. "Just for the record, I don't believe in anything I'm saying."

"So noted."

Eve cracked a smile. "It's like the stars are in alignment for your gift to reveal itself. Could be your instincts are kicking in, Mad. Maybe you were too stressed in New York to listen to the voices in your head."

"I do not hear voices in my head."

Eve hummed the theme song from the *Twilight Zone*. "Either that or vintage clothes talk to you because they have pasts and secrets to share."

I gave her a double take. "You think I stumbled on a secret from the past?"

"Hell no. But I have heard of people who get psychic readings when they touch old objects. They learn things about the object and the people who owned it. There's a name for that type of telepathy, I think."

"Aunt Fiona might know."

"I guess."

"Eve."

"What?"

"I'm scared."

"Being psychic is nothing to be scared of."

"I'm scared my sister will go to jail, nut job."

"Nut job? Me? Bit like the pistachio calling the geek a cashew, isn't it?" She poked me again, which helped me relax. Normal. That was what I needed right now. Normal. And look who I was trying to get it from . . . Eve. Hah.

"Police station parking on your right," she said, shattering normal.

"How did you feel when you found Jasmine's body?" Eve asked as I pulled in. "No visions, then?"

"Nope."

"How inconvenient."

"You're telling me."

The police station smelled musty, a combination of old books in attic trunks, rain-soaked dogs, hardworking men, and unwashed lawbreakers.

Werner met us at the door—a man who smelled, amazingly, of Armani's Black Code, a scent reminiscent of fruit, lavender, and a walk in the woods.

Silent, he led us down a barren institutional hall—top: cream, bottom: tan—separated by a bruised walnut chair rail. A dozen doors with knobby-glass windows revealed a slide show of sinister shadows.

He brought us to a sterile, pale puke green room where Justin and his family sat on backless benches along one wall.

As we joined them, the Vancortlands looked everywhere but at us, except for Justin, who came for Sherry and led her to a spot beside him, away from his parents.

Deborah surprised me. Aside from her feeble whine when Justin got up to meet Sherry, she was quiet. The Deborah I knew would be highly insulted and shrilly vocal about being made to wait in a dingy police station. This Deborah must be on tranquilizers. She wasn't even sporting puffy eyes. Maybe she'd gotten Botoxed this morning. At any rate, she looked more serene than she had last night.

Being so fond of Jasmine, you'd think she'd be in mourning, especially given the arrowed Morgue sign on the wall across from our open door.

It freaked *me* to know Jasmine's cold body lay just down the hall. I rubbed my arms to warm myself . . . in August . . . without air-conditioning.

Deborah's husband, Cort, sat a distance away from a wife who should need consolation, but didn't.

Were the Vancortlands on the outs, and was Jasmine the reason? After all, Cort had been visibly interested in the cake lady. Maybe he'd been just as smitten by Jasmine, which would give either of the Vancortlands a motive for killing Jasmine.

I sat, took out a small notebook, made a very rough sketch of the room I'd seen in my "vision," for want of a better word, and I handed it to Eve. Then I listed the details of said vision. On a roll, I took out the copy of the guest list that Fiona had given me and checked off anyone who might have had a motive for killing the girl. We had, unfortunately, provided the opportunity, the party, and the means, the veil. So I guess I needed to find somebody with a possible link to the girl.

The exercise served as a diversion until the uniforms came for us. They took us one by one, as if for a date with destiny, where one might expect to be shot by a dozen rifle-bearing officers speaking a foreign language, or so the maudlin situation made my overactive mind work, which *could* account for my "vision/hallucination/flight of fancy."

When Sherry and Fiona followed a detective from the room, Justin and I reached out emotionally, and he came to sit beside me.

Nobody who'd gone for questioning returned, so the room slowly emptied. Cue the *X-Files* soundtrack. Shiver. I grabbed Justin's hand.

The Sweets eventually joined us. Werner must have started early canvassing the neighbors.

Young Mrs. Sweet apologized for offering a hanging tree to lynch Jasmine "just last night, the poor dead thing."

Still poker-faced, Deborah made no sound, not even the pretense of a sniff.

"Mrs. Sweet," I asked the elder. "Were the two of you called in for questioning?"

"Of course not, dear. We're here to support Sherry."

"Bless your hearts."

They sat with us, improving the ambiance in the room with their smiles and signature scents of rose water and baby powder.

Werner came for me himself.

At first, he sat behind his desk, across from me, and sized me up—payback for the Wiener comment, no doubt. Then he shrugged, repeated last night's questions, after which I repeated my answers. While I did, he filled in the blanks on his computer screen, and printed the statement form out for me to read and sign.

"What about the autopsy?" I asked. "Any clues there?"

"You watch too much TV. We don't have the report yet, and if we did, I wouldn't be discussing it with *you*."

"I'm sorry," I said, relaxed now that my official statement had been taken.

"No problem. It's natural to be curious, especially when you're the one who found the body."

"No," I said. "I apologize for giving you that nickname in school. Kids can be cruel. I'm sorry I was a typical, cruel kid."

He looked at me as if he actually saw me, maybe for the first time, until his gaze focused beyond me . . . to a hurtful place?

Guilt skewered me, but Werner's sigh held a "c'est la vie" quality. "I like to think of that *episode* in my life as character building," he said. "Because of it, I learned to fistfight at an early age, work out regularly, and generally stand up for myself, which encouraged me to enter the police academy."

He shrugged. "Maybe I would have been a wuss, without your 'help,' and I use the term loosely." He shook his head philosophically. "Who knows, but for you, I might be a shut-in computer nerd, instead of a detective. I didn't like what you did, but I took what I could from it and threw the rest away."

"So you forgive me?"

His grin wasn't meant to be pleasant. "I didn't say that."

"Okay, so you're not a forgiving man, but you *are* a fair one."

"I am. I want the *real* killer, Madeira. I hope, for your sake, it's *not* your sister."

"It's not. Thank you." I turned to go back to the waiting room, but he took my arm and steered me around toward a side door that led to the parking lot.

My father and Cort were exchanging literary quotes in lieu of conversation.

Justin stopped pacing when he saw me.

"Where's Sherry?" I asked him.

"She and Fiona haven't come out, yet, and they went in for questioning before us."

"Baste it!" I swore. "And your mother?"

"She's not out yet, either."

Deborah came out almost immediately, but another fifteen minutes passed before Sherry joined us, and she'd been crying. I met her and took her in my arms, everyone crowding around us, but as soon as Justin broke through, Sherry moved into his arms.

"Are you okay, hon?" he asked, smoothing her hair back from her brow. She was looking down, so we couldn't see her face.

After a minute, Sherry pulled a bit away from Justin to address us. "Somebody told them that I called Jasmine a bitch and threatened her life."

Denial echoed around the group, with one exception.

66

"Deborah!" Cort snapped.

Justin growled. "Damn it, Mom!"

Deborah furrowed her brows attempting to look inno-cent. "The woman detective asked me if anybody had said anything incriminating. We were supposed to tell the truth, weren't we? Did you all lie when they asked you that? I mean this is a horrible scandal we're being dragged into." She slid her gaze to Sherry and away so fast, blame might not have been assigned, but it was. "I mean," she said, "it's all embarrassing enough without lying."

Cort looked disgusted with his wife, but the questions he shot at her revealed that Deborah had been the only one interviewed by the female detective who might, or might not, have asked about incriminating statements.

Deborah patted Sherry's shoulder in the way one might so as to keep from catching guilt cooties by association. "I'm glad you weren't arrested, dear."

Deborah turned to me with a smile. A smile, the stitch. "Madeira, you have something to drop off, don't forget. And dinner at our house tonight at seven." Deborah waved as she left, got into her powder blue Mercedes, and drove away.

Cort didn't look happy as he got into his taupe version of the same car and followed.

Justin and Sherry exchanged glances. "Eloping sounds good about now," Justin said.

"I can't leave the state," Sherry whispered.

"Screw work," Justin snapped. "I'm not leaving you to-day. Let's get out of here." He put Sherry in his car and they left together.

"I couldn't ask for a better son-in-law," my father said.

Given Justin's past connection to Jasmine, I sure hoped Dad was right.

Nine

Zest is the secret of all beauty. There is no beauty that is attractive without zest.   —CHRISTIAN DIOR

I touched Fiona's arm. "Aunt Fiona, can I follow you home? I'd like to talk to you."

"I was going to suggest it myself, dear. I'll make us some lunch. Eve, will you be joining us?"

"No, thank you, Fiona. Mad can drop me at home on the way. I need to go over to UConn. Get my paperwork settled. Scope it out for fall courses."

I made sure my dad was okay before I got in my car, and I let him leave first, so I could follow and make sure he got home all right. I dropped Eve at her parents' with a promise to call her after tonight's dinner at Deborah's.

Dad's car sat in our drive when I went by and I saw him walking down our sloping lawn toward the Mystic River. This must be hard on him, but he tended to suffer in silence, my dad, so who could tell what he was thinking?

I appreciated being home again with nature all around me. The house lots here in Mystick Falls were huge and staggered so that the riverside houses had a front-door view of the woods and the wood-side houses had a front-door view of the river.

Fiona's house looked more like a small Irish manor, mystical, inside and out, as if it belonged on a hillside surrounded by moors facing the Irish Sea. Not that I expected to see the occasional leprechaun, but I did find myself humming the theme song to the *Wizard of Oz* as I pulled into the driveway. Oy.

A tribute to her personality, her home spoke of her zest for life in all its intricacies, a quality I had always admired.

Perhaps because I'd seen that zest up close and personal during the occasional moon dance as a toddler? Add to that my formative years, during which I'd earned the right to walk in without knocking, a habit I took advantage of at this moment.

Aunt Fiona was on the phone and she signaled that she'd be another minute.

Inside, her textured earth-tone walls covered a spectrum of colors from clay to sand to Connecticut's wild honeysuckle. Celtic symbols adorned fabrics and artwork, even floor tiles . . . suns, moons, and stars dominating.

Candles—pillars, floaters, tapers, tea lights, gelled and jarred—occupied arches and corners, tables and counters. A few were lit, filling the air with the sweet summer scents of honeysuckle, sandalwood, and frangipani, my favorite combination, and Aunt Fiona knew it.

She loved thick, cushy upholstered furniture, so comfortable you could sink in and meditate . . . or fall asleep.

She hung up and hugged me, soothing all my ragged emotions without words. We didn't always need words, between us. I hadn't quite realized that until this minute.

"Seeing your house again makes me realize that over the years, ours has morphed from Mom's quaint Early American decor to Dad's tobacco-scented early faculty lounge."

"I've noticed," Fiona said, her Irish eyes smiling. "In other words, it's a house for a man's man."

"Well, Dad doesn't spit on the floors or anything."

We chuckled as we imagined something so vulgar from Harry Cutler.

From the mantel I picked up the picture of Fiona and my mother at their college graduation, arm in arm, both of them beaming. I touched my mom's face and missed her with a depth that caused an ache in my chest. I swallowed, cleared my throat, and replaced the picture.

The murder, the resultant stress, including the reminder of my mother's death in that house, and now the photo, pushed an old question to the front of my mind. "Why haven't you and my dad been able to get along since Mom died?"

Fiona looked up sharply. "That's not a simple question to answer."

"I guess that's between you and my dad. Forget I asked."

"Madeira, you and I have always shared a special relationship. The time you spent here as a child meant a lot to me. I used to look forward to you showing up with your latest sewing project. Back then, your questions were about your latest clothing design.

"It was a lot easier to tell you how to master a certain stitch than to talk about the past. I'll try to do justice to your question. It's valid. Just give me a little time."

I always wanted instant answers, but I forced myself to be patient. "Fair enough." I smiled as I remembered fondly all the time I'd spent with her when I was younger. "I grew up in this place, when you think about it, learning to make pot holders and latch-hook rugs, crocheting doilies, and best of all, sewing and designing."

She smiled. "You took the step from sewing to designing all by yourself, sweetie. I gave you fabric, needles, and thread, and you ran with them, straight to a sketching pad."

"Speaking of sewing, Sherry tried on Deborah's wedding dress this morning."

Fiona winced. "How badly did she hate it?"

"It's exquisite, a cross between my style and Sherry's, but I can turn it into Sherry's dream dress."

"So? Problem solved?"

"Well, that one is."

Fiona reached over and patted my hand. "I know. This morning is hard to call, but it could have been worse. I can't discuss the details with you. Lawyer/client privilege and all that, but Sherry can tell you."

"I'm gonna do some snooping on my own, so I'd appreciate knowing what might have happened between Sherry and Jasmine *before* Sherry became your client, or between Jasmine and anyone else in the neighborhood, before I came home. Can you think of anybody who'd want to kill her?"

"Given the bitch factor? Everybody."

"That's a big help."

"It's a fact." Aunt Fiona went to the kitchen.

I followed. "Can I help?"

"No, thanks. I've prepped something quick and easy."

I sat on a bar stool facing her as she made us each a plate of chicken and green grape salad on greens.

I stole a grape and popped it in my mouth. "Mmm. Did you notice anyone else, besides Jasmine and Sherry, disappearing toward the end of the party the other night?"

"Not that I can think of." She poured iced tea. "Deborah, maybe, for a short time. I noticed because of the lack of judgment in the room." Aunt Fiona popped a grape herself and winked.

I found it difficult to make small talk. My mind was too full of the mystery bride. "Aunt Fiona, something happened to me while I was working on the wedding gown this morning," I admitted with a rush. "Something spooky weird."

Fiona stopped scooping salad, rested her hands on the

counter, and looked up at me, ready to hear whatever I had to say. I'd told this woman when my "pet" toad dried up in the sun and when Nick dated somebody else for the first time.

Dear, wise Aunt Fiona always listened.

My hands trembled again, and I hid them in my lap. "I went into some kind of . . . trance, or I had a vision or something. I saw another woman wearing Deborah's wedding dress. A maid, I think. She was being fitted for the gown by a seamstress in a gorgeous room that belonged in a castle."

Fiona crossed her lips with a finger and looked at me as if she were trying to decide how to answer. Then she nodded, finished making lunch, wiped her hands on a dish towel, and brought our plates to her glass-topped kitchen table. We always ate in her sunny kitchen, leaving her antique oak refectory dining-room set with its carved chairs, hutch, and buffet for special occasions.

I grabbed our glasses of iced tea and brought them with me to the table.

"First," Fiona said, "if you want to know about *old* gossip, go see Mrs. Sweet's mother-in-law. Dolly Sweet knows all the juicy bits."

"Right. Thanks." I tasted the salad and sighed.

"Psychometry," Fiona said.

"What?" I put down my fork, my throat suddenly too tight to swallow.

"A psychometric can touch something and learn about its owner, or owners, or anything about the object's past. Works best with antiques . . . and, apparently, with vintage clothes, though that might take a specialist. You?" She opened her mouth to say something more and took a sip of her tea instead.

A shiver ran up my spine and the hair on the back of my neck stood to salute. "What aren't you telling me?"

She put down her glass of tea and released a breath. "You inherited your psychometric ability from your mother."

The clouds in my mind parted and the sun broke through. I felt close to my mother for the first time in eighteen years. "A long-dormant gift," Eve had called it. A gift from my mom. "Mom was psychic?"

My throat got tight again. I didn't know whether to laugh or cry, or run and hide. A frightening gift. Power, an accessory that I didn't ask for or want. What was the down-side of power, I wondered, but I knew instinctively.

Responsibility. I scoffed inwardly. God knew, I could deal with that.

Hands cupped my shoulders. Comforting, but not Mom's. I hadn't realized Aunt Fiona had come around the table. "It's a daunting gift," I said, turning to her. "I love it because it's from Mom, but—"

"Your father will kill me if he finds out I told you." She gave a small smile. "Sorry, bad joke."

"That's why you and Dad don't get along. You know things he wants to forget."

"Something like that." She sat down again and covered my hand with hers. "Madeira, I think the universe is trying to tell you something. Your mother would have thought the same."

"You two were a lot alike, weren't you? Dancing beneath the moon and all that?"

"Like sisters," Aunt Fiona said. "Soul mates, I believe. And I don't mean like she and your dad were soul mates. That was love, the real thing. I envied her that, but I was happy for her."

"He's a good dad."

"Harry? He's the best. The sad truth is that I fell for him, too, but he only ever saw Kathleen."

"Have you been carrying a torch for my dad all these years?"

"You tell him and I'll—I'll—"

"Turn me into a toad?"

"Let's save that conversation for when you're not on information overload."

"Bummer," I said, and she smiled.

"If I'm psychometric," I added, a conditional exploration of the gift settling in, "then I'm going down to the Underhill Funeral Chapel carriage house to lean against the outside wall and suck up all its secrets."

"That old shack. Why?"

"A shack. That's what Eve calls it."

"That's what everybody calls it. They say it's haunted."

An unexpected thrill of anticipation shot through me. "Haunted? Seriously?" Now why should that entice me? Maybe because I was already haunted by the bride of my so-called psychometric vision.

Fiona shrugged. "Who knows? What do you care about that old place?"

"I don't know, but it . . . appeals to me, always has, to be truthful. Do you know who owns it?"

"No, but I could find out. I hope it's because you want a tour. Maybe you could poke around a little. Though Goddess knows why you'd want to."

I'd heard Aunt Fiona say "Goddess knows" a hundred times, but I'd never quite picked up on it before. Neither had I surrendered myself so openly to the spiritual pulse in the air here. I couldn't define it, but it touched me. Today its warmth welcomed and consoled me. Mom, are you here?

Goddess knew.

Was it this house or was my newfound and dubious psychic ability coming into play?

Every house in Mystick Falls hailed from the nineteenth century, though ours was a century older, so we were talking living history here. Residual energy, perhaps. Entities from beyond this plane.

No, all our houses couldn't be haunted, though maybe Fiona's could. For the first time, I sought meaning in the Celtic symbols around me. I listened for their wise whispers and welcomed their comforting peace. One wall hanging in particular caught my attention—a spiral of assorted stars in bronze, silver, and gold—surrounding a mating sun and quarter moon.

I went and stroked the brilliant piece of folk art, feeling closer to my mother than I had in years.

"That was your mother's," Fiona said. "I took it off the curb where your father had left it for trash pickup and brought it here."

"It" represented more than a tapestry, it symbolized the kinship that Mom and Fiona shared.

Besides my troubling psychic ability, what else could I have inherited from my mother? What precisely had brought Kathleen O'Reilly Cutler and Fiona Sullivan, college strangers, together, besides their Celtic heritage? Was it their penchant for dancing beneath the moon?

I turned to ask Aunt Fiona how she and Mom met in college, but she'd left the room, as if she understood that I had puzzles to ponder and a mother to remember.

"I have a gift for you," she said, returning, cuddling a plump, bright little honey-colored fur ball.

"For me? Oh, Aunt Fiona, she? He?" I checked. "*She's* adorable. I took the kitten into my arms and something odd happened. "Aunt Fiona, I cuddled her and got the most amazing tingle in my middle and at the same time, joy and well-being seemed to fill me."

Aunt Fiona grinned. "She has an effect on your solar plexus? Isn't that interesting?"

"Why?"

"Because she's yellow and that's your yellow chakra.

When it's in balance, it brings a sense of well-being, positive thinking, and joy."

"It's like we're connected, somehow. Like she's supposed to be mine. What's her name?"

Aunt Fiona looked rather like the cat that ate the canary. "I call her Fraidy Cat, because she's afraid of everything. Your father doesn't want a watchdog; too big and too much trouble to walk, he says. I suggested one the other night. But Fraidy Cat frightens easily, and when she's scared, watch out."

"Why? What happens? She piddles on the intruder?"

"Wait, I'll give you a demonstration."

I presumed then that piddling *wasn't* the kitten's forte.

Fiona revealed the rubber mouse behind her back right before she squeaked it, and when she did, Fraidy Cat screamed like a banshee.

I jumped; I was so startled by the sheer volume in the capacious sound. "I can't believe that came from such a tiny kitten. Did it sound like she screamed a lengthy version of my name?"

"See? That's what I thought the first time I heard her," Aunt Fiona said. "She's all vocal cords, that one, the only kitten in the litter who is. Come to think of it, I've *never* heard a cat like her. When I got home last night, I scared her, caught the echo of your name, and knew she'd be perfect for you. Now I'm sure of it. She can be more than a watch cat; she can be your charm against negativity. When you feel nervous, stressed, or edgy, just pick her up, and she'll restore you to balance and well-being. I shouldn't be surprised. You gave me her mother when you went away to school in Manhattan. I'm glad you're back, but ticked that when you finally come home, there's a strangler on the loose."

"I haven't left New York for good," I said. But I wanted to, I didn't say. I snuggled the yellow kitten against my neck. "I need to name her. I was thinking about something to do with her yellow color like Citrine, but what do you think about Chakra, given her attributes?"

"Her attributes are yours alone, don't forget."

"Is that significant?"

"I think so, and you may agree with me . . . someday."

"I like both names," I said.

Fiona scratched the kitten behind an ear. "Then give the tiny little fur ball a name bigger than she is." She grinned. "Chakra Citrine."

"Given the names of the Cutler children, I should probably call her Dandelion Wine, after the wine my mother always made."

Fiona coughed. "Somehow, I don't think your father would appreciate that."

"I suppose, and I like Chakra Citrine Cutler much better."

"Your father will love her."

"Not. And you know it, but you take a perverse delight in annoying him, don't you?"

"Hey, I'm old. Annoying Harry is how I get my kicks. Cheesecake?"

I looked at my plate, surprised to find it empty. "I'd love some."

"Aunt Fiona. It sounds to me that annoying my father is how you get his attention."

She made a self-mocking sound. "If that's what I'm doing," she said, "shame on me for taking so long. I should drum myself out of Men Chasers Anonymous."

"Then you *are* trying to get his attention?"

"No. Maybe. Can I get back to you on that one, too?"

'Nuff said. I brought our dirty dishes to the kitchen and loaded the dishwasher. "Can I go up to the garage apartment when we're done? I'd like to grab some of my vintage summer clothes, maybe look through Mom's things. It's been so long."

Aunt Fee took a key from her kitchen drawer. "Keep it while you're home. I'm going out later, but it's the key to all my doors, so you can come back for Chakra Citrine before you leave."

"*You* lock your doors?"

"I do now. It's the twenty-first century. You can't be too careful. Even in Mystick Falls."

I thought of last night's murder with a shiver. "It's true but sad."

"And it's frightening."

"Hey, I'm a New Yorker; I'm always ready for the worst." Well, until I found a dead body in my childhood home, I amended in my head.

Half an hour later, from the apartment over Aunt Fiona's garage, I heard the crunch of gravel in the drive as she left. I hadn't told her that the apartment had no electricity, because I didn't want to make her late for her appointment. I simply left the door open at the top of the stairs to let in the sun.

Normally, I wouldn't think twice about it, but under the murderous circumstances, I slipped my pepper spray from my purse into my pocket . . . in Mystick Falls, no less.

I broke open a preservation box of my mother's clothes, knowing it was time, and in a way, I felt her presence as I did.

I hadn't realized that her taste in clothes mimicked Sherry's. Wispy and whimsical. I needed more whimsy in my life, I thought. I could take a lesson from them.

A whiff of White Shoulders, my mom's favorite perfume, made me look up. "Mom?"

No, of course not. Maybe that was her way of telling me she agreed with me. "Okay," I said. "I understand. More whimsy for Madeira."

I wrapped a trapeze dress—that I clearly remembered her wearing—around my neck like a shawl and held it to my face, my eyes closed as I tried for another vision, a peek at my mother *alive again*, the way I'd seen the illusory bride in the Vancortland wedding gown, but nothing happened. Yet I sensed Mom behind me, looking over my shoulder.

One way or another, I wasn't alone, and I took comfort in that.

I opened box after box and still no vision of Mom.

Disappointed, sleepy, full of cheesecake, and yearning for a glimpse of the past, I sipped the iced tea I'd brought up with me and sat beside the vintage treasures my father didn't know I owned. I'd better give him a heads-up when I decided to wear one of my mother's outfits. He thinks I gave them to charity, and I did. I donated them to the Madeira Cutler Vintage Clothing Foundation.

I'd been keeping them here at Aunt Fiona's with two antique Singer sewing machines and every other vintage outfit I'd bought over the years. Truth was, I'd probably mailed her a box a month, but only because I'd been *very* choosy.

Sorting through an old sewing machine drawer, a favorite pastime, I found bobbins, a thimble in a tiny glass shoe, wooden spools of thread, assorted needles, bone crochet hooks, a zipper foot, a strawberry pincushion, a bodkin for running ribbon through lace, and a darning egg.

I stopped stirring the delightful treasures when I heard a stair creak, a second . . . a third . . . footsteps coming slowly and ominously close to the landing. I put the drawer down.

Any of our neighbors would have called to Aunt Fiona or started talking halfway up the stairs.

This was no neighbor.

I slipped the mace from my pocket and crawled behind a sewing machine not far from the door, but I had to shade my eyes from the sun to see.

Quick as a sneak, a man appeared on the landing, gun raised.

Ten

In difficult times fashion is always outrageous.
—ELSA SCHIAPARELLI

The gunman hadn't spotted me. I elbowed the sewing machine so he'd look my way, and the minute he did, I maced him. A perfect stream for a dead hit, square between the eyes.

His gun clattered to the floor.

He followed it down.

His scream terrified me, until my wits returned, and then I was really terrified, because I recognized his voice.

Macing an assailant gave you time to run, and run I did, straight to the bathroom for a cool, wet towel.

Laboring to take a breath, the Wiener sat on the landing, his beefy hands covering his closed, swelling eyes. They must burn like hell. The ugly burgundy blotches growing by the second around his hands told the tale.

He couldn't see me, so I could jump over him and run, but he'd figure out who maced him, eventually, if not when he talked to Fiona.

On the other hand, would he want to admit that he'd been maced?

I fought to remove his hands from his face and failed, but managed to wedge the dripping cloth beneath them.

Surprised, he embraced the cooling balm. "Thank you," he said, congested and coughing up a lung. "Did you see who"—hack, hack, fur ball, hack—"did this to me?"

I huffed. "Aren't you supposed to announce yourself when you aim a gun into a private residence?"

My victim swore beneath his breath, the wet hand towel muffling his exact words, but I knew that at least three of them weren't "duck."

"I wasn't holding a gun," he muttered, searching the landing with his free hand, the other plastering the towel to his face. He found his weapon and opened his palm for me to see it.

"A trigger nozzle for a hose," he said, stating the obvious. "Pure bluff. I grabbed it off the newel post at the base of the stairs. Attorney Sullivan wasn't home, and the open door made me suspicious. There've been a few robberies in the neighborhood lately." He sighed. "Madeira Cutler, experience tells me that you're my assailant."

I said nothing.

"You might as well admit it."

"I come from *New York*!" I raised my voice in my own defense, my hands fisted, my fight-or-flight response deeply ingrained in the moment.

Werner stood as well, like a sloppy drunk, disoriented, stumbling, and reaching blindly. If he fell on me, he'd crush me; he was that big.

I shouldn't give him any ideas. I took another step back. "We've had enough murder in Mystick Falls," I said. "I'm outta here."

"Madeira, wait. I can't see. You have the advantage.

Don't go. I'm not angry. I've come to expect a certain . . . aggravation . . . around you."

"Aggravation?"

"Like fingernails across a chalkboard," he said, "slicing deep into my flesh."

"I see."

"May I have another cold cloth? The pepper spray warmed this one."

"I don't know where to find another. Let me refresh that one."

When he handed it to me, I saw the area around his eyes for the first time and remembered what *type* of spray I'd bought last fall. A burst of hysterical laughter escaped before I could clamp my lips together and cut off the sound.

"What?" he asked, stumbling over the threshold into the apartment, attempting to feel his way around the room.

"Stop!" I shouted.

He did. "Why?"

"Because the place is full of valuable vintage clothing and I don't want you to get blue dye on any of it."

The Wiener's jaw fell open. He turned to the wall he'd been using as a guide, fell slowly forward, bowed his head, and banged it. "Why? Why? Why?" A whack for every "why."

"It's a nice *electric* blue," I said, which didn't help at all.

The Wiener growled—well, he made a sound somewhere between a growl and a whimper. "The last time I saw a perp come in with a face this color, he stayed blue for three days."

"Blue perps *are* supposed to be easier for the cops to find."

"Police, not cops! Madeira, you were born to be the thorn in my side."

"*The?* You mean I'm your only thorn?"

"Yeah. Snort. My one and only."

"Why, thank you, Lytton. I'm honored. I think your perp probably stayed blue because he didn't bathe. There's a shower up here. Do you want to try giving your face a soapy wash beneath a stream of cool water?"

He relaxed and nodded at the wall. "I'd be eternally grateful."

Maybe I'd sprayed him for a bit too long?

"Which way to the shower? Walking blue-faced into the station," he muttered, "would be worse than overcoming the name Wiener for half my life."

Heat rose up my neck and burned my cheeks—poetic justice at its finest—so I took the Wiener by the hand and led him toward the bathroom, making a wide detour around my treasures.

In the tiny afterthought of a bathroom, too intimate by far, the Wiener suddenly seemed taller and broader. I used his hand to pat the shower stall door and shut him inside the small room.

"Where's the light switch?" he called.

"There's no electricity," I yelled back, "but you're blind anyway."

I heard another "duck," some Wiener-meets-the-wall encounters, a clearly stubbed toe, and a few more "ducks" before the peaceful sound of running water.

Nick walked in. "Hey, ladybug."

Scrap! "What are you doing here?"

"Nice welcome. But I have news."

"What kind of news?" I whispered.

"I've got a lead on Jasmine. Our medical examiner went to school with the Mystick Falls med—"

"Shh. Shh. Let's go out to the stoop." I tried to push Nick out the door.

"Wait a minute," he said, taking me in his arms and forcing me to stop pushing him away. "You smell sweet, like . . ."

"Orange blossoms, honeysuckle, and sandalwood? It's Red, my perfume. You've got a great nose for a Fed."

He cupped my bottom. "You've got a great as—"

"Ask and you shall receive?"

"If you're offering, I'm asking."

He smelled good, too. Too good. "Are you wearing Ultraviolet Man?"

"Yep!"

Yum. I was a sucker for ambergris, so sensual and manly.

Nick pulled me close for a hot and hungry kiss. I fell into it without my own permission, yet every nerve in my body sang.

"Does this place have a bedroom?" he whispered against my lips.

"Mmm."

"Lead the way."

I opened my eyes. "The way?" Past the bathroom. Down, girl. Get a grip. I stepped back and tried not to inhale seduction. Also tried not to listen to my libido: More Nick, more Nick, my body sang. "In case you haven't noticed, we're in the off-again half of our relationship. You slept on my sofa bed last night. Didn't that give you a clue?"

"Ladybug, we're spending all this time together, and you're *so* hot, and I'm *so*—"

"Horny? In lust. Deep like?" I suggested.

"Attracted, physically, emotionally, and intellectually, so I thought we'd be on-again sooner rather than later."

My body said, "Yes!" My brain said, "Not *now*!"

I tried pushing. He tried pulling. My body ended up plastered to his. Have mercy. I stepped back. "Later," I said. "Now let's go outside. This is no time to be spontaneous."

"You like spontaneous. Isn't that what we're all about?"

"Maddie," the Wiener called. "I can't find a towel."

Nick stilled. "What the hell?"

I started toward the bathroom, but Nick passed me and went in.

I turned my back, so I wouldn't see anything wiener-like.

"Hey!" Werner shouted. "I'm naked in here."

"And colorful," Nick said. "Here's your towel."

After Nick came out, I opened my mouth to explain, but I didn't have to.

"Did you mace him?" he whispered, his shoulders shaking.

I nodded and firmed my lips. I am not proud. I am not amused. I am a lowly *thorn* who—at the end of the day—owes some loyalty to its personal puncture device.

I took a large sip of my tea to keep my lips occupied and unsmiling, but mirth tightened my throat. Restraint became difficult. I couldn't even swallow.

One look at Nick's grin, and I lost the fight, laughed, and spit tea in his face.

"Argh."

When Werner emerged from the bathroom, his face a nice pale blue, he found Nick wiping his own face with an old quilt square.

"What'd she do, mace you, too?" Werner asked.

"Iced tea," Nick said. "All over my libido."

That made the Wiener grin. "Nice to hear I'm not her only target."

"Hel-lo, I'm here. And I'm busy, in case you haven't noticed. Take your toxic testosterone, the both of you, and *go away.*"

"Busy?" Werner asked, eyeing the disarray of overflowing preservation boxes. "Busy doing what? Opening a branch of the Salvation Army?"

"Hey, mock all you want, but you'd be surprised at the prime vintage you can find at Sal's."

Nick furrowed his brows. "Why *do* you keep buying vintage and parking it here?"

"Instinct?" I suggested, not sure myself.

The Wiener gave us a double take, his surprise landing on me. "You paid *money* for this junk?"

"It's not junk. It's vintage."

My off-again . . . *forever* and my personal puncture device with a death wish gave each other a "women . . . can't ignore 'em, can't score without 'em" glance.

I wanted to smack them both for good measure. "See the shoes I'm wearing? They're Manolos."

"Is that like Rolos?" Werner asked.

"Consider that a freebie, Lytton, since I owe you one."

"Two. You owe me two. Big ones. Huge. Gargantuan."

"Whatever. This is you, now robin's-egg blue and half paid off. Live with it."

Lytton raised questioning hands Nick's way. "Why do I feel as if I've been screwed and not in a good way?"

"She's no lightweight. Don't mess with her. She'll pin you to the mat."

"My hero!" I snapped, trying without success to herd them out the door. "My point is that these shoes sold retail for eight hundred ninety-five dollars but I got them at a vintage shop in the Village for two hundred dollars."

"Mystic Village?" Nick asked.

"No, dinosaur brain. Greenwich Village, New York."

He picked up a one-piece, bell-bottom playsuit. "Psychedelic orange? You? A famous designer? Bought this?"

"Faline is the famous designer. I'm her head assistant. But that's not the point."

I picked up the Day-Glo orange playsuit and held it to my heart. "*This* was my mother's. I kept her clothes after

86

she died, and now they're vintage. Then I bought more vintage. Fiona helped me get everything preserved."

Nick raised a brow. "Preserved . . . until?"

"Hell if I know."

Werner looked interested. "So you'd sell them cheap, because they're secondhand?"

Sell them? "No, the laws of supply and demand apply especially well to quality vintage. The fewer number of designer outfits or accessories made, the more valuable they become. These shoes are a recent Blahnik design. I could have bought them uptown for full price, so they're a bad example."

"But besides you," Nick said. "Who buys vintage, honestly?"

"Vintage is hot. All the rage in New York. Old is new again. Remember that old Mark Twain quote? 'Clothes make the man' (or woman). 'Naked people have little or no influence on society.'"

"Naked people? Oh, I don't know about that," Nick said. "I like naked people . . . of the female persuasion."

Lytton looked thoughtful for a minute and shook his head. "Nope. Nope, I think you're wrong. Naked women within *my* society definitely influence me. I'd like to be influenced more often, as a matter of fact."

"Pervert."

"Go for it; I've been called worse." He wiped his eyes once more, the sympathy hound.

"What did you want to talk to Aunt Fiona about?" I asked Werner. "I could give her a message."

He shook his head. "I was in the area talking to your neighbors, so I thought I'd stop in, rather than call. I'll call her later."

"If it's about my sister, you can tell me."

"No, I can only discuss Fiona's client with Fiona."

I shivered. "It's bad news, isn't it?"

Eleven

Fashion anticipates, and elegance is a state of mind . . . a mirror of the time in which we live, a translation of the future, and should never be static.　　　—OLEG CASSINI

By accident on purpose, or so it seemed, both men followed me into Fiona's house. Frankly—and this is weird because of this new sixth sense I'm trying on for size—I think neither of them wanted to leave the other alone with me.

Now maybe I'm full of myself. I often am. But I was feeling a major pissing contest coming on, and I had no intention of getting downwind of either of them.

It was only a hunch, mind you, but men were such easy reads. Not too many brain cells to muck up the works.

I turned on them. "Why are you following me?"

Werner stopped and Nick inched around him. "We're protecting you," Nick said. "We're law enforcement officers."

"Oh, so you *know* that you're both on the same side?"

They pretended they didn't catch my "tone" and followed me to the box with the litter of kittens, where they visibly relaxed.

"What?" I said. "You think you can take them?"

Okay, so I couldn't help myself. I'd worked in an industry ruled by men and a rare few big female cats. The rest of us were perceived as Barbies: right shape but nothing between the ears. I could be a formidable *biotch* for fun, sport, or sheer survival.

I'd won the gold in a particularly "cutting" triathlon once. Earned me a place with the cats. My signature talent: ball blasting, gonad gutting, cojon clipping; you get the picture. Sure, I'd toned it down for Mystic, but I got the power, baby.

I handed Nick the kitten and squeaked the mouse.

Chakra screamed.

The house shook.

Nick dropped her.

Werner caught her.

"Lytton! My hero!"

"Uh, you wanna go back to third grade and say that?"

I took my baby from the Wiener's arms. "Poor little Chakra Citrine, you scared Mommy."

Having lost the pissing contest, Nick frowned. "She's got vocal cords that exceed the sound barrier."

"It's not like she clawed you. You could have held on."

Werner scratched Chakra behind an ear. "Did she sound like she might have screamed 'Maddie'?" he asked.

Nick scoffed.

"Yes! You heard it, too. Isn't it wild? She can say my name. She's gonna be our guard cat and sleep on my bed." I gave Nick a pointed look, since, at the moment, he wasn't allowed on that piece of furniture.

Werner caught the exchange and turned his chuckle into a cough.

Before they could come to blows, I locked Aunt Fiona's house, and we each got into our separate cars. The dopes followed me until I turned into Mrs. Sweet's driveway. I parked and called Nick's cell.

ANNETTE BLAIR

"Jaconetti here."

"Jaconetti, you have info on the autopsy?"

"Yes and no. It's not finished. Something about a tox screen, but the Fed ME is going to let me know when he gets the report."

"A tox screen? Does that mean they suspect poisoning?"

"Could be."

"Poisoning and strangling? Why bother?" I asked. "Dead is dead."

"The tox screen may be routine, then again, maybe there were two attempts and only one success. It's also conceivable," Nick continued, "that if something toxic skewed or slowed Jasmine's instincts, she might not have been able to fight her strangler. Seems as if Jasmine ticked off half the town. Last night, they wanted to lynch her."

"Nick, that was like Sherry saying she wanted to kill her, a figure of speech."

"Jasmine was a raptor, who cut at least one local way deeper than the rest. Listen, I'm giving you her home address, almost against my better judgment, but I know you. I know that you have to be working on fixing this for your sister, under controlled conditions, or you'll run amuck."

"Thanks."

"Yeah, well, my ego's still a little bruised from your recent gentle handling. Anyway, I'd rather set you on a safe course than let you hurt an innocent bystander."

I opened my mouth to argue, but I'd be stupid to further alienate my personal information system.

Nick appeared to expect me to blow, because he sighed, as if with relief, after a minute. "Remember that this is a murder investigation, as in somebody died. Dead is forever, ladybug. Screw the word games. I want you safe. Hell, I just want you. Always have, Mad. Don't do anything stupid."

Oy, he was Madeira-mocking and I was getting the

warm fuzzies over it, darned close to flipping that relationship switch to on-again.

He cleared his throat. "I ran the Updikes through the system. No red flags, so go see what you can find. I know that's what you want to do. But, Mad, any other jaunts you feel like taking for the cause, you pass by me. Not for permission," he quickly added, "for backup. Got it?"

"Got it. And, Nick, thanks for watching my back."

"Well . . . I watch your front a lot, too." Husky voice, evocative tone, filled with tingly implications.

Seduction via cell phone. Who knew I'd be susceptible. Focus, Madeira, I told myself. "The address?"

"It's Two-two-seven Updike Circle, Wickford, Rhode Island."

I wrote it on the back of the guest list. "The Updikes live on Updike Circle?"

"Wickford used to be called Updike's Newtown. I'm guessing they're descendants."

"You'd think she would have been wearing real couture."

"What?"

"Never mind. Werner probably got the address from Deborah and gave Jasmine's family the news last night. I might go take a look around, offer my condolences."

"Mad, don't forget what I said."

"Which part?"

"All of it. Stay out of trouble."

"Some good-bye," I said, putting my phone away. With any luck, Wickford was as small and gossipy as Mystick Falls. Maybe I'd be better off pretending I didn't know Jasmine was dead. What would be the harm?

Scrap! If the police suspected two attempts on Jasmine's life, they wouldn't let Sherry off the hook, even if they did find another suspect.

I sighed and realized I was still sitting in the Sweets'

driveway. I took a few calming breaths before I got out of the car.

The Sweet house, two doors down from ours, had been handed down for generations; the current owners, however, had an unfortunate taste in colors. While Day-Glo orange looked great on a sixties playsuit, it did not suit a Victorian Lady.

Lucky for the neighborhood, old Oscar at the hardware store told young Mrs. Sweet that they were out of teal for the trim that day, and she settled on the pale peach he'd "just" put on sale. It toned down the shock factor and made the viewer only slightly queasy.

There are two Mrs. Sweets. Young Mrs. Sweet, only eighty, attended our party the other night. She rarely says an unkind word, except for that unfortunate incident at the funeral parlor when she'd publicly berated Mr. Sweet—comfortably ensconced in his brass casket—for leaving her to care for his ornery old mother, alone.

Old Mrs. Sweet, her mother-in-law, usually managed to hide her control-freak crunchy middle beneath a layer of I-only-want-to-please-you marshmallow cream. Either way, as a child I'd once imagined whacking the old lady with a broom. My guilt had passed at her son's funeral, however, because I understood her daughter-in-law's rage so well.

Both Mrs. Sweets had been extremely kind to us when Mom died. They cooked, baked, and showed up at most of our school plays and sports games, not to mention graduations, every one. If you multiply that by the four Cutler children, the sum is a hefty time investment.

It was nice to know that someone had been cheering or applauding when my father was off earning a living for us, and my mother was across the river in Elm Grove Cemetery.

Today, like many childhood days, I heard the two of them arguing before I rang the doorbell.

Young Mrs. Sweet answered. "Lordy me, Madeira, but Dolly's in a snit. Her hundred and third birthday party this afternoon with the governor, no less, and she refuses to wear her best dress."

I followed the daughter-in-law into old Mrs. Sweet's room. "Happy birthday, Dolly, dear. Why won't you wear your best dress?"

The centenarian pouted. "Madeira, you design clothes, so you'll understand about favorite dresses. I'm saving it for a special occasion."

The younger indicated the older behind her back with a jerky, exhibit-A, palm-out motion that roughly translated to: "Dead idiot walking."

At a hundred and three, Dolly must realize that her next special occasion would probably be her funeral, I thought, but wouldn't say. "I'll tell you what, dear. Wear your best dress today, and tomorrow I'll come back and measure you for a Madeira Cutler designer original. I'll make you a new best dress and you can pick whatever design you want. I'll even take you to select the fabric."

"Ethel," Dolly Sweet said. "Give me my best dress."

"Well, hurry, Momma. We have to leave in three minutes."

That's my work done for the day. I'd laid the groundwork for gossip over measurements and dress designs. "Tomorrow morning, then?" I confirmed.

"Come early, Madeira," young Mrs. Sweet suggested, "and we'll have tea first, like the old days."

"And cherry pie," old Mrs. Sweet added. She'd made us hundreds when we were growing up.

"Sherry thought you named the pies after her, you know."

Sweet the older winked. "Well, of course she did, dear, because I told her so."

I kissed them each on the cheek. "Oh, before I go,

Ethel. Did you notice anyone else go missing from the party last night, besides Sherry and Jasmine?"

"I saw Deborah go to the powder room, and you, Nick, your father, and Eve disappeared for a while, of course."

"Family reunion in the taproom," I said, wishing Sherry had been with us. "Thanks."

"Did you know?" old Mrs. Sweet said as I turned to go. "They think that girl might have been poisoned, too."

"I heard. How did you?"

"Tunney the butcher told me."

Son of a stitch. Clearly I'd gone to the wrong source.

Old Mrs. Sweet firmed her jaw. "And they say . . . she was in the family way."

"Pregnant? Jasmine was pregnant?" My stomach roiled. Who was the father?

And what the holy Harrods had Sherry told Justin to keep secret?

Twelve

In order to be irreplaceable one must always be different.
—COCO CHANEL

I drove the back roads from Mystic to Rhode Island and on to Wickford. Wildflower borders, old cottages with wedding-cake trim, manicured yards, and a farm with a colt nuzzling its mother all served to ease my anxiety and help me think straight.

All I could do for my sister was search for clues in the form of secrets, means, motives, or missing links to any of them, and to do that, I needed to keep a level head.

In Wickford, after a short stint on a secondary highway, I found number two-two-seven.

In a cul-de-sac, Wickford Cove surrounding it, Jasmine's home, a large architectural masterpiece, shed its paint in curls, grew its lawn to the knees, its shrubs like flailing aliens, and held its crooked shutters by disappearing hinges.

I turned in the cul-de-sac and parked in front of the house next door, where a woman knelt weeding the highly colorful flower bed along the wire fence separating her property from the Updikes'.

When I got out of the car, she stopped, straightened, and looked at me expectantly.

"Hello," I said. "Could you help me? I think I'm lost."

She stood and removed her gardening gloves. "If I can."

"I'm looking for the Updikes, Jasmine in particular."

No expression revealed any knowledge of Jasmine's fate. In fact, the woman smiled. "You're not as lost as you think. The Updikes live next door. Descended from the founding family, though not so uppity as I hear they used to be. I wouldn't know. I've never met them."

Jasmine's *very* old money must have run out, which accounted for her fake couture. "Thank you, I'll just go see if she's home."

My informant nodded and watched me take the sidewalk to the Updikes' porch steps, the giant man-eating shrubs impeding her view after that.

I rang the doorbell and realized how awkward this could be. What would I say? As usual, I'd acted first and now I thought, What the Hermès am I doing here?

A shabby-chic nurse answered the door, though her uniform tended more toward the desperate. Polyester double knit, a ridiculed retro. Very hard times.

"Can I help you?" she asked.

"Yes, I'm in town for business and I'm looking for Jasmine; she's an old college friend." Of Justin's, I finished in my mind, justifying the half-truth.

The nurse stepped back with no sign of sadness or surprise. "Do come in."

She led me to a small personal sitting room, while she held her uniform together at its side zipper. "I'm afraid you've missed her. She's off on another of her jaunts. I'm Mildred Updike, Jasmine's mother."

"I'm sorry to hear she's not here," I said, taken by surprise. She didn't know her daughter was dead, never mind that she'd been murdered. "Do you have any idea where she went?" I asked, feeling like a fool.

"She's off to see a college boyfriend, an old flame."

A flame? "I'm sorry I missed her. Will she be long? Can I wait?"

"She's on holiday, actually, and I have to leave for work soon, if I can ever get this zipper to cooperate."

"Let me see if I can help. I'm a seamstress," or I was, once, sort of. I tugged with no luck. "No, sorry. That's a vintage metal zipper and when those teeth are bent, they're gone, unless you have a hammer, and even that's dicey. I can give you a temporary fix if you get me a needle and white thread." I wanted a minute to check out the pictures scattered about the room.

As Jasmine's mother ran upstairs, I scanned the faces in the photographs hoping to find one of Jasmine and Justin—fat chance—but, lookee here, I did find one of Mildred Updike and Deborah Vancortland—major surprise. Friends arm in arm at a garden party in their late teens or early twenties.

Hmm. If Jasmine and Justin met in college, it might not have been by accident. It could have been planned by their matchmaking mothers, or by Mildred, herself, so Jasmine could catch herself a rich fix for the family fortune.

And why had no one told her yet about Jasmine's death? Surely Deborah had given Werner this address. Or better yet, why hadn't Deborah called Jasmine's mother herself if they were once such good friends?

Mildred Updike returned with a needle and thread so I could sew her into her uniform. "I'd say this skirt has served you well."

"Does it show? It's lasted forever. I'm behind on my laundry, but I figure the old lady I'm taking care of today won't know the difference."

"Fabrics are my business. Nobody else would notice.

Raise your arm so I can have some room to work. Thanks."

I slipped a hand beneath her skirt at the waist to get a grip on the zipper opening and hold the fabric together from the inside while I stitched it closed.

White spots danced before my eyes and when I opened them, Mildred had changed location and age.

A younger Mildred, wearing the same outfit, but new, with pricier shoes, crossed a luxurious sitting room to enter a gilded bedroom.

Deborah Vancortland, thirty years younger herself, lay tucked up like a queen in satin bedclothes, her face bright and excited. "Did you get it?"

Mildred tossed a sheet of paper on the bed. "I could lose my job for signing that."

Deborah grabbed the sheet, read it, and grinned. "Perfect."

A man shouted Deborah's name—Cort, out of breath, his footsteps on the stairs coming closer. At the sound of his voice, Deborah wilted, and moaned, and burst into tears, which is how Cort found her, Mildred's document pressed to a heart that suddenly seemed broken.

A doorbell brought me swirling back, and I found myself focused on Mildred Updike in the present, in her sitting room.

Poor woman didn't know I'd zoned. Another vision I couldn't decipher, but at least I'd recognized the players this time. I had goose bumps but quickly finished fixing Mildred's zipper.

"Excuse me while I get the door," she said. "I never have company."

When she disappeared, I slipped the picture of her and Deborah from its frame and turned it over. Scrawled on the back was "Deborah Knight and Mildred Saunders"—must be their maiden names—and "Day before coming-out ball."

I heard voices, put the picture back in its frame, and

had time to turn and face Werner—oy!—as Mrs. Updike ushered him in. She introduced me as a family friend, and Werner and I both pretended we didn't know each other.

The ice in his look told me I was in trouble, and I didn't doubt it for a minute. "Well," I said. "You have a guest. I'll drop by another time."

"No, stay. Miss Cutler, is it?" Werner asked. "Mrs. Updike could probably use a friend. Mrs. Updike, would you care to sit?" he asked.

"No," she said, bracing herself. "Why?"

Werner shook his head in regret. "Can you identify the woman in this photo?"

"Of course. That's my daughter, Jasmine, with Justin Vancortland, the young man she went to visit."

"In that case, I'm very sorry to bring you this news, but your daughter was killed last night."

"Jasmine?" The question revealed a veneer of shock but the woman took the news with a stoic lack of emotion, which might be her way. "Wild, that girl," she said, not really seeing us. "Never could stay out of trouble. Always wanted more than she could have. Reminded me of somebody else I knew once."

She glanced at the picture of her and Deborah, her gaze flying to me. With a raised chin, she reached out and straightened the photo.

Great, my first attempt at snooping and I move something in the home of an obsessive-compulsive . . . though her house and clothes didn't reveal the quirk.

Considering my recent "vision" of her and her glance toward the picture, I wondered if she meant that Jasmine reminded her of Deborah.

Werner opened his notebook. "Did your daughter have any enemies, Mrs. Updike?"

"A beautiful girl always has enemies," she said, "but no more than the usual."

"What you mean," I said, "is that she was so attractive that other girls' boyfriends tended to *gravitate* in her direction, and the girls blamed Jasmine?"

The woman gave a half nod.

Werner and I exchanged quick glances.

"I couldn't keep her in money," Mildred said, resentment in her tone. "She loved men, and parties, and fine things, but I had to fight to get her to work for them." Mildred rubbed her arms against a phantom chill. "Sometimes the easy way can lead to trouble," she said.

Werner cleared his throat and took notes. "Mrs. Updike, can you name any of the girls whose boyfriends strayed Jasmine's way?"

Mildred named nearly a dozen girls, but my sister Sherry wasn't among them. So Jasmine's behavior was a way of life, a slight Sherry shouldn't take personally. Cold consolation for a murder suspect.

Why had Werner said that Jasmine had been killed, not strangled? And for pity's sake, why didn't Jasmine's mother care how her daughter died? Unless she was in shock, and I didn't recognize the signs.

Were the Mrs. Sweets correct about a pregnancy? Maybe not. Maybe that's why Werner didn't mention it.

If there was a pregnancy, Justin *couldn't* be the biological father, I hoped, for Sherry's sake. But I didn't doubt that Jasmine had been cold enough to try to pin fatherhood on Justin like a life sentence.

Werner looked up from his notes. "This might be redundant after recent revelations, Mrs. Updike, but was Jasmine dating anyone special?"

"No one in particular. How did she die?"

The question should have come sooner. And where was her disbelief? Didn't disbelief normally come before acceptance?

Plus, she knew Deborah, so she must have known about Justin. "Where did she go on holiday and with whom?" I asked.

"I'll ask the questions, Ms. Cutler."

Oops. "Yes, Detective."

"You really should sit down, Mrs. Updike," Werner said, waiting for her to do so before he explained that Jasmine had been murdered, though he never used the word "strangled."

Mrs. Updike grasped her throat. "My poor baby."

Bit tardy for the baby bit, especially after the playgirl revelation, and okay, the throat thing seemed like more than a coincidence, but people did that.

Werner noted it, too. I saw it in his expression as he took to examining the room at large.

In one way, I wished I could hand him the picture of Mildred and Deborah. In another way, I wanted to figure out the relationship on my own.

I wondered why and realized that I wanted to be the one to save my sister.

"Excuse me," Werner said. At the sound of footsteps on the porch, he went into the foyer.

He came back with the officers who'd searched our house—was it just last night?—and a team of Rhode Island officers.

"I know this is a bad time to intrude, Mrs. Updike, but I have a search warrant," Werner said, producing it. "We're looking for anything we can find that might lead us to your daughter's killer.

"Start in the victim's bedroom," he told his men. "Mrs. Updike?"

She jumped as if surprised he was there. "Oh, third floor. The attic. It's wide open and all hers."

"I'll be up in a minute," he told the officers before

returning his attention to the dry-eyed mother. "We'll have to hold your daughter until the medical examiner completes her report."

"How will I know when to make arrangements?"

"You can make arrangements anytime." Werner eyed her like a bug under glass. "But you can't hold the funeral until you have the—until Ms. Updike is released."

He turned to me and I felt the temperature drop. "Ms. Cutler, I'd like to question you further. Wait for me outside, please. I'm sure Mrs. Updike would prefer to be alone with her thoughts right now."

"Maybe I should stay with her for a while. She's had such a shock."

She looked at the picture I'd moved and her eyes went hard. "My neighbor will look after me. We're great friends."

Werner accompanied me to the foyer.

"Am *I* under suspicion?" I whispered.

"Wait for me," he repeated beneath his breath as he opened the door and indicated my path through it.

I went but I wasn't happy about it.

Besides my car, there were now squad cars from two states and Werner's unmarked car parked outside.

The Updike house centered three mansions on the dead-end circle. The mansion on one side had been turned into a school, now closed. On the other, the neighbor who admitted that she didn't know the Updikes.

Why had Mildred Updike lied about knowing her neighbor? To get me the heck out?

I walked that cul-de-sac in an endless circle for the better part of forty minutes, making notes and trying to make sense of every weird detail, including my newest vision, before Werner and the officers emerged.

As I approached from the far side of the street, Werner spoke to his men. One of them got in Werner's car and drove it away. The squad cars followed.

Uh-oh.

When I got to him, his eyes hard and promising retribution, Warner opened his hand my way with a gimme motion. "Your keys, please?"

Scrap! "I'm not too drunk to drive."

"I'm driving. We need to talk."

"Fine!" I slammed them into his hand.

"Ouch!" He removed the keys, and I saw that the point of my scissors charm had punctured his palm.

He looked at the droplet of blood and didn't seem the least surprised.

I shrugged. "At least it wasn't a thorn."

"Oh, yes, it was." Shaking his head, he turned into a gentleman and tried to help me into my passenger seat.

"I didn't do it on purpose, and be careful not to get blood on my dress. This fabric is expensive."

He looked at his palm, then at my dress.

"Don't even think about it," I said.

On his way around the front of the car, he wiped his hand with his handkerchief.

Like a sardine in my driver's seat, he sat knees to chin, until he grunted and rolled back the seat.

I'm afraid I let a giggle escape.

Werner gave me the withering look I'd come to expect.

"Can I help it if you're taller? I'm not short but you're a giant."

He quirked a suggestive brow.

"Are you coming on to me? Because that might be against the law, since my sister is your prime suspect."

"You've got a hell of an ego, Cutler. I was silently intimating that you should have called me 'Giant' instead of 'Wiener.'"

"Oh." I played with the beading on my bag. "You know, you've really gotta let that go."

He whipped his gaze my way. "I tell myself that at least

once a week, right after somebody reminds me. 'Hey honey, you remember the Wiener? Want fries with that Wiener? Or ketchup, or onions, or mustard?' "

I slapped a hand over my mouth. No wonder I was so good at macho-mocking. I'd started really young. I wondered if it ever came up in the locker room—

Oy, blocking the visual of that pun!

Lytton sighed, started my car, and pulled away from the curb. I looked back at the Updike house. Jasmine's mother stepped away from an attic window and let the curtain fall.

"Mrs. Updike now knows that you and I must have known each other before we 'met' inside," I said.

"Good. There's something she's not telling us. Maybe if she thinks we were pulling some kind of sting op, she'll be more cooperative the next time I visit. Alone," he stressed. "Without you, unless you want me to charge you with obstruction of justice."

"How did you get the blue off your face so fast?"

"Changing the subject won't help. We'll get back to it, eventually. I found an effective face scrub."

"In women's facials?"

"Or I could haul you in now for interfering with a murder investigation."

"Touché."

His expression held a mix of anger and respect. "Why were you there, and what did she tell you before I arrived?"

"Why hadn't someone already told her about Jasmine?"

"No address. We had to run her through the system."

The FBI could do it faster, I thought. "But Deborah, Mrs. Vancortland, I mean—"

"Didn't know her address."

Weird, or a lie. Sure, Deborah and Mildred *might* have lost touch, but something—my new sixth sense, perhaps—

told me that it was more likely that Deborah didn't want the police near her old friend.

Werner looked at me, expecting an answer.

"I went because I wanted to find out why Jasmine came to Mystic looking for Justin. If she hadn't, my sister wouldn't be the prime suspect in a murder case."

Werner did a double take. "Precisely."

"I didn't mean it that way!"

"Again, what did the Updike woman tell you before I got there? You're not obstructing if you share what you know with the police."

I made a pretense of sighing so he'd think he won a hard battle, but truthfully I was dying to tell him. "There's a picture of Mrs. Updike and Deborah Vancortland in the Updike sitting room, so if Justin and Jasmine met at college, it probably wasn't by accident. Could be, given the state of the Updike house, that Mildred wanted Jasmine to marry up."

"Which has no bearing on the case," Werner said.

"It would if Deborah didn't think Jasmine was good enough for Justin."

"Where have you been?" Werner asked. "Deborah Vancortland adored Jasmine Updike."

"Have you seen Deborah shed one tear? You know the one thing I learned living in New York and working in the fashion industry?"

"Not to call people names, I hope."

"No, to survive, I actually had to learn to do *that* better."

Werner grunted in disbelief.

"I did learn two things. One: Let go of the past. Two: Life is a matter of straight pins, light filters, packaging, and hype. Nothing is as it appears."

Thirteen

When in doubt, wear red.
—BILL BLASS

Sherry came home late that afternoon no longer appearing innocent. A little grass on her shoes, a trail of beach sand, French twist hanging to her shoulders, and a self-conscious sprint to the stairs told the tale.

I stepped from the ladies' parlor, Sherry yipped in surprise, and the kitten screamed.

"Maddie!" Sherry held a hand to her heart. "You scared the hell out of me, and so did wonder kitty here." She reached over to pet my new baby, relaxing again into the comfort of my arms. "Yours?"

I nodded. "Chakra Citrine Cutler, a watch cat from Fiona. Go on up before somebody sees you."

"Dad?" She looked down at herself and ran.

I followed.

In her bathroom, I put Chakra on the floor to further investigate her new home. Then I leaned against the door and crossed my arms.

Sherry grabbed the hem of her white blouse and stopped. "What? Are you gonna watch me get into the tub?"

"Afraid I'll see the love bites?"

"Shut! Up! Mad!" That was a repeat of her first complete sentence, a family joke quoted regularly.

I took her black jacket off a hook and put it on a hanger. "What are you wearing to dinner at Deborah's?"

"My black—"

"No, Cherry Pie. You've worn enough black. Time to be a scarlet woman. Be bold. Shout your innocence to the world. Well, to Deborah Vancortland, at least."

Sherry let her veneer of bravery fall away as she threw herself into my arms.

Relief swept through me. My hard plastic doll had come to life again. Our bond, forged after the loss of our mother, would hopefully grow stronger in the wake of this nightmare.

I'd seen Sherry through every milestone, toddler to teen to teacher. But being a murder suspect was the biggest hurdle she'd ever encountered and hardly something that I could kiss better.

The floodgates opened and between us we released a waterfall of fear, confusion, and for my part: guilt for disliking Jasmine so intensely. Whatever our combined emotions, and there were plenty, I needed a good cry as much as Sherry did.

When we parted, Sherry wore a harder shell than the one she'd shed in tears. Scrap! A new sadness weighed me down as I offered her a tissue before I took one for myself.

Sherry may have firmed her spine, but if I planned to fix this, I needed to be stronger than her and smarter than the killer. Nothing a shot of tempered steel, and a boatload of luck, wouldn't provide.

I wondered if Aunt Fiona had a luck spell, if she worked spells at all. A witch, apparently. But spells? That question remained as yet unanswered.

Still, I'd always believed that we made our own luck. So be it. I cleared my throat. "What happened when you disappeared with Jasmine the night she died?"

Sherry tossed her tissue. "Jasmine went upstairs and I went outside."

"And?"

"And . . . nothing."

"You vanished?" I asked, being facetious.

"In a manner of speaking. Subject closed."

Vanished . . . in a manner of speaking.

How many ways could one vanish? In dreams, day or night. In . . . visions, I had recently learned. In music or the arts. In a feast for the senses—sex, alcohol, drugs.

Determined to force an answer, I stepped back, faced the question, and my sister, head on. But she looked so fragile with tear trails running through her peach blush, eyes like a raccoon—breakable, like fine porcelain—that I couldn't push her over the edge.

I couldn't *break* her, not when she needed to be strong enough to face Deborah this very night.

Whatever secret she and Justin were keeping, it couldn't be that bad, unless—No. No way. Impossible. Sherry and Justin had nothing to do with Jasmine's death. Of that I was certain.

Three hours later, I was still pondering ways to vanish when my father stopped his Volvo at a marble arch, guarded by twin lions and centered by gates too decadent to be heaven's. A proud sign read: Cortland House.

While I imagined shocking Deborah by painting the lions' lips and toenails red, a whirring, searching video camera from a pricey, albeit aging, burglar alarm system focused on us.

A hidden robot asked my father to identify himself, and after Dad did, a pair of gold filigreed gates began to part in clockwork approval, the reflection of the bright setting sun off the gilt temporarily blinding us.

As the gates opened, a central pair of kissing swans parted, breaking the heart made by their necks, and allowing us into a world where one *could* vanish.

Riding in the backseat, Sherry sat forward, probably looking for Justin.

We approached the monstrous waterfront structure with its glossy marble façade and tall, Gothic-arched diamond-paned windows that caught the setting sun in a sinister wink.

"Wooly knobby knits!" I said. "What the Hermès? Cortland House belongs in a horror movie." Despite a pastel flower garden, centered by an angel fountain, a rainbow in its mist.

I turned to Sherry. "Now, that's just trying too hard."

She actually smiled. "Justin's always been so embarrassed by it that in tenth grade, he told the whole class that his parents rented it for his birthday party. The day he got his trust fund, he bought a house downtown."

"We're poor in comparison," my father said, slowing, as if he'd rather turn the car around and forget the whole thing.

"Justin's not ashamed of *our* house, Dad. He feels more at home there than here."

I could see why. A third-world country could be fed for a week on the cost of gardening alone, as my sister Brandy would say. She believed that wealth should be shared with the needy, and I respected her for it.

Off to the sides, spiral sculptured shrubs and weeping cherry trees lived beside pristine gardens in symmetrical designs and showy colors.

As we approached the front door, and the uniformed valet waiting to park our car, I half expected my father to quote from Don Quixote about tilting at windmills as he charged through the portico and kept going. But to my surprise, he stopped, without quote, for Sherry's sake, I'm sure.

Looking embarrassed to have the car door opened for him, Dad cleared his throat as he handed the valet his keys. "Please tell the Vancortlands that their hapless future relatives have arrived."

"Dad!" I was both appalled and amused, but Sherry held her stomach as if she might be sick.

"You look spectacular," I told her. "More than good enough for this place. A real stunner, and the gown looks great, too." I'd talked her into wearing my new red, floor-length Versace with a basket-weave diamond-shaped bodice and basket-weave waist.

She didn't carry a bag. Sometimes, I couldn't believe she was my sister. But she wore my classy red pumps with a self-weave of their own and heels that left rosette imprints—Louboutin's self-proclaimed "follow me" shoes.

I wore a nineties Armani spiderweb gown, black with the web centered at the V neck, growing wider as it flowed to the hem. Originally see-through, I wore it over a slip I'd designed of imported gray liquid lamé. I stood tall in my black patent Yves Saint Laurents with diamond-studded heels and cross straps, and I loved my small sculptured bracelet bag by Will Hardy.

All in all, our clothes, if not our mind-sets and person-alities, fit the decor.

A maid waited at the door. "The family will be right down," she said. "Let me show you to the parlor."

We crossed a grand foyer, its floor worked in a French royal-blue-and-gold mosaic design. I pulled Sherry and my father close, one on each arm. "I'm surprised Deborah didn't have the gold fleur-de-lis replaced with dollar signs."

"Deborah, Cort, Justin!" my father called, greeting

them too loudly to be subtle as he tried to cover my catty remark.

Justin took Sherry on his arm, the red-faced apology for his gaudy home in his expression giving way to his appreciation of her beauty.

Deborah's mansion screamed "money and plenty," but it bypassed confidence to achieve a level of . . . swagger.

She gave us a quick tour of the main floor whether we wanted one or not. But I wanted to see it all, in my quest for a painting of the mysterious illusory bride.

I nodded, smiled, and made the appropriate—I hoped—sound of appreciation at the colorful Tiffany glass in the floral-scape windows. I wowed appropriately at the ornate fireplaces, one walnut-carved, one of Italian marble in claret with honey veins, another of imported Dutch tiles, yada yada.

A fireplace in every room. So what? We had a center chimney colonial with fireplaces off of it and another in the taproom. Some of them even worked.

Lace made by blind Belgian nuns, I thought, looking around, wishing Eve were here to see this.

Nick appeared at my side before I remembered Justin's morning invite—what a full day—and the prospect of the evening improved. In any stage of our relationship, taking Nick Jaconetti's arm sent a rush of pride and warmth through me. A shiver of lust, too, especially when he looked at me with that twinkle of appreciation and invitation.

Deborah cleared her throat, her look focused on us.

Nick and I were so busy flirting, we weren't paying attention to *her*. Properly chastised, we gave her our full concentration, though Nick's hands had an agenda of their own. Mmm.

Deborah referred to her house as a cottage, a clear ploy to have someone correct her.

Nick obliged—he was so full of it—but Deborah accepted his patronizing comment as her due.

Her hard-eyed "thank you" said, "You bet your ass it's more than a cottage. And her snide sidelong look at Sherry added a silent, "More than *you* deserve."

My protective big-sister instincts went into overdrive and I knew I'd give Deborah what *she* deserved for looking down her nose at Sherry, first shot I got.

Fourteen

We must never confuse elegance with snobbery.
—YVES SAINT LAURENT

During predinner drinks and hors d'oeuvres in the huge, opulent, and "intimate" east parlor, Deborah gave us the stats on the French ormolu eight-day clock, the Lalique chandelier, and all three Rodin bronzes.

Clearly, this was the French room. Come to think of it, each room had some kind of theme. I wondered where they kept the phantom bride's room. Because my vision could very well have taken place in *this* castle.

I have to admit that I fell for an inkwell, of all things, made from a pair of nineteenth-century glass slippers sitting on an ornate brass stand.

Nick winked and bowed like my very own prince, mocking me, when I gushed, but Deborah gave me a genuine smile for the first time. Then she clapped her hands for attention and signaled for us to sit.

Everyone but Cort obeyed.

"Now for our first surprise," she said, her Dior gown shimmering like gold dust.

Justin scrubbed at his face with both hands, his discomfort apparent, as maids carried in the tissue-stuffed wedding dress on a mahogany plank, or maybe it was an old door, and set it down like a stiff on the coffee table.

"Sherry, dearest," Deborah said, giving Cort a brusque "come and hurry" signal.

He stepped forward, chewing on his unlit cigar like it tasted of fresh lemons.

Deborah beamed and indicated the gown with both arms. "Behold the Vancortland wedding dress."

Gee, no trumpets?

"Sherry, the brides in our family have worn this gown to be married in for five generations, and I'm . . . proud . . . to have you represent the sixth."

Justin stood, raised my sister to her feet, and took her in his arms. "I'm proud of you, too."

Deborah's gaze wandered expectantly from Justin to Sherry and back.

Cort rubbed his hands together. "We're all proud. Let's eat."

"Wait," Deborah said. "Sherry, what do you think of the Vancortland wedding gown?"

The gauntlet had been tossed, and Justin had given no hint as to his thoughts on the subject of Sherry wearing the gown.

She left his arms and stepped closer to it. "I think it's classy, austere, and timeless." She stroked the fabric in the loving way she'd seen me do. "I'd be honored to wear it. Oh," she added, slapping her hand to her heart. "What a surprise!"

She'd botched the surprise act, by *ending* with it, but her appreciation came off as genuine.

"Mad," Sherry added. "Can you make it work for me?"

I joined her and examined the gown. "It looks big for you," I said, giving Deborah as good as she gave. "But I can take a few tucks." I turned to our hostess. "Deborah, it's genuinely exquisite. I've never seen anything so beautiful and I've seen the best. It's hand stitched," I said, fingering the peau de soie, "but so well done, it could be haute couture from Paris."

Deborah preened. "I did find something in a family journal that mentioned having it made in Paris."

"There you go." I'd managed to put her off guard for now. She could hardly make a scene about the altered design when Sherry walked down the aisle wearing it.

Sherry and I high-fived each other, and Deborah beamed as if we'd given her a personal compliment.

"I'm *still* hungry," Cort said, leading Sherry in to dinner. Justin took my arm, and my father took Deborah's, Nick bringing up the rear.

"Pardon the small dining room," Deborah said. "But we're all family. We save the state dining room for entertaining."

I counted twenty chairs around a table that served a family of three.

Justin avoided his mother's eye as he tossed a place card over his shoulder and sat beside Sherry.

Nick followed his example.

While a maid scrambled to retrieve the debris, Justin nodded toward the huge Majolica soup tureen in the center of the table. "What do you say, sweetheart? Think we could give baby Kelsey a bath in that?"

"Justin!" Deborah said. "You used to have impeccable manners."

"I'm outgrowing them?" He snapped his fingers. "Darn. My deepest apologies to everyone. I don't mean to ruin my mother's special evening. I mean, if a murder couldn't, why should I?"

He was right. The evening had proceeded as if Jasmine had never existed . . . or been murdered. Crass, really . . .

and wouldn't Deborah have a hissy if I said so. On the other hand, Justin just did, and she didn't get it.

Sherry raised her chin. "Justin, if you're upset about Jasmine, maybe we should postpone the wedding."

"Sweetie, I'd be upset no matter *who* got murdered at our engagement party."

Deborah raised a brow. "*Unofficial* engagement party."

"*Only* engagement party," Justin snapped. "And, Sherry, we're *not* postponing. As far as I'm concerned, we should elope."

Her face mottled, Deborah held her tongue . . . with white-knuckled fists, so to speak. Lips pursed, she nodded at a maid, and the salad promptly arrived.

Later, as we finished our Coquilles St. Jacques in relative silence, Deborah rose in a new bid for attention: "I have a second announcement."

"Of course you do," Cort said, indicating his need for a wine refill.

Deborah clapped like a child facing a toy store shopping spree. "Harry," she said, addressing my father, which surprised us all. "I've decided to save you the expense of the country club. We'll hold the wedding and reception here."

Cort emptied his newly filled glass in one tip.

Sherry gasped.

I gaped.

Nick rubbed his nose, his devilish dark eyes twinkling.

My father, ever the English lit professor, regarded Deborah as if she'd interrupted his lecture; in other words, as if she were a bug doing the backstroke in his soup.

Nevertheless, Deborah beamed. "I know you're overcome with gratitude, but you can't talk me out of it."

Justin covered Sherry's hand and squeezed. "Lesser men have died trying."

My father found his voice, more or less, but he had to

clear his throat twice before it emerged. "We, ah, hadn't considered the country club."

"No need now," Deborah said. "We'll host it here. Ceremony under an arch by the water, dinner in the state dining room—black tie, of course—and dancing in the ballroom."

Of course they have a ballroom. Doesn't every self-respecting gazillionaire?

And then I noticed Deborah's eyes. Void of emotion. Hard. Calculating. She wanted so badly for Sherry to argue, she might lose her own impeccable manners, if she wasn't careful.

She hadn't gotten an argument over the gown. So now she was poking a little harder. Deborah knew how every girl dreamed her wedding. She was stealing my sister's dreams to break her, so she'd blow like a cheap bottle of champagne.

Deborah wanted to force Justin to choose between them.

I didn't need a vision to see her scheme. I did need to do some snooping, though, and the suddenly loud and all-encompassing discussion going on around me would likely go on for some time.

Sherry could hold her own. Besides, Justin, Dad, and Nick were on her side, to the point that she was the only one *not* speaking.

I stood. "Excuse me, could someone direct me to the ladies' lounge?"

I needed to see if I could find a room where a different Vancortland bride might have been fitted for the antique wedding dress that I couldn't wait to redesign.

Ignoring directions to the first-floor powder room, I made my way up a wide, curving staircase out of *Gone with the Wind*, heart pounding, drums of doom in my head, accompanied by a silent-movie score crescendo signaling danger.

I chuckled to myself and acknowledged the "too stupid to live" heroine inside me, who was having a blast.

I stumbled across the library, quite by accident, and couldn't resist a quick search for wedding albums, but no go. Farther down the same hall, I opened the only closed door—quite the anomaly in a hall this long—and found the illusory bride's fitting room.

It looked nearly the same, except for the designer drapes. The three-way mirror had been taken away and a small piano brought in, as if to make it into a practice room. Ancient family pictures covered the instrument, but none were of the nervous maid wearing the Vancortland gown in my vision.

The gown itself had been brought up from the drawing room and was now being worn by a luxury mannequin of glossy black, the kind Faline bought in Italy. Nothing but the best in the Vancortland house. And why they hadn't brought the dress down on the mannequin was beyond me, except that the parade of gown bearers had been much more dramatic.

I removed it from the mannequin and sat in the mission-style rocker on which a maid's dress had once been draped—if my interpretation of the vision was correct, or even real.

Embracing the gown, I closed my eyes, hoping for another vision.

Rocking made me seasick, so I stopped, opened my eyes, and saw the mysterious bride once again, dressed in her finery, gorgeous and swan-like, all toffee-cream skin and thick, black waving hair, her lush figure one that any man would admire.

The door flew open and she jumped—we both did—and the bride touched her trembling hand to the pearls at her throat, gifts from the sea as flawless as she.

"What do you think you're doing?" Deborah snapped.

I came back to myself with prickles running up and

down my arms. "Deborah," I said, swallowing the nausea rising in my throat as I found myself in the here and now. "You scared me."

I could have used a musical crescendo of danger before that door opened, I'll tell you. I might have had a heart attack, never mind my confusion.

Had Deborah spoken in my vision?

In real time?

Or in both?

Fifteen

Haute couture consists of secrets whispered from generation
to generation . . .
        —YVES SAINT LAURENT

"What are you doing in here with Sherry's gown?" Deborah asked. "We keep this door closed."

I'd come back to the present with such a jolt that my
mind raced for old and new answers. "A closed door," I
said, probably too fast. "Precisely why I thought it was a
bathroom. Why was it closed? It's such a beautiful room."

Her gaze slid from mine toward some unknown distance
beyond me. "I've never been fond of this room," she said.

If I had truly seen the past just now, with Deborah in it,
had she once confronted the mysterious dark-haired bride,
jolting her with fright the way she'd just jolted me?

I mean, I had an empathetic heartbeat running like a
gerbil on its wheel at midnight.

I'd always known that Deborah was a force to be reckoned with, but she'd never been quite as terrifying as she
was at this moment.

"You're on the wrong floor," she said, acting normal, for
Deborah, and in the now again.

I brought the gown back to the mannequin to redress it and gather my wits. "I know. I got lost right away, and your gorgeous stairway beckoned. You shouldn't expect anything less in this showplace, Deborah. It was like I was swept into another world. I mean, it's all so luxurious and stately, like a beacon in a historic tapestry."

Scrap, I'd better stop kissing "class" before I ended up testing my gag reflex. "This room in particular seemed to call my name the minute I opened the door. I sat to rock and enjoy its classic atmosphere. And there was Sherry's gown just waiting for me to learn its *secrets*." I stressed the word "secrets" on purpose and watched Deborah for a reaction.

She didn't even blink.

"I know the *room* has secrets," I said, trying again.

Still no reaction, but her poker face gave away her need to hide her emotions.

"Well, dear, I can see why it called to you. This *was* once a sewing room, and you do take in sewing."

"I'm a designer. A world-class New York designer. Have you bought a Faline in the past five years? I probably designed it."

I was annoyed with myself for falling in with her verbal one-upmanship. And yet, why not make the best of it? "After I fit the gown to Sherry, I'll send Faline pictures of it, and get her to send me a dated Faline label for a side seam. That'll add to the gown's provenance and value." Only a slight truth stretch. With a vintage redesign, the label would only help the gown *retain* its value.

Deborah's eyes, like little slot machine windows, went *cha-ching*. I smiled despite myself. "You should have someone document the gown's history on acid-free paper so Sherry can keep the history with the dress when she has it preserved after the wedding."

Okay, so I was getting in another shot. The last bride to

wear the gown became its custodian, and its link to the next generation, which had apparently not occurred to Deborah before this moment.

"So," I said, to smooth her frown, "a Faline label. Good idea? You'll be able to say you wore a Faline wedding gown."

"Aren't you a helpful girl?"

As I stood, Deborah took my arm. "Is there anything else you'd like to see while we're up here?"

"As a matter of fact, there is," I dared, "and I think Sherry would like to see it, too. Will you show us the photos of the Vancortland brides who wore the gown?"

Deborah squeezed my arm; in friendship or warning, who knew? "I think that can be arranged."

We went back to the dinner table together, raising a few eyebrows when we walked in like BFFs. Yep, me and Deborah, best friends forever. What a hoot. I gave Sherry a look asking her to play along.

Her expression said she was willing but reluctant.

I'd told her about my possible psychometric ability and my visions as we got ready this evening. She didn't say I was nuts. She didn't say she believed me. She did say that she loved and trusted me.

Nick rubbed his nose again, clearly amused, because he knew me well enough to know that I was up to something.

"I'm so excited, Sis," I said. "Deborah is going to show us pictures of all the brides who wore your gown. Seeing them will help me fit you properly."

"What a great idea." Sherry didn't have to add "I guess" as she raised her glass. "Thank you, Deborah."

A tense moment ensued when I feared Deborah would ask Sherry to call her "Mother," but it passed when my father raised his glass. "To Justin and Sherry," Dad said. "May you find a lifetime of joy and the blessing of old age together."

Sherry teared up and I swallowed hard, both of us understanding his wish. He also toasted the Vancortlands for their generosity. I guess it was settled. The wedding would take place here, and for the moment, Deborah didn't seem to mind that she hadn't gotten her fight.

Made me wonder what she'd pull next.

After dinner the men went to the smoking room, even Justin and Nick, though they didn't smoke, but they planned to go to the billiard room after for a game.

"Wedding albums," I said, urging Sherry forward behind Deborah with a get-going hand.

"Imagine," I said behind her. "Pictures of all the brides."

I saw the light finally go on in her eyes as Sherry turned to me.

Forget the amazing staircase; we took an elevator to the third floor. The turn-of-the-nineteenth-century lift had brass filigree V's in a flamboyant script decorating its see-through doors.

Deborah left us in her personal sitting room while she went for the albums.

"Look at this place," Sherry whispered. "You'd think she was royalty."

"Well, it is the master suite," I pointed out.

"No, it's not. Cort's suite is on the second floor."

Separate suites on different floors. I filed the information into the growing data bank in my brain. I'd seen Mildred cross this very room on her way to Deborah's bedroom. At the time, there'd been no doubt in my mind that Cort and Deborah shared the suite.

I thought of the interested way that Cort and the cake lady had looked at each other at the party. But I was losing track of my purpose. Would the Vancortland wedding photos include the mystery bride? I could hardly wait to see.

Deborah brought a stack of wedding albums. "They're

all here except mine. I can't think where I put it. But don't worry, I'll find it eventually." She forced Sherry to move so she could sit between us on the French provincial settee.

We had to sit through four complete albums. Five if you counted Justin's baby album. Then we had to go and find the portraits of each bride, the first having married around the turn of the century.

Why hadn't I asked to see portraits instead of the albums? There went two hours of my life I'd never get back. Okay, so my disappointment had grown a sharp edge. No album or portrait of the bride that was becoming more illusive by the minute.

After what seemed like five hours, the men came to find us. As soon as they arrived, I asked Cort if any of the Vancortland men had ever been engaged to anyone other than the women they married.

Deborah and Cort went very still and avoided making eye contact between them.

"Nope," Justin said, taking Sherry's hand and tugging her beside him. "The Vancortlands marry their first loves and they stay married, right, Mom and Dad?"

Did he sound facetious?

His parents said nothing, but I didn't think a "yes" would fit on either count.

Who the Hermès was the dark-haired woman in the gown? Did people get false psychic vibes? Could I have picked up on a maid who'd daydreamed about a Vancortland, whose fantasies included the gown and the master of the house?

I didn't dare ask for a tour of the servants' quarters, given my prevalence of interest in anything Vancortland on this occasion. That would be too telling, but there was so much more to explore.

Eyeing Sherry, I let my gaze run from left to right, and back, hoping she'd read my "I want to see it all" signal.

She leaned into Justin like a cat seeking a stroke. "Show us more," she coaxed.

Justin tipped up her chin. "You're being polite. You don't really want to see the whole mausoleum?"

Deborah protested his disrespect.

Sherry ignored them both. "Every corner."

Shaking his head, Justin led Sherry by the waist, while Nick and I followed the same way. My father paid more attention to Deborah than her husband did.

We saw the indoor pool, and the outdoor pool, the gym-workout room and the *Sound of Music* ballroom. "That's it for the high points," Justin said.

"But I've never seen servants' quarters," Sherry said, her arm around his waist sliding toward his butt.

"No!" Deborah snapped. "That's where I draw the line. No one needs to go up there. I hate it up there."

"I like it up there," Cort said. "It's *genuine*."

Sixteen

I love the T-shirt as an anti-status symbol, putting rich and poor on the same level in a sheath of white cotton that cancels the distinctions of caste.　　—GIORGIO ARMANI

"Come, daughter." Cort stole Sherry from Justin. "I'll show you the servants' quarters. I made myself an office up there."

Deborah's gasp made Nick and I hesitate, but my father shooed us along. "I'll prevail upon Deborah to show me her hothouse."

"My orangerie," Deborah said. "I forgot that you like horticulture, Harry."

Good, my father would be in his glory and Deborah would be too busy to fume and collect mental darts for our return.

The servants' stairs were plain, serviceable, and immaculate. They smelled of lemon and family secrets. Tacked to the wall at each landing, near the servants' entrance to the family quarters, was a map of the rooms on that floor with occupants' names.

"I don't want to invade anyone's personal space," I said. "I just realized that people must live up here."

Cort shook his head. "Not an issue; employees don't live in anymore."

Employees, he'd said. Deborah would have called them servants.

He pointed to a name on the map on the second-floor landing. "Right . . . here . . . this was my mother's room."

Justin came closer and ran his finger over the name. "I didn't know that. I didn't even know her name was Elinor."

Cort's quiet pride was rooted in family. This was his home, but it was Deborah's trophy. His ownership was born of heritage, hers of self-indulgence.

Justin regarded his father with a new awareness. He might have grown up feeling rooted here, too, if he'd learned to think of this as more than a society prize or a gaudy showplace.

Cort had failed his son on that score, until now.

Unsure as to whether truth or conjecture filled my thoughts, I knew only that I saw more life in Cort at this moment than in any of the other times we'd met.

Today, I liked him.

He squeezed his son's shoulder, held for a minute, let go, and led the way up another flight. The higher we went, the bigger the secrets. I felt them in the air around us, thickening it, making it heavy, weighing me down with a need to fix problems I didn't know.

"My grandmother's name was Elinor," Justin said to Sherry. "What do you think about Elinor for a girl's name?"

Cort faltered, but didn't look back. Nevertheless, he straightened, shoulders back, a new pride in his gait as he continued leading the way.

On the top floor, his office took up one simple room with a round window that looked out over the back lawn and the greater Mystic River beyond. A room pulsing with life.

A small plain bed sat tucked under the eaves, a hand-crocheted rosette coverlet in lilac giving the room life and substance. Beside the bed, a delftware pitcher and bowl of lavender wands sat on a small dry sink.

Cort reached over and squeezed a wand to bring out the faint scent of lavender. He relaxed as he breathed deeply.

A man's worn plaid robe lay across the foot of the bed. A pair of slippers sat perfectly aligned on the floor beside it.

Cort chucked me under the chin. "It gets chilly up here in the winter, and yes, sometimes I nap up here. Just to get away," he whispered. "But I don't live up here. This is not the doghouse. It's quite the opposite."

I smiled, listened for the secrets, and ran my hand over the coverlet, hoping for a vision. I saw nothing but the present.

Cort neatened the papers on his desk. "I come here to work in peace."

He took pride in Justin showing Sherry and Nick a railroad map. The Vancortlands had made their money in railroads years ago but diversified soon enough to save the family fortune. They now owned excursion trains in several countries in addition to North America.

I stood back to take in the room at large, and that was when I noticed the framed photo on the wall by the door. My heart beat a hopeful tattoo, because I couldn't believe my eyes, so I went to examine the old photograph more closely.

When I got there, elation shot through me.

Oh my Goddess! The illusory bride herself, young, happy . . . guileless.

"Mr. Vancortland," I said, trying to give the impression of polite interest, my heart now running a marathon, my palms starting to sweat.

"Cort," he said. "We're about to become family, Madeira . . . if I may?"

I nodded. "Cort and Madeira it is." He *could* be a

charmer, I thought. "I couldn't help but notice the wonderful vintage coat in this picture," I said, pretending that the photo of the wearer *didn't* make me want to Snoopy dance around the room. "I'm sure you don't know, but vintage clothes are a passion of mine."

"Well, I know you're a fashion designer," he said, "so it stands to reason that the history of fashion appeals to you."

"Thank you, Cort. You're the first Mystic resident who's made my passion sound sane."

He chuckled.

I returned my attention to the picture. "Despite the black-and-white photo," I said, "I can tell you that the model is wearing a wool gabardine coat, probably blue, so the velvet and braiding on its bertha-type collar would be burgundy. It's a great example of the forties style."

"I'm impressed," Cort said. "You got the colors exactly right. The coat used to be my mother's."

"She had excellent taste. My compliments. Is this her in the picture? She's exquisite."

I'd seen his mother's wedding pictures. This was not her.

Cort slid his hands into his pockets and rocked on his heels. "The wearer's name is Pearl," he said. "The coat was a hand-me-down by then. Pearl was my nurse's daughter and my best friend growing up."

"She'd been playing in the snow, I see."

"*We'd* been playing in the snow," he admitted.

"Is she still on staff?"

"No." He seemed to look back for a minute. "She quit one day and left no forwarding address."

"I'm sorry to hear it. Maybe she went back to where her mother came from."

"New Orleans," he said, "but I went looking once. Her uncle said that Pearl wasn't there."

I could sense Cort sinking, sinking into the past, or into grief.

"You were playing in the snow together," I said to pull him back. "So did you take the picture?"

My ploy worked. He saw me again. "I did, and it's always been a favorite."

"She's naturally photogenic, but really, she looks like a young woman in love."

"It was the camera," Cort said. "Pearl always made love to the camera."

"Judging by her expression, she cared a great deal about that camera."

"You think so?" His voice cracked.

I pretended not to notice. "I'd love to sketch the coat at some point. It's such an exquisite example of the times. Would you mind? I'd do it when you weren't working here. You name the day and time."

I did want a sketch of Pearl, because I got the strangest feeling that learning about her would tell me something about the murder . . . and here I'd been pronounced sane only two minutes ago.

I also wanted to take the picture from its frame to see if there was anything written on the back, like on the photo in the Updike sitting room. Somehow, in my skewed psychometric mind, it all seemed connected. Or, to quote Eve, I was a nutcase.

To my utter shock and delight, Cort took the picture off the wall and handed it to me. "Take your time with it, Madeira, but I would like it back when you're finished."

"You've got it," I said. "Thank you so much. The sketch of the coat will make a wonderful addition to my vintage fashion portfolio."

Nick, Sherry, and Justin, it seemed, had been eavesdropping, for I don't know how long, and waiting to go back downstairs.

Nick grabbed my arm as we started down and held me back so we'd be the last to go down. "You're coming home with me."

I scoffed. "You smooth talker, you."

He gave me a look of pure Italian exasperation. With very little effort, I can make him swear an Italian blue streak. Or would that be a red, white, and green streak?

"I mean that I'll drive you home," he said, "so we can talk in the car."

"Pity," I said, chuckling and running ahead of him down the stairs.

Well, what good was a boy toy if you couldn't taunt the scrap out of him? Besides, I was celebrating. I had not only found the illusory bride, I had her picture. It was a perfect size to slip into Nick's pocket when he caught up with me.

After my sewing-room vision, which Deborah quite possibly interrupted in the past *and* present, I didn't think Deborah would like to see me with a photo of Pearl.

A dessert buffet waited for us on the patio. Coffee, tea, hot and iced, after-dinner drinks, and quite the assortment of French pastry.

"Did you get this from the cake lady?" I asked, choosing from the decadent morsels.

"Of course not," Deborah said. "Our pastry chef is perfectly capable of making dessert."

Ah, I'd fallen out of favor by touring the servants' quarters. I raised my éclair in a salute. "Yummy. My compliments to your pastry chef."

Werner walked in—or out—to the patio from the house, and he had two uniformed officers with him.

My heart went into overdrive, and I scanned the room to locate Sherry safe in Justin's hold. "Joining us for dessert, Detective?"

Please don't be here to arrest Sherry.

"Honestly," Deborah said, turning on my sister. "I wish

you'd keep your scandals to yourself. I don't need you bringing all of Mystic's gossip and scrutiny down on *my* head."

Justin and Cort turned on *her*, literally, and she raised her chin, a clear case of false bravado, though none of them said a word.

Werner tilted his head. "Is there some reason you prefer not to be scrutinized, Mrs. Vancortland?" He studied her as he slipped his hand into his inside breast pocket. "Look to your own house," he added, as he removed his notebook.

Deborah stepped back, absently clutching her emerald-cut diamond pendant, though she no longer held Werner's attention.

I sidled over to peek at his notes from behind—a list of those present. He turned and tilted his head my way, so I lowered myself to the chair behind me as if that had been my intention all along.

He didn't buy it.

I didn't care.

He turned to my sister. "You still can't leave the state, Ms. Cutler," he said. "Young Mr. Vancortland, you can't, either. I'm here to ask you some questions, and I suggest that you cooperate."

Deborah hit the floor in a dead faint.

Sherry shouted, "No!"

For a surreal moment, half a second, we all stared down at Deborah, then everyone moved at once to get her into a chair.

Werner told one of his officers to call 911.

Deborah came to and gave me such a look of hate, I stood up and moved away from her.

With his mother settled, Justin hooked an arm around my sister. "It'll be okay." He turned to Werner. "There must be a mistake."

Sherry, however, trembled like the last leaf of winter in a Mystic River breeze.

Cort got his wife's maid to tend her and he came to stand by Justin in a show of solidarity, his hand on his son's shoulder. "May I ask why, Detective?"

"Jasmine Updike died pregnant. Your son could very well be the father."

"No," Sherry said. "She couldn't—I mean it isn't . . . wasn't Justin's. They hardly knew each other. They haven't seen each other since they were study partners years ago." Sherry's voice broke on the last.

Doubt and calculation grew and diminished, circling the room like a saw-toothed gargoyle on clay feet while Sherry begged Justin, with a pleading look, to confirm her faith in him.

He tightened his fist around her hand, his knuckles going white.

"I understand your loyalty, Miss Cutler," Werner said, "but Justin Vancortland and Jasmine Updike lived together for two years while they attended college."

Seventeen

With a cry of dismay, Deborah fainted again, but she was already in a chair, her maid wielding smelling salts.

Sherry tore from Justin's arms, and though he tried to pull her back, she stepped from his reach, shaking her head, her eyes overflowing with horror and disappointment.

I wanted to go to her, but my own shock held me captive.

Werner cleared his throat to recapture Justin's attention. "Where were you at eight fifty-five p.m. on the night of Miss Updike's death?" Werner asked.

Justin gave Sherry a speaking look.

The secret!

"He was with me," my sister said, a weak alibi at best, given their relationship.

"Doing what?" Werner asked, "and where?"

"Justin," I said. "Don't say another word. I'm calling Aunt Fiona." I hit speed dial with success. After a short conversation, I clapped my phone shut, symbolically putting

134

period to the free-for-all. "Attorney Sullivan's on her way. Take a break." I gave Werner a half nod.

"I should have thought to call a lawyer," Cort said. "Forgive me, son. Shock and all that. Thank you, Madeira."

Deborah moaned as she came to, her maid wiping drool off her chin, a humbling moment for the self-styled head of Mystic society.

Deborah sipped from the glass of water her maid held, acting weak, but not too weak to send eyeball daggers my sister's way.

When it came to an unplanned pregnancy, everyone usually blamed the girl, especially the boy's parents. So why wasn't Deborah blaming Jasmine?

All Sherry did was agree to marry her son.

So Deborah blamed Sherry for what? Saying yes? Did the pending wedding, ah, or the announcement, bring Jasmine to Mystick Falls?

Speculation, I reminded myself, did not a murder solve, and I had enough speculation to muck up the facts but good. I'd do well to separate my "clues" into two columns, "speculation" and "fact."

Frustrated by the number of questions without answers and by the charged silence, I offered Werner dessert and coffee.

"Thanks," he said, accepting both and taking them down to the river.

I offered the same to everyone, and most accepted coffee, at least. Even the Vancortland maids were in shock, because they didn't move to action until I handed one of them an empty pastry tray.

Deborah was clearly not herself or she would have been snapping orders.

Fiona arrived in less than fifteen minutes. Werner saw her and crossed the yard to the patio. With his help, we caught Fiona up on what she'd missed.

Ready to resume questioning, Werner checked his notes. "Now, young Mr. Vancortland, can you tell me where you were when Jasmine Updike was murdered?"

Sherry raised her chin. "We'd had a misunderstanding and we were making up in my father's boathouse."

"We were making *love* in her father's boathouse," Justin countered.

Ah. Sex. That kind of vanishing act. Bummer. I'd thought of that and dismissed it. I needed a brush-up course.

Nick raised a speaking brow, as if offering his services. I rolled my eyes and he shrugged.

I should have figured it out, but I'd discounted the possibility, because they were keeping it a secret. Everybody expected an engaged couple to have a sex life. There was hardly anything incriminating in the admission. But were they telling the truth? That particular location was a pretty dicey alibi.

While some boathouses were actually buildings, ours was more like a three-sided shack, the open side facing the river and any boaters who happened by. A hard pill and all that.

Werner definitely had trouble swallowing. "You'll pardon me," he said, "if I'm skeptical, under the circumstances. Any witnesses?"

"That's a kinky damned-if-you-do and damned-if-you-don't question," I snapped.

Werner raised both brows my way.

Sherry covered her face and started to cry.

Justin grinned. "A boatload of tourists. A riverboat full."

Sherry all out wailed.

Werner kept his head down as he took notes, but I'm sure I caught the corner of his mouth turn upward for an instant. "We'll see if we can trace any of the riverboat passengers who were on that tour," he said.

Justin grinned. "The tourists did plenty of cheering, hooting, wolf-whistling, and clapping. I'm sure there are a few snapshots out there as well. I don't care if you plaster my face, though maybe it should be my bare ass, all over the six o'clock news, just find us a witness."

Deborah looked ready to faint again, but she rallied, her gaze snapped my sister's way.

Maybe I should worry about Sherry's safety.

The paramedics arrived and took Deborah's vitals, pronounced her fit, and left. Deborah would always land on her feet.

Nick pulled me aside. "Why didn't Sherry tell us where she and Justin had been?"

I straightened his Hugo Boss tie. "She's mortified."

"I wouldn't waste those bragging rights."

Neither would I. "Meet me at midnight." I winked.

"Date." He rubbed his nose. "Wear your lucky panties," he whispered.

I got closer. "Which ones?"

"Hot lips."

Ah, white silk and lace with mouth prints in red "lipstick" and "Kiss My Sass" on the back. "Done."

"For what it's worth," Nick said, "I think Justin and your sister are telling the truth." He grinned. "You can't make up something that kinky."

"I'm glad you have faith in them."

"And I admire them, too."

I tugged Nick off the patio and around to the side of the house. I couldn't wait any longer to ask him for a favor. Werner's latest round of questions had shot my sense of urgency into overdrive. I needed to do some serious investigative work.

"Why wait till midnight?" Nick asked, pulling me into his arms. "Let's give Cort's boathouse a practice run."

With both arms, I elbowed my way out of Nick's hold

and stayed a safe distance away. "You have a one-track man-brain. How *do* you solve FBI cases?"

"I'm normal . . . when you're not around."

"Glad to hear it. Now try being normal when I am."

"It was worth a shot, and Cort's got a great boathouse." I huffed. "I need a background check."

Nick aped my huff. "Fine, a background check on who?"

"Anything on a maid who worked here about twenty to twenty-nine years ago. Her first name was Pearl. She grew up here and stayed to work for a few years. Her mother was Cort's nurse. I don't know their last name but her mother came from New Orleans."

"Nurse? Was Cort sick as a kid?"

"No, she was his nanny. You know, she took care of him in the nursery. It's a rich-people thing."

"Gotcha. Why do you want to know about this Pearl, precisely?"

I cringed inwardly at the question. Fiona believed the universe sent me information for a reason. I wasn't sure what I believed. My visions came from the wedding dress, though, and solving Jasmine's murder seemed somehow linked to my sister's wedding or the dress. In any case, I wasn't ready to tell Nick about my psychic visions. I might never be. "Let's say I'm playing a hunch."

"That sounds like you," Nick said. We returned to the patio with his hand at my nape and my mind on our midnight date.

Werner stood front and center with Justin as his target. "How can you explain a two-year lease for an apartment in walking distance of Harvard signed by you and Jasmine while you were both enrolled there?"

Justin's guilty expression begged Sherry to understand. "You had dumped me, Sherry. I was mad and on the rebound. Our relationship—mine and Jasmine's, if you can call it that—didn't last a week, but she was on scholarship and her credit sucked." He shrugged. "I cosigned as a 'thank you' to her for tutoring me in Bio."

"Bio! Great," Sherry snapped. "I'll bet you aced it and got stuck for a bundle. Oh!" She started to cry again. "You cheated on me."

"You broke up with me. I wanted to get you back, but I only hurt myself. One week out of a six-month breakup. It was awful being with anybody else. I only wanted you. Sherry, you have to believe me."

"I don't know if I can. I'm not sure there will be a wedding."

Deborah perked up at that.

Sherry's stubborn Cutler chin came up. "*Was* Jasmine's baby yours?"

"Of course not!"

My sister was not a crier, but she'd been weepy since the murder. True, she had reason; the Jezebel trying to steal her fiancé had died in our house, and Sherry was the prime suspect. Now she finds out that her true love once lived with the Jezebel.

"I didn't live in the apartment with Jasmine," Justin repeated for Werner's sake, while he fought Sherry to take her hand. "I spent one week dating Jasmine, but I didn't spend one night, not one minute, in Jasmine Updike's bed, car, hammock, boat, or boathouse. Ever."

Nick snapped his fingers. "Hammock," he whispered. "Nice."

Sherry turned to leave but Justin sprinted after her and caught her up in his arms despite her struggle to get free. *"You,"* he said. "I love you."

Werner closed his notebook. "Then you won't mind coming down to the station with us right now, Mr. Vancortland, to answer a few more questions, make a formal statement, and give us a DNA sample."

Eighteen

The most courageous act is still to think for yourself.
Aloud.   —COCO CHANEL

Early the next morning, I opened my eyes and realized that I was trying to hit snooze on my cell phone.

When I focused, I read the caller's name and opened my phone. "Aunt Fiona, what's wrong now?" I asked, sitting up, not sure what time I'd been roused from sleep.

"Everything that was wrong yesterday, dear, I'm sorry to say, but nothing new. I do want to tell you that your father, Sherry, and I stayed with Justin at the police station until one. Your father couldn't have gotten your sister home until after two, and she was still upset about Justin and Jasmine, so if she finally fell asleep, don't wake her."

At least I didn't have a boathouse tryst to feel guilty about. How could I have followed through with my sister in such a state? But I had taken a rain check.

I fell against my pillows. "You woke me to tell me not to wake my sister?"

A chuckle that I loved smoothed my not-so-ruffled feathers. "Forgive me, sweetie, but I seem to remember you making a breakfast picnic out of watching the sun rise."

"There is no sun in New York, but there are plenty of all-night clubs. I morphed."

"Ah, well, maybe you'll morph back while you're home. At any rate, I did have another reason for calling. You asked me about the Underhill Funeral Chapel carriage house and I wanted to tell you where to pick up the key so you could take a look at it."

My heart took on the beat of a parade drum. I sat straighter, a John Philip Sousa march in my chest, probably because I was home in Mystic, Americana to the core, where I'd watched so many parades from the sidewalk beside that very building.

Home. Maybe deep down, I wanted to stay.

"Who, where, when?" I lowered my legs to the floor as I sat on the side of the bed.

Had the building enticed me even then? At parades where I shunned shorts and wore ruffled dresses with shiny Mary Janes, held the perfect purse for the perfect outfit, while devouring cotton candy, my hand in my mother's?

In memory, it seemed so.

"Let me grab a paper and pencil," I told Fiona.

"Certainly, dear."

I looked at the phone. She'd sounded . . . sarcastic. I grabbed a pencil and aimed it at a notebook. "Shoot."

"All right, listen carefully, because it's complicated. Take a right out of your driveway, drive a tenth of a mile, and get the key from old Mrs. Sweet."

I fumbled the phone and caught it halfway to the floor. "Aunt Fiona, are you there?"

"Yes, dear."

"Old Dolly Sweet owns the Underhill Funeral Chapel carriage house? Is she a granddaughter or something?"

"Something. It was a juicy old scandal when I was a

girl. She had an affair with Underhill, who was years older than her at the time, and to make matters worse, he left her the property."

I grinned. "Goddess bless the Mystick Falls gossip mill! Can we have a scandal sleepover sometime, you, me, and Eve, and you can dish up the dirt?"

Fiona chuckled. "Maybe if you stick around long enough, you'll unearth some dirt of your own. Take your father to see the building with you, dear, and bring a flashlight. It's falling down. It could be dangerous. Have a nice day and let me know what you think."

I smiled, sat back against my pillows, and wallowed in anticipation. Okay, don't wake Sherry. Good thing I had faith in her love for Justin or I'd feel guilty about doing something for myself, like touring the carriage house, for a couple of hours.

I hit speed dial. "Eve, wake up," I said when she mumbled hello. "We're touring the Underhill carriage house today. Just you and me."

She hung up on me. That's the kind of friends we were. We could flip each other off—metaphorically speaking— and still be BFFs.

A half hour later, my phone rang as I stepped from the shower.

"What time?" Eve asked when I answered.

"Eleven. I have to fit old Mrs. Sweet for a new dress and—"

Eve growled. "You woke me at dawn so I could meet you at eleven?"

"Okay, make it ten. I'll go right over to the Sweets. They'll feed me breakfast."

Eve did that metaphorical thing again with a mumbled "up yours," which of course meant she'd be there.

In New York, morning communication, which ranked right up there with taxicab- and commuter-eze, had no bearing on the language used by the working population during the rest of the day. Evidently we'd brought a mild case home with us.

At the Sweets, I followed the scent of cherry pie to their back door and knocked on the screen, though I could see them drinking tea and bickering, their favorite sport.

They'd been up for hours, the ambitious old things, and by the scents and clay flowerpots lined up out here, one had been gardening and the other baking.

My breakfast consisted of vanilla hazelnut tea and cherry pie. Yummers. Old Doll tried to feed me a lemon square in addition, but her daughter-in-law slapped her hand. "Leave her be, Momma. I'm sure she wants to keep her figure to find a man."

I nearly spit out my tea and ended up having a coughing fit. More tea was their prescription. By the time we finished breakfast, I had enough caffeine in me to fly over the Underhill building.

In her bedroom, afterward, I made old Doll strip to her slip, so I could take her measurements. "Now what kind of dress do you want?"

"I want one like Katharine Hepburn wore in *The Philadelphia Story*."

I sat back on my knees. "Which scene?"

"The wedding scene, of course."

"Of course," I said, remembering a pale pink swath of silk organza in my collection, a gown she might like better than a stylish new dress, but I measured her anyway. Might as well be sure the vintage layered pink confection would fit. "Mrs. Sweet, do you remember *all* the brides who wore the Vancortland gown?"

She chuckled. "I'm old, but I don't have amnesia. The first bride to wear it married the year I was born, cupcake, but I remember the rest, and I've seen pictures of the first."

"Deborah showed us pictures of them last night, but,

you know, I have the strangest sense that I didn't see them all."

"You saw five albums?" she asked as I made her raise an arm.

"I did, but one of them was Justin's baby pictures. Deborah couldn't find her wedding album, but we saw the rest."

"Well, it's five brides with Deborah. Far as I know, only one other girl might have tried on that dress."

Hel-lo! "How long ago was that and who was she?"

"She was the maid who ran away. Bit of a scandal, that."

I looked up from the floor, measuring tape forgotten. "Why?"

"Because she was Vancortland's first love. Vancortland Four, I mean—Cort—not your Sherry's man. I think her name was Ruby or some such. She and Cort were engaged and she broke his heart when she left. He married Deborah on the rebound. Maybe that's why she's so sour."

Okay, okay, suspicion confirmed, but what did it mean and how did it fit into the murder—if it did fit into the murder? I added this new information to the scraps I'd snipped from various sources since Jasmine's death. So far all I could do with them was make a crazy quilt.

I got off my knees. "Measurements finished. Want to look at dress designs, though I didn't bring any that look like Tracy Lord's wedding dress."

"I really had my heart set on that one."

"Fine. I've got a couple of design ideas and I'll bring them around later. I have another errand to run first, though. Did Fiona tell you I was coming?"

"No, sweetie, you told us you were coming."

Sharp as a tack, my father called her, and with good reason. "Okay, did Fiona tell you that someone was interested in the Underhill building?"

"Yes, and how stupid are they? It's older than me,

though my memories of it are as vivid, glorious, and sweet as ever."

Okaay. I cleared my throat. "It's me. I'm the stupid one. I mean, I fell in love with the building when I was a little girl. I found myself going right to it the night I came home."

"You want Dante's building?"

"Dante?"

Dolly's eyes went all starry. "Dante Underhill, the undertaker's son who became the undertaker."

A sweet-talking undertaker, evidently, one she still missed. "I don't know if I want the building yet. I do know that I need to look at it."

"What would you do with it?"

"I'm not sure, but I'm thinking vintage clothes might play a role."

"You mean like for a museum?"

Hmm. "I hadn't thought of that." But I shouldn't dismiss it. Some of my finds were museum quality. "Maybe. Why? Does what I do with it matter? I mean, if I was interested, I'd *buy* it from you."

"Oh, I understand that. I'd have only one stipulation to the sale. It was in Dante's will that I never tear it down, and I'd want to sell it with the same stipulation."

"Oh, it's too beautiful. I'd never—" I stilled. "Why? Is there a body buried under it?"

Old Dolly laughed so hard, I had to help her to a chair. When she caught her breath, she cupped my face. "You think it's beautiful." She'd spoken with awe. "Everybody else thinks it's an eyesore. A shack. I've fought for years to keep it there. I kept it up to building and electrical code standards, so it wouldn't be condemned. Pissed off the Mystick Falls town council once a year. A real perk!"

Her grin was contagious. "You mean it has electricity and running water?"

"Sure does."

"Why is it boarded up, then?"

The old girl blushed and giggled. "To keep kids from breaking in and using it for a love nest."

Oh, Lordy, I wanted Dolly Sweet's old love nest.

Nineteen

Success is often achieved by those who don't know that
failure is inevitable.   —COCO CHANEL

I expected it to be hot in the carriage house without air-
conditioning. So I wore a cool, peach Louise Goldin barely
there mini, with a cutout circle baring my midriff. One of
those desirably funky outfits that made you look like a
crew member on a starship. I loved it and paired it
with Blahnik raffia beaded mules and a woven-straw flow-
erpot bag.

When I arrived, Eve's car sat empty in the cracked ce-
ment lot outside, but my black-garbed friend was nowhere
to be seen.

Two boards lay on the ground out front, and about the
time I noticed how they would fit the design crossing the
door, Eve opened it and stepped outside. "Welcome to
the shack." She looked me over and rolled her eyes. "Chill,
Mad. The fashion police are not waiting inside."

Eve had a gift for snark.

"My outfit isn't about what I look like, Meyers. Yes, it's
a fashion statement, but I couldn't care less about what

anybody else thinks; it's about how I feel. Cool. Awesome. Inspired. Confident. Speaking of which, when did you go platinum blonde, and how did you get inside?"

"I went platinum yesterday. Makes my black clothes more striking, don't you think?"

"Yep, just what you needed. A little color in your life. Snort."

She stuck her tongue out at me. That's how long we'd been friends. "As for this place," she said, chin high, leading the way. "I broke in."

"So much for Dolly's theory about keeping out the riffraff. I'll have to get an alarm system."

"Riffraff?" Eve rounded on me. "You? You'll have to do what?"

I heard the echo of my own words the way she must have. "Gee. Don't know where that came from."

"What are you up to?" She followed me inside.

I flipped on a light and fell in deep doo-doo, otherwise known as . . . love at first sight.

Talk about secrets. A current of anxiety and expectation crackled around me. I swear that I heard the combined mourning of a century, a humming wail in a sad and unending jumble of loss and death. But beyond that was a thread of celebration and new beginnings. How odd.

The hair on my arms stood up, while silent cries shifted the air in subtle, sweeping currents, both soft and taunting.

I shivered and Eve chuckled. "Pretty tucking beautiful for a shack," she said, borrowing my designer vernacular.

So beautiful, it should be listed on a historic register, not that I'd suggest it. Under those guidelines, it'd be hell to remodel.

Remodel? Did I want to do that? Oh, I hoped so. Somebody had to take care of it after Dolly . . . "No wonder Dante and Dolly insisted on preserving it. It's beautiful."

"It's ginormous," Eve said. "Bigger than a barn, though it smells like one."

"The smell can be fixed." I ran my hand along the front wall. "How many barns have you seen with polished mahogany walls? I have to say, there isn't much damage, considering."

"Not that you can see," Eve cautioned. "Don't discount concealed damage. It could be rotting from the inside."

"It'd still be worth fixing." We'd come in through a people door, but the huge double-wide barn doors, two sets, one to the right and one at the front, opened wide enough for a team of horses to pull a hearse out.

Speaking of which, not all the "car" stalls were empty. Color *me* wigged.

"Nice hearse." Eve gave me a wink, wink, nudge. "Museum quality?"

"Talk about vintage. I wonder if Dolly knows it's here."

"Dolly?"

I told her about old Mrs. Sweet and Underhill.

Eve hooted. "Dolly and the undertaker. Talk about strange bed partners."

At that moment, near the hearse, I saw a shadow brighten . . . or . . . materialize. A vision, a different kind, a man . . . wearing a top hat? I turned to Eve. "This is the new millennium, right?"

"Did you have another vision?"

"Guess not." Ghost not, I hoped.

The vision disappeared before I could confirm it, but I pretty much had my answer. Top-hat guy didn't scare me as much as the general atmosphere when we got here. And even that had eased to near-comfortable.

"Move it, Cutler. Let's scope out the joint."

"Wait. Dolly drew me a map." I took it from my purse, studied it, and refused to look in the direction of my apparition.

"Speaking of stalls," I said, excitement erasing unease. "Follow me." I led Eve around behind the stairs, built against an inner wall, and stopped to take in the sight. "Horse stalls," I said. Gorgeous, with curly black wrought-iron corners and brass trim finials fronting each stall.

"Would this not make an excellent fitting room? All I'd have to do is clean it up, and the stalls would need full-height doors."

Eve placed her hand on my brow. "Not running a fever. Fitting room for what, Cutler?"

I faced my conscience, raised my chin, and threw back my shoulders. "It's all coming together, Eve. I believe I want to open a vintage clothing shop. Something so great that I'll have New York collectors driving north on weekends."

"What will you call it?" Eve snapped. "Mad . . . as a Hatter?"

"Hey, good one. I thought of another possibility on my way over. Mad-Vintageous."

"Mad's Outrageous fits the situation better. Come on, Mad, you gotta think longer than three days and one murder on this."

I ignored her. I was good at that. "Let's go look around upstairs."

I hit the light switch at the bottom of the stairs and the second floor lit up as well. Great for now, because I wasn't ready to come face-to-face with a shadow wearing a top hat in the dark.

"Note to me for the future, though: 'Have circuits split.'"

We climbed the enclosed stairway, pushing each other ahead, until we reached an elbow-to-elbow stalemate at the top, Blahnik mules and Doc Martens hot glued to the last step.

Finally we agreed to emerge together on the count of three. And we did, pulling, clutching, and tripping each other like cowardly scarecrows.

I didn't know what to focus on first, the wide-open floor space, its size and potential—for storage and maybe a couple of apartments—or the selection of vintage caskets displayed on pedestals along the back wall.

Eve marched toward the front of the building. Gun boots were great for marching. "What the hell is this?" She toed a huge, dull silver, oval metal tub, quadruple the size of those big, old copper boilers, like the one my great-grandmother once washed me in.

I went closer to examine it, squeaked, and backed up.

Eve hadn't gotten as close, but she backed away as well.

"You figured it out, didn't you?" I asked.

"Nope, I'm following your lead on general principle."

"Fine," I said, "imagine it skirted and filled with ice blocks and sitting in the middle of a Victorian parlor."

Eve nodded. "Okaay."

I gave her a double take. "With an occupied casket on top?"

She jumped back. "Holy crap!"

We turned to run, but we stopped short at the sight of the caskets—light pine, ruddy cherry, golden oak, and dark walnut—with that old-fashioned shape—six-sided but elongated, dead-body style.

Ancient caskets. All sizes.

Eve sighed. "They're closed."

"So?"

"Sooooo, do you think there's a body in any of them?"

"Of course not."

"Well, undertakers don't know when they're going to die, do they?" Eve whispered. "The last one could have been in the middle of . . . somebody."

Yeah, like Dolly, I thought. "Don't you think the deceased's family would have collected the body?"

"If the deceased had a family." Eve nodded. "It's our duty to open them."

"You brat, you're dying to open them."

Eve shivered. "I am?" Her sober expression turned to a grin. "I am. I *am*."

I chuckled. "Go for it."

As she tiptoed over to the first one, my left side got cold, then my neck, same side, but I refused to turn toward the source of the chill. Obviously Eve didn't see anything, because she'd just shot me an animated grin.

An icy draft chilled my ear, like a breath of winter that made me want to cup it to warm it, then . . . "Hello, there" loud in my ear.

I screamed.

Eve screamed.

We ran smack into each other and fell on our asses.

Eve caught her breath. "I'm gonna get you for scaring me like that."

"Mouse," I said.

"Yeah, well, if you're gonna buy this shack, get used to them." She scrambled to her feet and tiptoed back to the caskets, as if, after our screams, she could possibly disturb anyone.

"Gee, thanks," I said, wiping dust from my hands as Mr. Gorgeous and See-Through appeared facing me, arms crossed, enjoying the view.

I froze, knees up; his dimpled smile was so wide, I squeaked and scrambled to my feet. Of all the days to wear a pair of lucky panties—mint green silk briefs with clusters of clovers and "Nice Shamrocks" written on the front. "That was rude," I told him.

"Hey," Eve said. "Sometimes you need to hear the truth."

"I guess." I'd been talking to McShadow, of course, but she didn't know that.

I went to look out over Bank Street and, as I expected, a freeze rolled up my right side. No more putting it off;

I turned toward the chill, and icicles shot through me. "Dante?" I whispered beneath my breath.

He tipped his hat. "At your service."

"I don't think so."

"Nice panties."

"Peeping Tom."

"Even a dead man needs the occasional thrill."

"Afraid to come and watch?" Eve called, goading me.

I turned to her. "Believe me, I'm not squeamish. Go ahead. Open one. I dare you."

"I will. Okay, I am. Now." She pulled the cover up about a quarter of an inch and sniffed.

My bark of laughter echoed through the cavernous top floor.

Eve shot me a disgusted look and threw the cover back so fast, she screamed like a maniac. When she stopped, she looked inside. "It's empty."

"I'm going to look around downstairs a bit more," I said. "Scare yourself silly."

"Okay, I will."

I headed back to the fitting room—I mean to the horse stalls—where bits of hay still lingered. Dolly obviously had the exterminator in regularly, because I *hadn't* seen a mouse. Otherwise, the horse stalls would be overrun with them and the place would be in much worse condition, if only from vermin, termites, and carpenter ants. I'd have the building inspected, of course, but I thought it looked pretty sound. More so than I could have imagined.

I turned to find Dante leaning against a stall, like a playboy of old, though I could see a brass finial through his shoulder. Handsome as sin, he exuded charm in his tux with tails, top hat, and gray pinstripe pants.

Eye candy.

Maybe Dolly's mention of *The Philadelphia Story* colored my thinking, but between his twinkling blue eyes and the gray at his temples, Dolly's ghost sure made me think of a certain dimple-chinned icon. On the other hand, maybe Dante was the reason Dolly loved *The Philadelphia Story* so much. "She never forgot you," I said. "Dolly, I mean."

"I never forgot her. Where did they plant her?"

I couldn't help my smile. "She celebrated her hundred and third birthday yesterday."

"She's still alive? Good for her. Give her my best."

Yeah, right.

"I thought sure she'd passed the torch when you showed up."

"I'm thinking of buying the place. You have someplace else you could haunt?"

"No. I can't seem to get out of here."

"You probably left something undone."

"Dolly?"

A witty, slightly bawdy ghost. I smiled despite myself. "The ghosts I live with don't talk. How come you do?"

"Undertakers make peace with death. No sober hang-ups about where I am or what state I'm in. I know I'm dead and stuck here, but it's been too quiet. What do you plan to do with my carriage house? Something that'll get the place humming, I hope."

"I'm thinking of opening a vintage dress shop. This would be a ladies' fitting room. Could you live, er, exist with that?"

He gave me a bold and thorough, eye-twinkling once-over, the same way he'd looked up my skirt, stroking me, literally, with his gaze. Wow. I couldn't believe he saw my lucky panties.

"Love your shamrocks?" he asked, brow raised.

"What are you, a mind reader?"

"No, but I'm aces at reading panties. And I must say if that's an example of what women are wearing these days,

I'm sorry I'm dead." He reached toward my circle of bare midriff but I shivered from the cold and stepped back.

"Your customers won't have much to take off in this dressing room," he said, "but I'm game. The truth is: You may never get me out of here." His chin dimple deepened.

I wasn't really having this conversation, I told myself, until Eve screamed again, reminding me that I must be. Two caskets open.

"Dante, how much do you know about murder?"

"I never killed anybody."

"But you must have buried a few people who were murdered."

"More than a few."

"That doesn't instill confidence. Are you the only ghost in residence?"

"For the most part. The others, they come and go, and they don't say much. Me, I miss people. Conversation."

I'd lived with spirits for years at home and taken the gift for granted, until my mother told me that not everybody saw them, and if I mentioned it, people might not believe me. I could as easily live with them here and say nothing about it.

But a talking ghost? New territory. Dante would certainly pose an interesting, if not a seductive, challenge. "I'm investigating a murder," I told him. "My sister is the prime suspect. I don't really know where to start."

Dante rubbed his square chin, his dimple deep. "The killer is in the details," he said.

"What?"

"In my undertaking days, I tracked plenty of investigations waiting for the police to release the bodies. The cops, they start with the obvious suspects, but the fact is, it's never obvious. Start at the bottom and work your way up. Let the tiniest details string together like links in a chain that will get stronger. That's my take."

"Pretty insightful, if you ask me. Then again, I'm the kind that usually tries to go for the quickest approach; starting slow will drive me crazy."

Oh, Lordy, his grin. Be still my heart.

Eve screamed again. Three caskets open.

"She nuts or what?" Dante asked.

"Eve, she's brilliant. A computer geek."

"A who what?"

"Never mind. I'll explain another time." Oy. What am I, nuts for promising to explain computers to a ghost. "Why can't *Eve* see you?"

"You have the sight. One plumber in the last seventy years saw me, and when I said 'hello,' to him, he dropped dead of a heart attack. I can't hurt you. Just talk to me. I can't even touch you, and you look pretty damned touchable."

Hmm. A ghostly compliment. "I understand. Our house is haunted. Never bothered me, but you and I, we can only talk when nobody else is around. Got that?"

"Deal. Now, when are you moving in?"

"I'm not . . . at least, I don't think I am. This place would be for my shop."

He winked. "Think about moving in."

Wooly knobby knits; I must be nuts for being flattered to have a ghost flirting with me. I'd best talk to Aunt Fiona before I thought another minute about buying the place.

I heard Eve coming down the stairs and went to meet her. "Did you open them all?" I asked. "I didn't think I heard enough screams."

"Yes," she croaked, pointing to her throat. "Sore."

"No wonder. Any bodies?"

She shook her head in disappointment.

"Hot tea with honey and lemon would help your throat." I was thinking of all the places to start from the bottom. Tunney's butcher shop. Bartleby's, the Harp and Hound,

Mermaid's Cove, and Whyevernot, to name a few. Then there was the Cake Lady. All very unlikely places, but the cake lady had one thing we needed. Hot tea. "How about we grab tea and pastries at the Cake Lady while I ask a few questions?"

"Why the Cake Lady?" Eve rasped.

"To see if she saw anybody disappear from the party the other night." I could hardly explain McShadow's suggestion to start from the bottom suspect of the list during a murder investigation, now could I?

I didn't believe that I was taking advice from a ghost.

Twenty

It's all about good taste.
—GIORGIO ARMANI

The Cake Lady served pastries filled with meats and cheeses, tiny ones, so you could get an assortment that included dessert pastry and make orgasmic noises through the whole meal if you wanted.

The place smelled of almonds, chocolate sin, honeyed nuts, and strawberries. The soft ambiance welcomed customers with pastels . . . in the icings, the pastry box ribbons, robin's egg walls, the multihued check-print valances, and the wildflower bouquets on each round table.

You could see your reflection in the curve-top glass case. If you concentrated, you could also feel the expansion of your girth and the clench of your arteries hardening.

Nevertheless, Eve and I both wore our invisible pig-out bibs. Their presence had to do with a look neither of us could pinpoint but we recognized in each other, and when we wore them at the same time, watch out.

I went up to the counter and ordered the patisserie sampler for two. Oink. "Oh, and tea, hot tea right away, please. My friend's throat is raw."

"Tea with honey, then," the cake lady said.

I hated that I couldn't remember her name, but it would be rude to snap my fingers to get her attention later.

"I'm sorry," I said when she brought Eve's tea, "but I don't remember your name from the other night."

She straightened. "The other—oh, that's where I met the two of you, at the murder house."

I reeled at the statement and bit my tongue on the two-word answer that came quickly to mind. "Well, it's my house, I mean my father's, but I grew up there, and since that was our first murder, we've decided to keep calling it the Cutler house."

"Of course," she said. Either she had a poker face or she was dumb as a doorknob. I couldn't tell if she'd caught my irritation or not. "We've met," I repeated, "but I don't remember your name. I'm Maddie Cutler and this is my friend Eve Meyers."

"Everybody knows me as the cake lady." She held out her hand. "Amber. Amber Delgado. Nice to meet you both. I'll be right back with your lunch."

"She seems nice," I said.

Eve held her throat and reserved judgment.

Amber returned quickly with our food.

"Amber, can I ask you a question about the other night?" I asked, digging in to the pastries with gusto.

"Sure."

"While you were serving the cakes, did you notice anyone leave the party or go into another part of the house?"

"Only Mrs. Vancortland. She went into the bathroom, and when she came out, she went toward the back of the house. Nobody else that I can think of, besides you and your family. I could see that was a reunion, of sorts, though Mrs. Vancortland wasn't with you."

Wow, same answer every time. Deborah? Nah.

"Too bad, isn't it," Amber added, "about the murder and the Vancortland brides?"

"What about the Vancortland brides?"

"They certainly seem doomed to getting married pregnant or dying that way."

"What?"

"Well, everybody knows that Mrs. Vancortland was pregnant when *she* got married and now her son's bride—"

Involuntarily, my fists closed and my shoulders straightened. "No, I think you're wrong about her son's bride." No matter how fast the gossip mill ground, I knew Sherry would tell me first. Well, after she told Justin, that is.

"No," Amber said. "I'm sure I heard that Jasmine was pregnant."

Eve sat forward. "Jasmine wasn't the—"

I'd kicked her under the table.

Eve's jaw snapped shut and she gave me a look that promised retribution.

"How did you hear about Mrs. Vancortland?" I asked Amber. "She works really hard to keep that bit of history quiet." So hard that I'd never heard it. Sherry didn't know about Deborah's pre-wedding pregnancy, either, or I would. Justin might not even know. "Mrs. Vancortland hates to be talked about," I said.

"Tunney the butcher told me," Amber said, bringing Eve another cup of tea. "He says that gossip is good for business." She shrugged. "I suppose, being new in town, I should get to know the locals, like Tunney suggested. But I like keeping to myself. I don't even get the newspaper. Who needs more bad news? Maddie, would you like some tea or coffee?"

First, I would *like* to go home and grill Sherry; then I wanted to roast Tunney on a spit over an open fire for spreading that rumor about Deborah. "No, thanks. Amber, you met Mrs. Vancortland and her son's intended when they came in to look at wedding cakes, didn't you?"

Eve opened her mouth and shut it again.

"Yes," Amber said. "Hard to believe the poor girl's dead." The cell phone in her apron pocket rang and she glanced at it to identify her caller. "Excuse me. It's my nanny. My daughter's, I mean; *she's* the center of my little world. No wonder I'd rather not step out of it."

Eve waited for Amber to disappear into the back room before she kicked me. "Now can I talk?"

I pushed a mini meat pie around my plate. "She has a little girl," I whispered.

"Why is she so confused? And why couldn't I straighten her out?"

Aware of how far away Amber's voice had gotten, I spoke in low tones. "There's been a murder and I don't think we should share information. She thinks Jasmine was supposed to marry Justin," I said, "because Deborah and Jasmine, the stitches, didn't bring Sherry with them to look at wedding cakes."

"Well," Eve said, "she'll figure it out when somebody orders a Vancortland cake."

"Sure, when Deborah does."

"Hey, that's retro about her being preggers before the wedding. I mean she acts like she's made of twenty-four-karat gold, instead of flesh and blood like the rest of us. What did you say about Deborah and the cake?"

"I'll tell you on the way to the butcher shop."

"You can't still be hungry?"

I rolled my eyes and pulled Eve from her seat by the shoulder of her Hells Angels jacket.

"Hey, watch the finery." She dusted herself off.

"I do wish you'd wear a color, any color, other than black for a change." I remembered my father once describing Eve in Jonathan Swift's words: "She wears her clothes as if they were thrown on with a pitchfork." He'd been joking, of course, but he hadn't been able to keep from sharing a quote that so perfectly suited her.

"You always look like you're in mourning," I said. "Or ready for a street fight."

"I *color* my hair. That's enough for me, and the black clothes haven't exactly been a detriment," she added, a grin blooming as she focused on the door.

My brother Alex's hockey jock buddy, Ted Macri, came in, ignored me, and kissed Eve with a great deal of enthusiasm.

I couldn't get over how fast she could reel a man in.

Reluctant, Ted pulled from the kiss. "When I saw you, I thought maybe I could catch you for lunch." He slipped an arm around her. "Looks like I'm too late. Hi, Mad."

"Ted." I looked from one of them to the other. "Did I miss something? Were you two an item before we came home from New York?"

"Nope," Eve said. "We had our first date after we left Sherry's party."

Ted gave her a speaking wink. "An evening sail. What's the matter with your voice?" He knuckled Eve's throat. "Sore?"

She crushed his shirt front with a fist and pulled him breath-teasing close. "I'll tell you . . . tonight."

Turn your back one minute and your BFF has a new guy and a new twinkle in her eye. Though I shouldn't be surprised. Eve was a man magnet.

Ted ran a hand through his short, shaggy hair. "Forgive me for running, hot stuff," he said, giving her a quick kiss. "Since lunch with my girl is out, I have a date with a Zamboni, paperwork I was trying to avoid, then a hockey-camp peewee game." He kissed Eve *again* before he left.

I sat down and waited for him to shut the door. "'Scuse

me, Mizz Meyers," I said, snooty as could be. "But aren't you a fast worker?"

"So's Ted, but he's slow when it counts."

I nearly choked. "Whoa, TMI."

Eve grinned. "You're jealous."

"I know I am. I need a life! Let's go castrate the butcher." I stomped out of the cake lady's shop.

Eve followed, chuckling. "Aren't you and Nick on-again yet?"

Nick wasn't the problem. I was. "He hasn't gotten me the info I need, so can you surf the Net for me, you computer genius you?"

"Cut the crap. I just ate. You'll make me spew. You know I will."

"Thanks. Find out what you can about Amber Delgado aka the cake lady. She might not be a gossip at heart, but she took some satisfaction in spreading that piece of information about Deborah."

Eve snorted. "Probably can't stand her any more than the rest of us can."

I had to give her that. "Check out Jasmine and Mildred Updike—daughter and mother. Oh, and I can't forget Pearl."

Eve stopped. "Who's Pearl?"

"Vancortland's ex-fiancée."

"Oh, ho. Being home is like living in a soap opera."

"Tell me about it. Also, run a query on Deborah Knight and Mildred Saunders together. Those are maiden names for Vancortland and Updike, by the way. I suspect that they might have gone to the same school. As for Pearl, her mother came from New Orleans and was Cort's nanny." Remind me, I'll bring you a copy of the sketch I'm doing of her."

"Where are you going with all this?" Eve asked. "I need details."

"I have no idea," I admitted, "but anything you find could help give me a direction."

"I told you to think about putting yourself in the driver's seat," Eve said, "but I didn't mean you should drive yourself crazy. What are you going to do with your life, chase down clues, sell vintage clothes, or go back to New York?"

"Damned if I know, but we haven't been home a week yet. Don't you think that's fast to make such a big decision, even for me?" I was faking. I pretty much knew what I was going to do, if I could afford to.

Together, we entered the best butcher shop this side of the Mystic River. You could buy more groceries at a truck stop, but that didn't matter. The draw here was meat, the spices to go with it, and a handsome butcher to flirt with.

You could find the finest cuts for the discerning palate or buy the cheapest cuts and learn how to make them taste like the best. Tunney not only cut the meat, he told you how to cook it so it tasted divine. On the side, he knew everything about everybody, mostly because he charmed the hell out of them.

"Mad, Eve!" Tunney said, wiping his hands on his white, bloodstained apron. "Good to have you two patronizing and annoying the locals again." He winked.

We'd grown up living for Tunney's winks. "We're glad to be here. But we're not buying today. We came to find out if you noticed anyone disappear from Sherry's party the other night?"

"I don't keep track of people."

He so did.

"Come on, give."

Tunney packaged the man-sized rib eye he'd just cut. "That Jasmine girl, poor thing, and your Sherry's Justin. Sherry, too, come to think of it."

"Nobody else?"

"You all went into your father's den. Everybody knew that."

Guess we weren't very good hosts, I thought. Everybody had mentioned it. Maybe if we'd paid better attention to our guests—No, not even a good host quizzes guests who want to leave the room. *Where are you going?*

To the powder room.

What are you going to do there?

Besides, there's no containing guests when you've got as many rooms on the main floor as we have. Nope, regret and hindsight never solved anything. Not even a murder. "Okay, Tunney, thanks. Now, what's the scoop on Deborah Vancortland being preggers when she married Cort? Sounds like old news to me."

"Old cat out of a new bag," he said. "I heard the info came from an old family friend."

The family friend's timing stunk like a dead herring. I needed to know where it came from, though Tunney rarely revealed his sources. "And the family friend's name? *Please.*"

"Not this time, cupcake, because I don't know who the old friend was."

"Here's one question you should be able to answer," I said. "When did the cake lady open her shop?"

"About six weeks ago."

"Has she lived in Mystic long?"

"No, she's a transplant from New York. Kind of like you, but in reverse. We're all glad you're home to stay."

"Who said I was staying?"

"We just assumed, with you buying Dolly Sweet's building. 'Bout time it got a face-lift."

"I don't know if I'm buying it yet. Gimme a break and try to squash that rumor. I'm sunk if Dad hears I looked at it before talking to him."

Apology filled the meat cutter's expression.

"Dad knows?" I turned to Eve. "My father knows."

Tunney raised his hands, as if to say, "that's life." "The good news is that your father bought a rib roast for supper. The bad news is that he came in right after Ethel Sweet."

"That's it. I'm in the soup."

"Throw some squash and cinnamon in. You'll go down better."

"Mystic River is what I'm going down, without a paddle."

Twenty-one

History is the key to everything: politics, religion, even fashion.
                                        —EVA HERZIGOVA

I knocked on Aunt Fiona's door without having called ahead, but she was happy to see me. She led me into the parlor . . . my father uneasily ensconced in one of her easy chairs.

"Madeira!" he said, jumping up, as if I'd just caught him climbing down the getaway tree. "What are you doing here?"

I raised a brow. "I might ask the same question."

"He's worried about his daughters; both of them," Fiona said.

Dad ignored her and kept his focus on me. "And I might ask what you're doing changing careers and buying run-down shacks on a whim," he snapped, turning the tables. "If I've told you once, I've told you a thousand times to think before you act. 'A hasty judgment is a first step to recantation.'"

"What great writer said that?"

"Publilius Syrus."

"Dad, you're making that up."

"No, he was a Latin writer of maxims and a famous improviser in the first century."

"An improviser? Hah. Which means that he made his living using hasty judgment." I wrote in the air. "Madeira, one. Dad, zero."

With a quick hand to her mouth, Fiona muffled her chuckle.

My father shot her a look.

"You find some weird quotes, Dad."

"Years ago, that quote made me think of you. I knew when you were a child that hasty judgment would one day be your downfall. That day has arrived."

I led him to Aunt Fiona's kitchen table and sat across from him, my elbows on my knees, my hands prayerful—as in: praying for him to understand my weird obsession with a . . . well . . . shack.

"Dad, I've been fascinated by that place since I was a kid. We always stood just there to watch parades, remember? It's strange really how it always seemed to whisper my name, but that's not the point. I've been unhappy in my job—not my work, or craft, or the clothing industry—but in my present position with Faline."

"I'm sorry to hear that, but—"

"Here me out, Dad. There's a lot about New York I'd miss if I came home, but every new beginning must have some kind of an end. Mine would be bittersweet, it's true, but something shifted in me when it was time to bring Eve home. I didn't want her to go. While she shared my apartment with me over the last couple of years, she made it easier for me to put up with my job. She knows I need to make a change."

I moved my chair closer to his. "I love the Underhill carriage house . . . though by no means have I made an offer . . . yet."

Dad opened his mouth—to protest, I'm sure—but I covered his hand and he firmed his lips.

"As long as I'm confessing, you should know that I've been collecting vintage clothes for years. A friend's been keeping them for me."

"*I've* been keeping them for her," Fiona said, coming up beside me and drawing my father's ire her way, "in the apartment above my garage."

"I might have known." Dad rose in judgment.

"Harry Cutler. I picked up a ten-year-old child to help her take her mother's clothes to a thrift shop, and she sobbed all the way. She didn't want to give them up. She wanted to wear them when she grew up, so I turned the car around and we brought them here. So sue me."

My father's eyes filled. He excused himself and went to the sliding doors to gaze toward the woods and beyond. After a minute, he took out his handkerchief and wiped his eyes under the pretense of needing to wipe his nose.

Aunt Fiona held her hand over her heart as she watched.

I went to lay my head on his shoulder. "I compounded matters, Dad, by buying vintage whenever I found a stunner. I've sent Aunt Fiona some awesome clothes over the years for my . . . I don't know . . . nest egg or . . . collection."

He put an arm around me. "You can wear your mother's things anytime you want, Madeira. She'd be pleased."

"Thanks, Dad. I don't know what Mrs. Sweet wants for the building, or if I can afford it, but I'm . . . thinking . . . of opening a vintage dress shop there. Thinking," I repeated.

Fiona applauded. "Brava. I wondered when you'd figure that out."

"Fiona, please," my dad said. "Madeira, nobody buys old clothes."

"You're a great English lit professor, Dad, but you know nothing about fashion. Enough people collect vintage for me to make a living, because I know what I'm doing. I know where to advertise and I've been compiling a database mailing list of collectors for years. Vintage is big in New York. I'd get the collectors coming up here. Greenwich, Connecticut, and Newport, Rhode Island, are full of wealthy collectors. Dad, I've been working in the heart of the fashion industry. I've learned a lot, not only about design and making clothes but about style, marketing, and customer relations."

My dad cupped his neck; he always did when a debate wasn't going his way. "Show me the building."

We piled into my car, Dad in the front seat, Fiona in the back, because I invited her.

"Where's your car?" I asked my father.

"I walked over."

I gave him a double take. "Do you do that often?"

"Only when one of my daughters is suspected of murder and the other is about to commit career suicide."

In other words, never . . . until today.

To say they were impressed with the Underhill carriage house would be a blatant lie. They hated it at first sight. Then I opened the front door and turned on the lights.

"Oh, my; the outside is a total fake out," Fiona said, running her hand over the fine wood molding. "I've only ever seen carriage houses this beautiful at the Newport mansions."

My father went over to the hearse. "I don't know about vintage clothes, but I believe there are people who collect these."

"Yeah, well, I don't know if Mrs. Sweet realizes it's here. She may want it."

My father gave me a second look. "I don't think any centenarian wants a hearse, honey."

Aunt Fiona raved over my idea for a fitting room while my father grunted noncommittally.

The caskets stopped them both in their tracks and though they stood closer to each other than they had in eighteen years, they didn't touch.

I entertained them on the way home by telling them about Eve scaring herself by opening them.

Aunt Fiona laughed so hard, she caught my father's begrudging attention.

Maybe, with Sherry getting married, I *shouldn't* move home. Maybe, without his children to distract him, Dad might turn his mind to settling this feud between them.

Before going up to Aunt Fiona's garage loft for the dress I thought Dolly Sweet might like, the one that loosely reminded me of the wedding dress from *The Philadelphia Story*, I kissed Dad and Aunt Fiona good-bye.

Dad grunted and walked back toward our house without a good-bye for either of us. Stubborn, that man.

With Dolly's vintage gown in a preservation box beside me, I drove to the Sweets'.

As I parked, Dolly appeared on the opposite side of the front screen door. Despite the wiry white hair escaping her bun and more than a century's worth of wrinkles, she looked as eager as a girl.

We had so much to talk about, I didn't know where to start, but when she let me in, she kissed my cheek and invaded my space. "Did you see him?" she whispered.

I fell back against the doorjamb. "Who?"

"Dante, of course. Shh. Ethel's out back."

Dolly hooked her arm in mine and led me out the front door. "Let's take a little walk. Slow," she added. "And you have to do the steering."

"Yes, ma'am."

"You've always been such a dear girl."

This from the woman who'd wanted to whack me with

a broom once. "Seems to me I made you frightfully mad when I was a child, but I don't remember why."

"Hah. You picked my prize roses. I expected to win a blue ribbon for them and you picked them so I couldn't enter the competition."

I gasped. "No wonder you were spitting mad."

"What possessed you?" she asked.

"My mother wasn't recovering from her accident the way we hoped, and I wanted to see her smile. It worked."

Mrs. Sweet squeezed my arm. "Then they went for a good cause." We walked in silence for a minute, each lost in thought, until she turned to me. "So, did you see him?"

She couldn't possibly mean what I thought. "I don't know who you're talking about."

Her gaze caught mine and held. "Yes, you do. Top hat, black tux with tails, and gray pinstripe pants. That's how I thought Cary Grant should have dressed to marry Katharine Hepburn at the end of *The Philadelphia Story*. It's a perfect movie, really, except for what he wore to marry her. Don't you think Dante looks like Cary?"

"Looked," I said. "Past tense. He's dead."

"Hah. You had to see him or you wouldn't be agreeing with me about his looks. After I inherited the building, I went to close the place up and he showed himself to me."

"I so hope you mean that he appeared to you."

Twenty-two

Fashions fade, style is eternal.
—YVES SAINT LAURENT

I learned something from Dolly in that moment. After your hundredth birthday, don't try to laugh, breathe, and walk at the same time. Her amusement brought on a fit of coughing and some major imbalance.

My heart raced while I sat her on a neighbor's wall so she could breathe, please God. I might very well have killed her with that joke.

When she caught her breath, I released mine. "Are you all right?"

"This is the most fun I've had in years, but you can't tell anyone that I saw a ghost," she said, "or Ethel will put me in a home. You'll keep my secret, won't you, dear, about my hottie ghost?"

"If you keep mine. He *is* gorgeous. He said he still thinks about you."

"Oh." She covered her trembling mouth. "You've made an old lady very happy."

"He congratulates you on your hundred and third birth-day."

My God, Dolly glowed. She must really have been in love. She wagged a finger at me. "You should be honored. He doesn't appear to just anyone."

"I know. Eve didn't see him and he was standing right beside me."

"Are you interested in buying the place? You shouldn't wait too long to decide. I'm not getting any younger."

"I'd need to have it appraised, and inspected."

"No, dear, don't have it inspected or valued. Your taxes will skyrocket. Let them think it's still a shack until you turn it into . . . what *do* you want it for?"

I explained my idea, details emerging as I did.

Dolly tilted her head. "You know, I always thought there were fashions that could have stood the test of time."

"Precisely. But, Dolly, there are valuable antiques in your building."

"What? The hearses?"

"One hearse."

"When you got to the top of the stairs, did you go left?"

"I couldn't because there's a wall there."

"Right, because the door is cut into the wall toward the front of the building. You'd have to be looking for the cuts to find it. The key I gave you opens it. It leads to a storage room over the horse stalls."

"Of course. I hadn't accounted for that space upstairs. Another hearse?" I asked.

"At least one and some other stuff. Odd things. I forget what exactly. The hearses were outdated, but Dante's father had loved them, so Dante stored them away."

"Is Dante as nice as he looks?"

"He is."

No, he was, I thought.

Dolly smiled like a dreamy-eyed schoolgirl. "Did you

notice the names of the horses in brass at the back of each stall?"

"No, I didn't."

"One brass plaque says Dolly. Dante named his favorite filly after me. It's a sound building."

"Seems scary not having it appraised or inspected, but I see your point. My dad seemed to think it was sound, too. How much do you want for it?"

"I've been thinking about that ever since you left. I'm out of the kind of time and energy I'd need to spend the money I have. Dante left me money, too, you know? Lots of it. Ethel will get most of that. I mean she's put up with me all these years. I haven't always been easy, but neither has she. She thinks you'll need to spend fifty thousand, maybe more, to fix the place, and she could be right. I haven't been inside in years."

That amount shocked me, but I tried not to let it show. Her selling price would be the deal breaker then. But I could get a mortgage on it if I had to.

"With expenses like that, you can't afford to pay much," Dolly said. "Would ten thousand dollars be too much?"

I wasn't sure I'd heard her correctly, then I shut my mouth so I wouldn't catch flies, as my nana used to say.

"Too much," Dolly said. "I knew it. Five thousand then."

"No, no, I don't want to take you to the cleaners, Dolly. That's a prime piece of commercial property. A corner lot. I could turn around and sell it for . . . a bundle."

"But you won't. Dante will have his home and you'll have your dream."

"How do you know it's my dream?"

"Everybody knows you kept your mother's clothes at Fee's and bought more."

Of course everybody knew, everybody except my father, until today.

"Cupcake, you love vintage." Dolly covered my hand

with hers. "I want you to have it. You brought up your sisters and brothers like a little mother when you should have been out playing. You had no childhood. I've lived a good long life. Bet I've had more fun than you. I had that fling with Dante, not unlike yours with Nick, I guess."

My jaw dropped.

She chuckled. "I can see that tree from my back bedroom on the second floor. You started young. I was a bit worried about you back then, but you've held your own and you were due for some fun."

She tilted her head. "Still, I don't think your Nick is as attentive as Dante was. Always going off on assignment. You should make him stay home more."

"I can't believe you've known about me and Nick since the beginning. Does the whole of Mystick Falls, including Mystic proper, know how long we've been . . . together?" Sort of.

"Of course not. Not even Ethel. I know when to be discreet. Nobody knew about me and Dante, either."

That's what you think. Scrap!

She patted my knee. "To hell with the money. I'm deeding Dante's carriage house over to you for the cost of this year's taxes."

"Oh, I couldn't just take it—no, wait, how much are this year's taxes?"

The old lady cackled. "Reasonable for a prime piece of commercial real estate on the corner of West Main and Bank. Sell one of the hearses and you could pay your taxes, maybe for more than a year."

Right. I'm sure there are loads of hearse collectors out there. "Are you certain about the hearses?"

"Nobody my age wants a hearse, believe me."

"That's what my father said."

Dolly grinned. "I have no attachment to the building or its contents, only to the man who owned them. And I love you for saving me the cost of taxes. Open your shop. There's no price between friends."

We started back toward her house, me doing the steering. "Can I keep the key for a couple of days so Nick and Alex can see it?"

"Of course, dear, and I'll have Fiona draw up the property transfer papers. The title will be clear, I assure you."

I got Dolly home safe and sat her on her sofa. "Oh, wait. I brought you something. Almost forgot in my excitement."

I fetched the gown from the car, and then I had to break it out of its preservation box. "It's a 1937 Chanel," I said, opening it in front of her, "and quite reminiscent of Katharine Hepburn's wedding dress."

Dolly applauded when I removed it from the box and then she got silent as it unfolded itself from the waist down. I shook it out. "Pink froth and layers," I said. A pricey prize of a gown, but nothing compared to the Underhill carriage house.

She tilted her head. "How much would I have to pay for that if I was a collector?"

"There's no price between friends."

She nodded. "No need to make me a dress. This is the one."

I nodded, too, because I knew it. "You can wear it to next year's birthday party with the governor."

"I don't know about that, dear, but I'll certainly be wearing it when I leave to join Dante on the other side."

Twenty-three

In fact . . . fashion was also inspired by history.
—CHRISTIAN LACROIX

The next morning, I drove to Deborah's to pick up the wedding gown we'd forgotten at Vancortland House in the excitement of the Wiener raid the other night. I needed to get serious about fitting Sherry and redesigning the gown because time was running out . . . in the event there would still be a wedding and not an arrest.

No, I refused to buy into the fact that nothing had gone right since I came home. Instead, I'd *make* it right. I'd alter the gown and envision a wedding. Never mind that I might be the next murder victim when Deborah saw what I did to the gown.

I chuckled, imagining her expression when Sherry and my dad walked up the aisle.

I turned my mind to figuring out how to keep the gown's train, given the new design. Two possibilities came to mind: attaching the train where the skirt swirled out from the fitted body at the thighs or removing the original train and making Sherry a cathedral veil from the same barely there gossamer lace as the coat.

I'd had some lace catalogs overnighted from New York and found an amazing Bruges lace—known as Binche or magic lace—from an artisan on the coast of Belgium. There was no question. Magic it would be.

As I gave my name to Deborah's surveillance robot, I thought about Dolly Sweet, who knew she'd be wearing her Katharine Hepburn dress for her funeral.

Seriously, what hundred-year-old wouldn't? And yet, she'd fooled me into being happy for her. Probably because she thought of going to Dante as something more like a wedding.

It also creeped the scrap out of me to think I might eventually have two chatty ghosts in residence at the carriage house, because Dante *wasn't* "on the other side," though maybe he'd leave the building if Dolly was finally waiting for him. Who knew? Maybe she *was* what he'd left unfinished, after all, and they were meant to be together for eternity.

One could only hope.

Then there was the matter of telling my dad that I had actually acquired "the shack," as he calls it, for the nebulous price of taxes.

Cortland House looked less ostentatious the second time around, without the last bright sunburst before dusk gilding it. The dozen or so police cars out front did not add to its ambience.

Son of a stitch! What now? Had Justin's DNA matched the fetus? I didn't want my sister to be the prime suspect, but I didn't want her heart broken, either.

Deborah met me at the door by throwing herself into my arms. *Huh?* "Madeira, you're just the person I'd want beside me at a time like this."

"A time like what? Why me?"

"Because you tried to help when I fainted last night."

"But you wouldn't let me."

"I was embarrassed," she said.

Lucky me. A red-letter week: on the downside, a dead body, a sister with a broken heart, and an exasperated father. On the upside, two new friends: a hottie ghost and a strutting society peacock. Or peahen, I supposed. However, knowing Deborah, she'd surely appropriate her mate's colorful plumage.

With no other choice, I slipped an arm around her and went inside. "What's going on?" I asked, watching two policemen upending vases in the foyer as if searching for drugs.

Deborah huffed. "They have a warrant!"

"How dare they!"

Her head came up and I tried to look innocent.

"Did they say why?" And did they plan to stay for a week, because that's how long it would take to search the place. A month, maybe.

"No, they showed Cort the warrant and invaded. When I protested, Cort told me to—" Her eyes filled. "He told me to 'be quiet.' He's never spoken to me like that before."

About time somebody did, but maybe not Cort. "Is Detective Werner here?"

"I'm right here," Werner said, coming our way.

Deborah snubbed him and walked away.

Werner scratched his chin as she did. "Did you want me for something, Madeira?"

"Maddie might not," Justin said, "but I do. Why are you searching Cortland House?"

"The deceased could have had something that somebody wanted badly enough to kill for, something she might have hidden here where she stayed. That's the scenario we're exploring. I have a full team in her room."

Justin's eyes narrowed. "You have a full team in my mother's room, as well."

Werner failed to respond. He knew something we didn't. Scrap!

One of the maids approached me then, and Werner took the opportunity to disappear. "Mrs. Vancortland wanted me to tell you, miss, that she found her wedding album and left it for you in your favorite room."

Deborah's album. Yes!

After the maid left, I hugged Justin on a whim and pulled as quickly away. "Sorry. I'm just so glad that they haven't arrested you."

"I *knew* my DNA wouldn't be a match, Madeira."

"I'm sorry, Justin. Sherry knew it, too. I'm just in panic mode. I never thought that any of this could happen."

He hooked an arm around my neck. "You're forgiven, Sis."

Aw. Now if he put me in a headlock, he'd feel like a real brother. "That's you off the hook. Now we can concentrate on getting Sherry off. Stay positive."

"Is she with you?" he asked, failing to hide his longing.

"No, I came to pick up the gown. I have to get moving on the alterations."

"If Sherry will still have me."

"Go and convince her that she will."

"The police want me to hang around," Justin said, "so I called her. She'll be here any minute."

"But I need her for a fitting. Never mind," I said at his disappointment. "I'll fit her here in the sewing room, but you—" I poked him in the chest with my index finger. "You have to get lost while I do."

"We have a sewing room?"

"Sure. Your mother usually keeps the door closed, but the wedding gown's in there, so stay away."

Justin turned toward the doorbell. "That'll be Sherry.

Let me have her for a while, Mad, before you start fitting her? I need her to forgive me."

I waved him away. A minute later, I found Werner in the sewing room examining Sherry's gown.

He looked up in surprise.

I crossed my arms. "Lytton, if you take that gown as evidence, I'll beat you."

"Threatening a law officer, Madeira?"

"My sister will be wearing that in less than a month to marry Justin. Seriously, tell me it's not evidence."

"It doesn't appear to be, but the Vancortland museum is enough to distract anyone."

"Even a detective?"

Werner raised his chin and I knew enough to shut up. "What are you doing here?" he asked.

"Fitting my sister for that wedding gown."

"So where is she?"

"She and Justin are making up after last night, I hope. They're in love, but they'd be happier if Jasmine Updike had never shown up."

"Jasmine would be happier, too." Werner checked his notes. "She showed up the week after the announcement of your sister's engagement hit the society pages."

Whoa. Jasmine and the cake lady had come to Mystic around the same time?

Was there a connection?

Twenty-four

Fashion is gentility running away from vulgarity and afraid
of being overtaken.   —WILLIAM HAZLITT

Werner went back to searching the sewing room, probing
and examining objects while I got ready to fit Sherry.

"I'll bet the news of your sister's engagement to Vancortland the Fifth hit every society page in the country,
knowing Mrs. Vancortland."

"I'll take that bet. I saw it myself in the New York
papers, and though Deborah was never fond of Sherry, she
certainly shouted that engagement far and wide."

"Well," Werner said, "she hadn't met Jasmine yet. And
methinks the lady likes publicity." He pointed to a framed
newspaper clipping of Deborah's wedding announcement
on the wall.

I hadn't noticed that before. Was Deborah trying to im-
press an old ghost? I wondered. "Deborah likes publicity,
but not gossip."

"You were right; she isn't in mourning." Werner took
a book from the shelf. "If you ask me, she seems
relieved—"

We locked gazes, mine of surprise and Lytton's of regret, probably for his slip. Could Deborah be the killer? "Lytton, what are you really looking for?"

"You know I can't discuss an open case."

"But I helped you. Does it have anything to do with the picture of Deborah and Mrs. Updike together as girls? Because that tip came from me, don't forget."

"For that, I thank you; *great* lead, which is more than I *should* say. Have you learned anything else that might help?"

"Oh, so I can share with you, but you can't share with me?"

He shrugged. "We're both trying to free your sister of suspicion. Isn't that enough?"

"You got me, but all I have is homegrown gossip."

He sighed. "I've had Mystick Falls gossip to my armpits. Why don't you leave the investigating to us?"

"In case you hadn't noticed, my sister got screwed out of a mother, and preparing for her wedding *should* be the happiest time of her life. Sherry needs to catch a break here."

"You did good by her, Mad, mother-wise."

"I'm your thorn and you're being nice to me. I don't know how to deal. Cut it out. Anyway, I want her to have the wedding of—" I sighed. "Deborah's dreams."

Werner chuckled. "Mrs. Vancortland is a force to be reckoned with."

"Why, thank you, Detective," Deborah said, walking in on us. "I'll take that as a compliment."

Humble *and* dense.

She put her arm through Werner's. "Tea is being served in the drawing room, but it's being delivered to your men on the job, assuming they're not allowed to stop ransacking. We hoped you'd join us, Detective. Madeira?" She offered me her other arm.

"No, thanks, really."

Werner gave me a "help me" look as Deborah escorted him out the door. He probably only acquiesced for a chance to grill Deborah, who'd loved Jasmine one minute and forgot she existed the next.

I jotted down the date of Deborah's wedding, embossed in gold on her album, so I could compare it to the date of Justin's birth, which I'd get from Sherry later.

In Deborah's wedding album, I found angle shots of her in the gown. I grabbed my sketch pad, and sketched the dress, old and new, fully prepared, if I heard footsteps, to slide the pad into my '93 Jean Paul Gaultier "Bag of Biblical Proportions."

As I sketched, it came to me. Deborah had been slim as a reed. The gown hugged her torso from cleavage to thighs. I knew body styles. Her stomach was concave, never mind convex.

So the gossips were wrong. Not pregnant at her wedding. What an odd coincidence for the gossip to come out now, as if it mattered . . . now.

And who started it?

The doorknob turned, and that fast, my sketch pad was in my bag. Sherry slipped in through a sliver of a door opening.

Justin tried to charm her into letting him in, but she blew him a kiss and locked him out.

I chuckled. "Bit hard to get away?"

"You have no idea."

"I guess I don't. I take it the wedding is still on?"

"Sorry, Mad, I didn't mean to sound smug."

I hugged her. "Happy. You sound happy, which makes me happy."

"You're the best."

"Strip. I have to start pinning. Why you insisted on

getting married so soon—" I stopped and examined her figure.

Sherry put her hands on her hips and huffed. "I'm not pregnant. I'm in love. It's getting harder to sleep alone."

"Which is why Justin spends half his nights at our house."

She played coy. "Hardly the same. It isn't *our* house."

"You're moving into Justin's downtown Victorian, I take it?" I slipped the gown over her head.

"Yes, and I love what I'm doing to make it mine. Changing curtains and rugs, redecorating the master suite, and making Justin sleep in a spare room when he's not at our house, so we can use our decadent new bedroom for the first time together as a married couple."

"It sounds wonderful."

"After you open your shop, you can come to lunch during school breaks. We'll be just around the corner from the carriage house."

"Hmm. Guess my shop is old news, and I haven't seen the paperwork yet."

"Yep, everybody knows. I'm happy for you, Mad, but I'm selfishly happy for me, too. I've missed you something fierce since you went to New York. Dad, too, though he'll never admit it. And Nick, he's probably doing cartwheels in his rigid FBI-controlled mind."

I chuckled as I buttoned her into the gown.

"Why haven't you and Nick tied the knot?" she asked.

I shrugged. "Neither of us is ready to step into the inferno."

Sherry paused and then nodded her head in understanding. "The minute you get close to the heat, you both pull away?"

"Bingo! I like to think of it as fire dancing. Nick is my perfect partner."

"Don't worry," my baby sister said. "You'll know when you're ready."

"I'm not worried. I'm enjoying the dance. And I'm really excited about my *potential* new shop. You know, this gown is a little tight in the breasts for you. You're bustier than Deborah, so I'll have to adjust the darts—but I have plenty of material. You also have a smaller waist and trimmer hips."

Sherry began to hum "Get Me to the Church on Time," like the happy bride I wanted her to be, but when I finished pinning the gown's torso and moved up to pin the pouf from her sleeves so she could see what they would look like, my world shimmered. Once again, I saw a different bride in a different time, but in the same place.

Pearl was all decked out. Gown and veil, pricey necklace and earrings.

The gloves covering her work-worn hands seemed to give her confidence. She held herself straighter and looked taller, hands relaxed at her sides.

She looked down at her seamstress. "I'd like the shoulders plainer with less pouf."

Ah, Pearl had an eye for style.

"Yes, *miss*," the seamstress said with a bite in her tone, a resentful staffer forced to treat a peer as her better.

The door flew open and hit the wall, startling everyone, even me.

Deborah in a snit, a sight to behold. "Get out," she snapped at the seamstress, who was only too happy to comply, and fast.

Deborah stared at Pearl. A definite if-looks-could-kill, poison-dart look. Oy. Lucifer's mistress, her toxic smile revealing a side of Deborah I'd only suspected. "Take. Off. My. Gown."

Pearl raised her chin. "It's my gown," she said, way less

confident than she pretended, her shoulders no longer as straight, one hand on her heart, the other clutching her pearl necklace. "Cort is marrying me. He *loves* me."

Deborah smiled. "Not enough to keep him from sleeping with me at the country club, where—you'll notice—he *doesn't* take the help. Cort is marrying me, not you.

"*I'm* carrying his child."

Twenty-five

My role is that of a seducer.
—JOHN GALLIANO

When I roused from my light-headedness, Sherry smiled with relief. "Are you okay, Mad? I waited for you to come out of it on your own. What did you see?"

A shark and her prey, for one thing, and a familiar pair of earrings, though I didn't know why they looked familiar.

I mentally frowned at the universe. I need a hint here, please. "Sis, can I tell you in a few? I need to talk to Cort."

Sherry grabbed my hand. "You won't hurt him . . . with memories, I mean. He's such a good man."

I squeezed her hand. "And he's getting an incredible daughter-in-law." I grabbed my Bag of Biblical Proportions and slipped it over my shoulder.

"Oh, before I go, when is Justin's birthday and how old is he going to be?"

"He'll be twenty-seven on September fifteenth. Why?"

"Tell you later. Lock the door behind me until that dress

is back in its garment bag, then take it out and put it in the trunk of the pimpmobile, will you?"

Eyes twinkling, Sherry agreed. I heard the lock click into place behind me.

Deborah hadn't been pregnant with Justin when she married Cort, and they'd had no other children, so either Deborah lied or she had a miscarriage.

"Deborah," I said, joining her guests in the drawing room. "Do you know where Cort went? I need to talk with him."

"Is it something I can help you with?" she asked, clearly curious and maybe a little miffed at being kept out of the loop.

"No, it has to do with our tour of the servants' quarters." I'd purposely brought up her personal taboo, and—if there was justice in the world—her worst nightmare, just to see her reaction.

The way she stilled spoke volumes. "He's around somewhere," she said, dismissing me in a way that only Deborah could.

So much for being her friend.

I climbed the back stairs to the servants' quarters and called Cort's name as I did.

He looked down from the top landing. "Madeira?"

"Can I talk to you?"

"Sure, come on up."

Back at his desk, he waved me in. "I never have company," he said, "and now twice this week. Deborah rarely comes up here." His smile became a grin, then a chuckle.

The poor man had to run away from home in his own house.

I opened my bag. "Here's your picture of Pearl. Thank you for letting me borrow it. My sketch of the coat came out great. And, I hope you don't mind, but I took the liberty of making a detailed sketch of her face and getting it framed. I thought you might like to have it."

He ate up the sketch with his gaze, ran his hand over the old photo, and slipped that into a drawer. My sketch, he hung on the wall in its place.

I knew that I'd managed to catch the love in her eyes.

Cort swallowed as he examined it. "This means a lot to me, Madeira. Thank you."

"I signed the drawing," I said, "but I'd also like to write her name and the date on the back for posterity. May I?"

He took the sketch down and handed it to me.

I slipped the backing from the frame and took a sketching pencil from my bag. I wrote "Pearl" and then I looked at him to supply her last name.

"Morales. Pearl Morales," he said.

I wrote her last name and the date, put the frame back together, and offered the sketch to him, but he seemed to be gazing beyond me, to better times, perhaps.

Maybe he and Deborah were happy in their own way. Who was I to judge?

On the other hand, if I'd been in Pearl's place, that volley of Deborah's about Cort not taking me to the country club would have sent me running.

Deborah was a slick operator.

"When did you go to New Orleans looking for her?"

"Before I married Deborah. Madeira, I put all that behind me. I'm sure Pearl has, too. Obviously, or she wouldn't have left me."

"I'm glad it's behind you, Cort."

He touched the sketch on the wall as I left. Sure, he'd put it behind him.

I hadn't meant to bring up old hurts, but I needed to find out why the universe had shown me these things. Why had I seen Pearl in the gown, Mildred as Deborah's nurse, yet no glimpse of the past when I fitted Dolly for *her* vintage gown?

There must be a reason that only certain pieces of vintage clothing spoke to me.

I wasn't sure I liked the idea of being played by the universe like a puppet. I needed to speak to Aunt Fiona about that. Besides, I hadn't told her yet about meeting Dante.

When I left the servants' wing and stepped into the house proper from the back stairs, I interrupted Werner and several of his men.

He raised a hand to them, putting the discussion on hold. "Ms. Cutler."

I nodded. "May I speak with you, Detective? In private?"

"Certainly. Carry on with your search, men."

Lytton followed me toward the sewing room but stopped just short of my destination. "Mad, you could have talked to me anytime during the last mile."

"Not without anyone hearing, I couldn't." I grabbed his wrist, pulled him into the sewing room, and shut the door.

"Why, Maddie Cutler, how impetuous of you." He stepped closer.

"Back up, buster."

"I will, if you stop manhandling me."

"Oh, sorry." I let him go.

Werner tugged on his cuffs. "Forgive me for teasing you. Just don't manhandle me in front of my men, okay?"

"You called me Ms. Cutler for their benefit."

"And for yours, and you used my title in return. I appreciate that. You wanted to talk to me?"

"Two things. Have you found any boat tourists who might have seen Sherry and Justin in the boathouse?"

"We're checking on the ones who used credit cards to buy their tickets that evening. We'll only put Justin's ass on the six o'clock news as a last resort."

I smiled. "I'm sure Deborah appreciates that." I took a deep breath. "I think you should search her papers." For the one that Mildred Saunders signed, I thought, but didn't dare say.

How could I? Visions, indeed.

"Because she seems relieved Jasmine's gone?" Werner asked. He quizzed me with his look.

"I don't know, but I think maybe Deborah's hiding something." And if she wasn't, my suggestion couldn't hurt.

Twenty-six

A search for new values led to "Flower Power" and the Hippie movement, as well as interest in the occult . . .

—GERDA BUXBAUM

Where had I seen those pearl earrings before? Scrap! It could have been at a vintage shop in New York years ago or at the butcher shop on a local yesterday, for all I knew.

I checked the pimpmobile's trunk to make sure the gown was in there before I left Cortland House while several police cars came and went.

The swans on the estate gates as they parted reminded me of the earrings, kissing swans with pearl bodies and diamond eyes. Cort might have had the earrings commissioned, but I wouldn't ask. Sherry was right. He had painful memories.

I'd never seen Deborah wear anything like those earrings. Too sweet. Innocent. Her tastes ran to large sparkles of the diamond variety, pieces just short of neon signs flashing her worth. Mrs. Moneybags, my father had taken to calling her since our dinner here the other night.

My cell phone rang. "Hi, Eve, got anything juicy to report?"

"Not exactly, but I learned that Mildred Saunders and Deborah Knight were classmates at the same finishing school."

"No surprise there. Anything else?"

"That's it. What about Pearl; did you get a last name?"

"Just got it. It's Morales. Feel like going to New Orleans with me? I found an address on the back of a photo Cort has."

Eve sighed. "I'm giving a class twice a week. When did you want to go?"

"First thing in the morning. Want to see if you can book us a flight?"

"I can't go tomorrow. I can't miss the first class."

"Bummer," I said, sincerely disappointed. "I'll go by myself then. It can't wait."

"Madeira Cutler, you are *not* trying to solve a murder by yourself?"

"I've had a couple more visions and I need answers."

"I'd like to go on record as saying that I don't think you should go alone, but it's too late to cancel my class."

"I'm going. Book me a flight?"

"I'm not your computer secretary, but of course I will, as usual."

"You're a keeper, Mizz Meyers. Do you need my credit card number?"

"No, I have it memorized. I use it all the time."

I scoffed. "I wouldn't mind if you did, for something besides your black fighter-pilot look."

"In your dreams. I am who I am."

"Whatever you say, Popeye. Thanks."

My phone rang again before I had a chance to put it back in my biblical bag. "Hello, Aunt Fiona. What's up?"

"The title on the Underhill-Sweet property is clear. Are you sure you want to go through with this?"

"Do you think I shouldn't?"

"What I think doesn't matter. If you're ready to move on this, you need to come and sign a few things before I can process any more paperwork. If you're not sure, I think you need a sounding board. I'm here, Madeira."

"I won't kid you. It's moving fast, even for me," I said, "and I do need to talk. I'm leaving Cortland House now. Can I come right over?"

"See you in a few."

Aunt Fiona sat on her front porch waiting for me with iced tea and a frown.

I took the garment bag with the gown from the trunk. "Can I hang this inside while I'm here?" I asked, coming up the walk.

Fiona stood waiting for me. "Is that Sherry's wedding gown? Do I get a peek?"

"Sure. You want to see what it looks like now? Or do you want to wait and see what it'll look like when I'm done with it?"

"Madeira, you're not?"

I tried to look innocent. "I'm not?"

"Deborah will have a cow." Aunt Fiona waved me away. "We never had this conversation," she said.

"Fine with me." I let her screen door bounce off my backside as I went inside to hang the gown.

When I came out, she handed me a glass of iced tea. "How's our little Chakra Citrine?"

"Afraid of ceiling fans and cell phones, as well as people, though she fearlessly battles house slippers and the dust bunnies beneath my bed. She especially likes to perch on the top of Dad's bathroom door and swat him when he goes in. She also happens to love *live* mice and baby snakes to the point that she brings them home as gifts." Dad found a tiny green garden snake in his bed the other night.

Fiona clapped a hand to her mouth.

I grinned. "I don't know how Chakra will feel about Dante when we move into the carriage house."

"You changed your tune fast. You *want* the carriage house then? Rewind—move into? You? And who's Dante?"

"Dante Underhill, Mrs. Sweet's old lover. He's a ghost and comes with the building. Why can I see him and Eve can't? I've had enough surprises, Aunt Fiona. Why are all these psychic activities happening to me since I came home? Conversing with hottie ghosts, visions of the past, messages from the universe?"

"Really, you talked with Dante? Can I meet him?"

"You think you'll see him?"

"I know I will."

I made the porch swing go faster. "Why me? Why now?"

"I don't know. Sometimes these talents develop late."

"Okay, so that's the when. So now the why. Who am I to have such gifts . . . if they are gifts?"

"They are, sweetie, if you want them to be. As to who you are; you're your mother's daughter. She, too, was open to what the universe asked of her."

"My uptight mother was a witch?"

"Your father wouldn't be happy if I answered that question. But yes, and I can tell you that she wasn't uptight with the craft. By the way, she used dandelion wine for her rituals, which is why your dad wouldn't have liked the name for your kitten."

I chuckled. "Was Mom Wiccan?"

Fiona looked toward the heavens, as if trying to decide whether to answer. Eventually, she sighed in resignation. "Your recent experiences tell me that you need to know this, but woe to us both if your father finds out that you know."

I crossed my heart.

Fiona did, too. "The Wiccan tradition comes with a set of rules, and your mother didn't want to be bogged down by rules. Sound like somebody you know?"

I raised my hand. "Me."

"You're more like her than you know." Fiona took my hand. "Kathleen liked the earth-based Celtic tradition. She studied different paths and practiced what felt right to her. Sweetie, your mother was an eclectic witch."

"I guess you have to be pretty open-minded to practice witchcraft."

"It's like a calling."

"I can't believe I'm like her. I thought she was uptight and you were the free spirit. Now for the big question. Are you a witch, Aunt Fee?"

"I started as a solitary like your mother, then in college, we found each other and a couple of other like-minded individuals, and we practiced together."

"But why become a witch?" I asked.

"It's a belief system, sweetie, a spirituality linked to nature. Have you ever seen the quote 'You call her mother nature; I call her Goddess'? I don't know who said it first, but that's it in a nutshell. I love the words "blessed be" and "bright blessings." I believe if everybody understood that whatever they put out there came back to them times three, they might think before hurting others. Like your mother, I'm an eclectic. I listen to the universe and to the beat of my own heart."

"You and my mother, you practiced this 'respect for nature' together, didn't you?"

"We did, to your father's dismay."

"Can you do magic?"

"Within the realms of my belief system, the rules of nature, and magical ethics. To start, as I said, whatever I send into the universe comes back to me times three, therefore, the words 'and it harm none' are, in some form, part of any spell. I can't change the free will of another; if I try, I'm failing to grow psychologically and spiritually."

"What can you do?"

"I can cast a spell so you find a solution to a problem, but no spell will *solve* your problem. *You* have to work at that. By the same token, I can do a spell so you find the right job, but if you don't go job hunting, my spell is useless. I can cast a spell so you obtain your heart's desire, but be careful what you wish for. Your heart's desire may have a cost you're not willing to pay."

"Wow, so how does magic work within the rules of nature?"

Aunt Fiona smiled. "I can't make a pot of rosebuds bloom before our eyes. I can't cast a spell so you win the lottery, though there are spells for luck. I can't turn a person into a toad."

"Or vice versa?" I asked.

We laughed together.

"How did Dad feel about Mom's beliefs? Witchcraft doesn't sound like something an academic would embrace, especially as sober an academic as my father."

"Harry tolerated the craft until we had a car accident on our way home from a midsummer celebration."

I stopped the swing. "I didn't know you were with Mom when she had her accident."

"Your mother saved my life by pulling me out of the car before it caught fire. We didn't know she was bleeding internally. We thought I was hurt worse than she was, but we were wrong."

"What about you and Dad; why the feud?"

"I think I remind him of what he's lost, so he avoids me. At first, he blamed your mother's death on our beliefs, and then he blamed himself for not driving us, in protest of our beliefs."

"Oh, no. Poor Dad."

"I know. Now, I think he's trying to make peace with destiny."

"Trying but not necessarily succeeding?"

Fiona shrugged.

I sighed and straightened my purse. "I'm not ready to tell Dad about my new gifts," I said. "I may never be."

Aunt Fiona patted my knee. "That's up to you, dear. Just remember that he'll love you no matter what, the same way he loved your mother."

"Thank you, Aunt Fee. Because this scares me, this new . . . power? Insight? Witchcraft? Insanity?" I shivered. "Is there such a thing as being a natural witch?"

"I think some of us are born to the nature of the craft, though it takes time to settle into it."

"Did you and Mom take me moon dancing because you thought I had a natural affinity for the craft?"

"You saw the house ghosts like we did. We thought it was possible."

"But I can embrace the craft or not. It's my choice."

"You're in communication with the universe; it hasn't rushed you yet, has it?"

"Whew. Good. Because I'm not sure about any of it."

"You wouldn't disappoint anyone if you didn't embrace it."

"I'm glad to know that. Do you think Dante is a natural part of the universe communicating with me?"

"Possibly."

"Suppose I don't want to communicate."

"If you weren't open to communicate, you wouldn't have seen Dante."

Scrap! Of course I wanted the gift; the visions and the hot, chatty ghost, in the same way that Eve wanted to open those caskets, screaming with the thrill of adventure.

The witchcraft? I wasn't so sure. "Why doesn't *Mom* appear to me?"

Fiona smiled. "I've often wondered the same thing. She may have gone to the other side right away. The power of love can do that. Nothing left undone. She'd honored and respected the universe and gave it four gorgeous gifts, you, your sisters and brother."

"So once you go to the other side, you can't come back?"

"Not necessarily."

"Wow, you're full of information."

Aunt Fiona chuckled. "I'm sorry, dear, but some of this you'll just have to learn for yourself. As you embrace your gifts, answers will come to you."

I sighed. "I'm flattered that I'm like you and my mother," I said. "Scared, but honored. Dolly's building is like a gift from the universe, too, isn't it?"

"You tell me. The universe always has something to say. Listen."

I listened, hard, but I didn't hear a darned thing, beyond birdsong, the wind in the trees, the river licking the shore, and the whisper of butterfly wings.

Fiona took a folder from the small, white, wrought-iron table beside her rattan porch chair and cleared her throat. "Change of subject. The carriage house, ghost and all, do you want it?"

"How much *are* the yearly taxes on it?"

She shuffled through her papers and showed me an amount.

I whistled. "I can afford to keep that building for five years without making a profit."

"I think the contents might help with that, though there's no official inventory." Aunt Fiona took off her glasses. "But as far as your design talents are concerned, what about creating private designs under your own label . . . in addition to selling vintage? You have a magic flair with clothes. A unique style to market."

A magic flair with clothes . . . Bling! The last piece of the "what Madeira wants" puzzle fell into place. Vintage *and* my magic designs. Vintage Magic!

"Aunt Fiona, I think the universe wants us to celebrate." I ran down the porch steps to a sunny patch of grass on the side of the house near her star-shaped herb garden. Duh! Her pentacle-shaped herb garden. "Hurry up."

She followed me, her smile growing, took my hands, and we twirled and laughed, like schoolgirls at a playground.

My father stopped in his tracks at the sight, with Chakra Citrine pulling against her leash. "Are you two crazy?"

"Are we?" I asked. "Are you? I thought you didn't want a dog to walk but now you're walking a cat."

"The point is that I'm not *required* to walk her . . . unless I want to. What's going on here? Ah, you're the image of your mother, right now, Madeira, with the sun shining on that hint of paprika in the dark brown sugar of your hair. Your hazel eyes are so bright, greener than gold right now, and you look . . . happy."

"I am happy. This is a celebration." Fiona and I twirled one last time to show him, and my father chuckled, a rare and cherished sound.

"What are you celebrating?" he asked as we met him halfway.

"Dad, I'm accepting Mrs. Sweet's building . . . for the price of taxes. I'm coming home from New York to stay. Congratulate me. I'm the proud new owner of Vintage Magic, a shop for designer vintage and designer magic originals."

The way my father cupped my cheek, I sensed a quote coming on.

" 'In words, as fashions, the same rule will hold, Alike fantastic, if too new, or old: Be not the first by whom the new are tried, Nor yet the last to lay the old aside.'" He shrugged. "Who am I to argue with Alexander Pope?"

I threw my arms around him.

He'd just given me the greatest gift of all . . . his approval.

Twenty-seven

I was among the first to board the noon plane to New Orleans, because Eve had gotten me a first-class ticket. I should have told her I'd fly coach, but I hadn't thought of it. In future, I'd make a dollar go further, now that I was starting a new business.

I'd given Sherry a talking-to before I left about taking charge of her wedding and not letting Deborah do it *all* her way. Sherry perked up at the rebellious possibilities and I felt better leaving her in good spirits.

I'd dressed in a navy vintage Nicole Farhi pinstripe narrow jacket, with a knife-pleated crepe skirt by Betsey Johnson, the Connecticut-born designer to the stars.

An inveterate people watcher, I enjoyed the parade of diversity boarding the plane, and I thought again about my carriage house.

My carriage house . . . be still my racing heart.

The transfer/closing was scheduled for this coming Monday, but I might die of panic beforehand at the thought of the renovations I would have to do before I could open . . . well, okay, so the panic was also shot with a thick ribbon of wild anticipation.

Aunt Fiona had succeeded in getting everything rushed through because of the seller's age. Young Mrs. Sweet approved of her mother-in-law's generosity, but she didn't want to get hit with an inheritance tax on a building they were giving away, so the transfer was moving fast. The only thing that bothered me was that everybody expected Dolly to leave us at any moment. That, I would not buy into.

I looked for my cell phone to turn it off and realized that I left it at home connected to the charger. I really hated when I did that. Sherry said if I didn't switch purses all the time, it wouldn't happen so often. She keeps hers in the purse she uses for *everything* and never forgets her phone.

I rolled a pillow beneath my nape and closed my eyes, feeling the seat shift with the arrival of my seat mate.

Plane rides were a dicey business. You never knew who you'd get stuck beside, but at least no five-year-old was kicking the back of my seat every twelve seconds.

I tried to get a sidelong glimpse of the guy wearing the yummy aftershave, but he was leaning forward, facing away from me, trying to shove his carry-on beneath the seat, his scent making me miss Nick.

I adjusted my carry-on to give the guy room and we bumped heads.

"Careful there, ladybug." He rubbed my sore spot.

"Nick! No wonder I liked how you smelled. What are you doing here?"

"Eve didn't think you should be chasing a murderer by yourself. And neither do I, so I had her get me the seat beside you. You like how I smell?"

"You know I love Ultraviolet Man, you interfering beast."

"I do, you impetuous beauty."

205

"Shush. I have a book to read."

"Fine, I have an autopsy report to read."

"What? You have it?"

Already I wanted to smack the Italian studster for his cocky wink.

"Want to take turns?" he asked. "Me first? Or do you want to read it together?"

I stifled my exasperation, only because I wanted to get my hands on that report. "Together."

"That's my girl."

In a way, I did belong to him, but in another, neither of us belonged to anyone, and sometimes I missed the intimate daily connection with another human being, emotionally and physically. Even spiritually, though I wasn't sure quite what that meant to me anymore after Fiona's revelations and the possibilities they entailed.

"No need to try and charm me," I said. "I know you too well."

He tickled my ear with his breath. "The way I know you."

I elbowed him. "Shush."

He grunted, took out the report, and held it between us.

I read for a few silent minutes. Pregnant, I knew. The toxins in Jasmine's system were common antianxiety drugs. Not enough to kill her, but if she wasn't used to them, they could have taken the edge off her ability to struggle. Cause of death: strangulation. But the markings on her neck weren't consistent with the bridal veil as a murder weapon.

I picked up the picture of Jasmine's bruised neck and examined it closely. "What would make a mark like this?" I asked Nick. "It reminds me of a fancy dress trim."

"Nobody's figured that out yet."

"Any residue?"

"Yeah," Nick said, pointing to the report. "Olive oil."

I read it twice. "That's helpful."

"Not yet, it isn't."

I shuddered and gave him the picture. "Gruesome."

Nick withheld comment. As an FBI agent, I was sure he'd actually seen gruesome.

I read ahead and lifted page corners before he was ready, then I sat back in my seat. "We know the rest."

"You skimmed, as usual." Nick pointed to a line in the center of a long paragraph.

"Pearls?" I asked. "Jasmine had pearls in her mouth? You mean, like the pearls on the floor around her?"

Pearls . . . like the ones Cort had given Pearl. "Nick, could this be about vengeance?"

"Every murder could be about vengeance. Why?"

This was Nick. There were certain people in your life that you trusted to know the real you. Eve and Nick loved me, faults and all. How could I not come clean with Nick, my hero, who'd come on a greased pig chase to keep me safe.

I bit the bullet and told him about my visions, as corroborated by Fiona, about seeing Pearl Morales in the gown, and why I was going to New Orleans.

Nick pinched the top of his nose. A total stalling tactic. "Ladybug."

"Shut up," I said, keeping my voice low. "I see that you think I'm a fruitcake. Holy Harrods, I do, too. Do you imagine that this has been easy on me?"

"I know that you believe you've had—"

"Cut the psychobabble. There's no point in debating whether I did or not. Just listen. Eve got back to me last night with an updated address for the Morales family, so we won't have to dig as much as I expected."

Acting before thinking had worked in my favor. *This time*, I could imagine my father adding, and he would have been right.

Nick took my hand. "Fine, ladybug, let's say that you had a vision—"

"Several."

"Fine. Let's also say that what you saw happened at one time or another. There's no motive for murder. If it had to do with Deborah stopping Pearl from marrying Cort, why would somebody kill Deborah's houseguest, thirty years later, and not Deborah herself?"

"I don't know. Isn't this like following a lead? We don't have answers, just clues."

"Right, except that the clues are all in your head."

"Shut up and listen. Suppose the killer thought Deborah loved Jasmine, and they wanted to hurt Deborah by killing Jasmine?"

Nick shook his head. "A convoluted long shot, Mad, and Deborah's hardly in mourning."

"Which you don't find weird?" I asked as the flight attendant picked up our trash.

Nick took a last sip of his coffee before giving it up. "You're right. It *is* weird."

The seat belt sign went on as the flight crew prepared for landing. "Wow, that was fast," I said.

Nick tickled my ear with his whisper. "Don't ever say that to me in bed."

Hardly likely. He knew how to take his time. "There'll be no more of that, mister, if you keep calling me a nut."

"I didn't. You did."

"You didn't deny it."

He nibbled my ear. "There will be more, and you'll love it."

"You're such a . . . man."

He grinned with a cocky pride. "Did you check any suitcases?"

"I've got everything right here." I pulled my carry-on from beneath the seat.

We took a limo to a pricey hotel of Nick's choice. "Mr. and Mrs. Jaconetti," Nick said, checking in. "We have reservations for a king suite."

I opened my mouth to protest, but the man behind the counter shook his head. "No, your secretary called to fix that, Mr. Jaconetti. Ms. Meyers specifically asked me to tell you that she corrected the error."

I chuckled, and Nick gave me the evil eye.

The desk clerk pulled our reservations up on the computer. "I have a single for Mr. Jaconetti on the seventh floor and a single for a Ms. Cutler on the first floor, both charged to Mr. Jaconetti's credit card. Correct?"

"Correct," I said.

"Eve," Nick muttered, shaking his head as I signed in first.

Yes, Eve, I thought, still protecting me from the worms and still sticking it to Nick.

I kept quiet until we got on the elevator. "Mr. and Mrs. Jaconetti. Hah."

"I'm FBI and this is a murder investigation. I'm trying to protect your identity."

"I know your game. A room with a king for two."

"With a balcony overlooking Bourbon Street," he said. "Now who's sorry?"

I hated that I found the skeptic so adorable. But I hardly believed in my visions, so why should he? In my room, I let him back me up to the bed. We liked playing games, the two of us. Nick's anticipation and amusement reflected my own.

I saw the kiss coming. Wanted it, dodged it.

His heady ambergris scent, mixed with the jasmine, peach, and musk in my perfume turned us into a lethal and combustible combination. Nick clutched a gentle handful of my hair in one hand to hold my head still; the other cupped my face.

A shiver shot through me.

I liked giving him some control so I could find ways to thwart him, except when we wanted the same thing. My knees grew weak as I welcomed his mouth against mine, open and hungry . . . a waltz of tongues, a rise of awareness and appetite . . . until the phone rang and pulled us back to our surroundings.

There was no sound quite as jolting as the ring on a hotel room phone.

I answered and recognized Eve's chuckle. "Just calling to make sure you got the right room."

Nick nibbled my free ear, his hand sliding down my spine.

"You're a sneaky but ineffective bodyguard, Mizz Meyers."

"Hey," Eve said. "You behave yourself."

Nick took the phone from my hand. "Bye, Mizz Meyers." He hung up on her and glanced at the bed. "A king would be better, but this will do."

"Nick." I put the flat of my hands on his chest. "Sherry is counting on me."

Regret marred the carved angles of his features. "Of course she is."

"What my sister needs, more than we need a fire dance, is for us to take a quick cab to this address." I pulled a slip of paper from my pocket.

He read it and stepped away from me. "Stubborn, I can fight," he said. "Admirable wins every time. I promise, ladybug, that we're destined to be on-again any second now."

I sensed that. I might even be ready for it. Maybe.

"You're right, there's a murderer on the loose. And he might be getting antsy as the police close in. Time is an issue."

"You mean you were thinking with the wrong brain?"

"What can I say? I tend to favor it."

I scoffed. "Ya think?"

In the center of the city, we found the address we were looking for, a garden apartment off a fountain-centered courtyard with a live oak draped in moss. A world away from Mystic.

The apartment belonged to Antonio Morales, Pearl's younger brother, or so Eve had believed when she gave me the information.

I told Mr. Morales that we were from Mystic, Connecticut, and that we'd like to talk to him about Pearl Morales.

He tried to shut the door in our faces, but Nick showed his badge.

In the Morales living room, the man sat across from us shaking his head and refusing to answer each question until his anger got the best of him. "Pearl came home from Mystic broken," he snapped. "Somebody there owes her. She brought home two things, a hatred that destroyed her mind, and a baby in her belly."

"Pearl has a child?"

Morales nodded. "And a grandchild, so I hear."

"How is Pearl?" I asked.

"Come," he said, "I will bring you to her."

We left his home and walked several blocks in silence, the clicking heels of my Lagerfeld spectator pumps slowing me down a bit. The scents and sights of Bourbon Street and beyond called to me, lifting my spirits, until Morales entered a cemetery and wove his way through a maze of mausoleums.

I knew then where we would find Pearl.

Inside the Morales mausoleum, I froze as he ran his hand over her name carved in pink granite. Pearl Morales Delgado.

A shiver ran through me, fear and awareness melding into a stream of ice flowing through my veins. "Delgado? Do you know an Amber Delgado?"

Mr. Morales stilled, hesitated, and ultimately nodded. "Amber is the name of Pearl's daughter."

"Nick, we have to go home."

"We have a return flight in the morning."

"No, I mean we have to leave *now*. Sherry's in danger."

Nick took both my arms and looked into my eyes as if I might be under the influence or something. "Madeira, what are you talking about?"

"Amber Delgado is the cake lady."

"Who?"

"She served the mini wedding cakes on the night of my sister's party—"

I obviously hadn't gotten through, or so Nick's confusion said. "The daughter of the bride from your vis—from the Vancortlands' past?"

"Exactly," I said.

Morales swore in Spanish. "The Vancortlands; they ruined everything."

Nick stood straighter, listening, really listening after Morales echoed Amber's likely sentiment.

"The daughter of the woman Vancortland jilted was at his son's engagement party," I repeated. "How weird is that?"

"You have my attention."

"Amber thought Jasmine was the Vancortland bride; she told me so herself."

"Ladybug, you're talking too fast and you're not making any sense."

"Who cares? This morning, I talked Sherry into picking out her own wedding cake, and I forgot my cell phone at home."

"That sounds serious," Nick said.

I wanted to kick him, except that I knew my words must be as scattered as my thoughts. I took a deep breath. "A couple of weeks ago, Jasmine and Deborah went to pick out the wedding cake without bringing Sherry, so Amber *assumed* Jasmine was the bride."

"Oh," Nick said. "That puts the picture in focus."

"Damn straight. What if Amber wanted payback for what Vancortland did to her mother and got it by killing the next Vancortland bride . . . except she killed the wrong one? My sister could walk into the pastry shop any minute and correct that misconception. Is that clear enough? Gimme your damned phone!"

"Madre de Dios!" Mr. Morales wiped his face on his handkerchief. "Not *murder.*"

I looked at Nick's phone and blanked. Who remembers cell phone numbers with speed dial to fall back on? I thought I was sunk, but we'd bought our phones together, all of us at the same store, same time, for the family minutes, and our numbers were close.

I found Sherry's on the third try, but she was either out of range or her phone was off. I left her a message. "Sweetie, I don't have time to explain, but don't go pick out your cake today. It might not be safe. Stay with Justin. Lock the doors and don't open them for the cake lady." I clapped the phone shut and held it so tight my knuckles hurt. My father was at UConn, like Eve, teaching a last summer course and prepping for the new semester. Fiona would be in court and tied up for the rest of the day.

I had no justification for asking Werner to protect my sister. None.

Thunder rumbled in the distance.

"I'll try Alex," Nick said, repeating my actions, but he shook his head after letting it ring for a minute. "He must have turned off his phone for the meeting I'm missing."

"It was Amber's mother," Morales said, recapturing our attention. "Pearl, she poisoned Amber's mind, filling it with every detail of her short-lived joy and bitter emotional pain. But it's not Pearl's fault, either. It's the fault of another,

213

though Pearl never said who. I wondered if Amber knew who hurt her mother, or who her father was, especially when she . . . when her mind snapped."

"*Amber's* mind?" I asked.

Morales nodded with sadness. "Always a loner, that girl, in her own world nurturing dark thoughts. She did better under the doctor's care," Morales added. "She was improving, but she left the psychiatric facility four years ago without being discharged. We never knew where she went. About two years ago, she sent us word of her daughter and told us she was better. I think since you are here, she was wrong about that."

"Deborah could be in danger, too, Nick. I don't know her number, but doesn't Amber's mental state give us justification for calling Werner?"

Nick nodded and made the call.

"See if you can get him to take Amber Delgado in for questioning. Tell him that she owns the Cake Lady shop. Ask him if he can hold her until we get back. Tell him that Sherry's in danger and that we'll catch a quick plane out."

I turned to Pearl's brother and offered my hand. "Thank you, Mr. Morales." I smoothed my fingers over Pearl's name. She'd died at twenty-five, a fate she didn't deserve.

I pictured her in the Vancortland gown, saw her fleeting happiness and her love for Cort.

Sorrow rose up and tightened my throat. "Rest in peace, Pearl. We'll see that Amber is safe."

Nick got off the phone. "Werner agreed to bring Amber in and hold her for questioning, but he said he wouldn't be able to hold her long."

"Why not?"

"He thinks he made a breakthrough on the case."

"How can that be?"

"He arrested Deborah for Jasmine's murder."

Twenty-eight

I love old things. Modern things are so cold. I need things
that have lived.   —BARBARA HULANICKI

We picked up our bags at the hotel and drove to the airport
in a thunderstorm, which delayed our flight. Before we finally boarded, Nick was able to reach Werner and give him
our flight number and arrival time, asking again for him to
hold Amber until we got there, but she hadn't yet been
found. Her shop was closed when it should have been open.

Panic gripped me and my imagination ran wild. I tried
Sherry again with Nick's phone while the rest of the passengers boarded. When I failed, I called home.

Sherry wasn't there, either. I hung up and called again,
to key into our home voice-mail system.

One message: "I called your cell phone, Sis, and when I
did, I heard it ringing in your bedroom. I'm tellin' you, one
purse makes life easier. Anyway, congratulate me; I'm on
my way to take matters into my own hands. I'm going to
listen to bands until I find one *I* like, and then I'm going to
pick out my own damned wedding cake."

Oh, God, she had left that message hours ago. "Sherry's

in trouble, Nick, and it's my fault. Amber might know by now that my sister is the next Vancortland bride. Sherry could be—she could be—"

"Calm down," he said, putting up the seat arm between us to hold me. "Sherry will be fine. You're hyperventilating on conjecture. We've already sent Werner looking for Amber and Sherry. And there's no physical proof that Amber's the murderer."

Physical proof. Physical proof. Why did the words make me nauseous?

I needed to distract myself or I'd go mad. So I decided to sketch my visions to see if I might have missed the smallest of clues. I took my sketchbook from my satellite bag and began to put my visions on paper.

Sketching was a part of designing that usually brought me peace, but today my hands were no more steady than my heartbeat. Nonetheless I brought the scenes to life.

Life. That's what we were down to. Life and death. That's why putting the smallest details in each sketch was important.

I did every one, including my vision of Mildred as the nurse caring for Deborah.

Since I needed to keep busy or scream, I added a sketch of Deborah and Mildred at finishing school and the head shot I'd done of Cort's picture of Pearl, but I did this one with the pearls and earrings he'd given her. She must have taken her bridal jewelry with her when she left.

Despite the no-cell-phone rule after takeoff, I furtively tried calling Sherry several more times between sketches, but with no luck. If I got caught, I figured Nick could flash his badge.

My sketches were rough, and a bit shaky, but they were detailed, and who knew, they might serve a larger purpose than helping me work off a nervous breakdown's worth of energy.

I sketched through the flight, the storms that dogged the plane seeming like an omen of doom—my sister's doom—which only made me concentrate harder on every detail of each scene.

Nick respected my concentration, though I felt the seat beside me shift often. I wasn't the only passenger filled with angst.

He didn't ask to see the sketches until I sighed and said they were finished, and even then, I hesitated.

"Ladybug. You know you can trust me."

I put them in chronological order and handed them over.

I identified Pearl in the first. Nick whistled, gave me a look of speculation, and examined the rest with quiet focus. "I didn't mean to be derogatory when you first told me," he said after going through them. "Visions, really? I won't say it's not hard to believe, but these sketches speak volumes."

"Gee, thanks. You think I wanted a gift that would make me sound like a pathological liar?"

"Nevertheless, ladybug. Be ready to deal with the naysayers. Most people will think your story is fiction, that you're nuts, to use your word, but I know you better than that. Is there a trigger?"

"Trigger? What do you mean? Like the trigger I wanted to pull when you made me feel like a mental case for telling you about my visions? The clues are not all in my head. They're right there. On paper."

Nick winced. "Do the visions come when, say . . . a bell rings, or a clock strikes? Do they generally come to you only when you're with your sister? Or when you're working on her wedding gown?"

"When I'm working on *clothes*. Any clothes."

"Fine," Nick said. "So you had visions all the time in New York?"

"Never."

"So it happens only when you're in Mystic working on clothes?"

"No." I shuffled the sketches. "I had that vision in Wickford, Rhode Island. It's *vintage* clothes, I think. It seems only to happen when I'm working on clothes with a past," I said, excited to pinpoint the lowest common denominator . . . except for Dolly's gown. Bummer.

That couldn't be right. Well, maybe I was half right. No need to make Nick any more skeptical. "Fiona says it's called psychometry, knowing things about an object's past by touching it."

"Only old clothes talk to you?"

"Not all of them do, as it turns out, and I don't like your tone. I'm sketching my psychic visions. Live with it."

I was jumping out of my skin with the worst possible scenarios running through my mind by the time we arrived at the Providence airport, and as if the flight hadn't been long enough, we had to circle before we could land, because of the weather.

Thank the Goddess, we didn't have any luggage to claim. "Now we have to wait for a bus," I said, hearing the whine in my voice.

"No, we don't," Nick said as we cleared the gate and his phone rang. After a brief conversation, he hung up. "Werner's waiting for us out front."

"That's bad, Nick. He wouldn't be here if he didn't have bad news." My eyes filled as I imagined Sherry in Jasmine's place, strangled on a cold floor somewhere.

The darkness inside me was like the darkness outside where Werner stood by a patrol car waiting for us. "Get in, Mad," he said. "We need to talk."

I didn't move. "Sherry's dead, isn't she?"

"No, Mad, she's alive, none the worse for being locked in Amber Delgado's bedroom for a few hours."

My eyes filled from sheer relief. "Locked in Amber's bedroom?"

"Sherry said that shortly after she got to the cake shop, Delgado asked for a ride home. Said her car wouldn't start—she was waiting for a mechanic—but her daughter had taken ill."

I could see Sherry, the kindergarten teacher, falling for that.

"At her apartment, Ms. Delgado got Sherry to go in with her, in case the little girl needed medicine, so Sherry could go and get it."

Yeah, Sherry would fall for that one, too.

Your sister thought she was going to meet the child when she entered Delgado's bedroom, but the door shut and locked behind her. No windows in the apartment bedrooms, so Sherry picked up something heavy and waited at the door for Delgado to return. She said she heard Delgado making calls to find a sitter."

"That's odd," I said, not that Amber Delgado wasn't odd from the get-go.

"We took Delgado in for kidnapping, and I asked her about finding a sitter. She said the strangest thing. She said, 'The mind poison stops here.' That make any sense to you?"

"In a way, yes. She didn't want to poison her daughter's mind the way her mother poisoned hers. I'm thinking she probably didn't want to kill Sherry with her daughter in the house." Again, my tears threatened.

"That's a stretch, Mad," Werner said.

"Because you don't know the facts."

Werner rocked on his heels. "Suppose you tell me the facts, then."

"Let me call Sherry first."

Werner sighed, and I got into the police car and called Sherry. She heard my voice and burst into tears. I joined

219

her but composed myself quickly, told her that I loved her, and that I was on my way home.

Nick put our bags in the trunk of the police car. "My car's in the lot," he said, getting into the front seat, "but I'll come back for it."

"Why didn't you offer me a ride this morning?" I asked. "I had to take a bus."

"I needed to catch you by surprise, didn't I, if I wanted to go with you?"

"Right."

Werner joined me in the backseat. "Billings, drive," he said. "It's time, Madeira, the facts as you know them."

"As a child Cort was cared for by a nurse/nanny who had a daughter named Pearl Morales. We spoke with Pearl's brother today. Pearl and Cort grew up together; they were best friends. Cort told me that himself."

"I'm listening."

"Cort was engaged to marry Pearl when Deborah got in the way, effectively put an end to the engagement, and sent Pearl running home to her family. Pregnant. Amber Delgado is Pearl Morales Delgado's daughter, possibly, no probably, by Cort. Morales never knew Amber's father's name, but he believes that Amber did."

Werner sat straighter. "Now there's a skeleton I hadn't found. Does any of this comes with evidence?"

"Depends on what you consider evidence," I said, thinking of my visions, rather worthless when you came right down to it. "Pearl's brother said that Pearl called herself 'the throwaway bride' and until her death, she relived her every minute at the Vancortland estate, filling her daughter's head with hate."

Werner reopened his notebook. "I'm listening. I'm not saying I'm buying it, but I'm listening."

"After Pearl died, her daughter kind of lost it. Amber spent time in a psychiatric treatment facility, probably while she was a teen, judging from the time frame her uncle suggested. She ran away from the facility without being discharged, and her uncle lost track of her."

"You got that from the uncle today? Will he testify?"

Nick nodded. "We didn't ask but I think so. Delgado's a reasonable man and family obviously means a great deal to him. I believe he'll do what's best for his niece." He seems to think that Amber Delgado has all but lived her mother's experience at the Vancortland house. My guess is that she needs her ghosts brought out in the open to put them to rest."

"I agree," I said. "Don't forget that both Amber and Jasmine came to Mystick Falls shortly after Sherry and Justin's engagement hit the society pages. Suppose they came because of the announcement but for different reasons."

Werner kept writing. "If Amber Delgado is mentally unstable," he said, speaking as if to himself, "a Vancortland wedding announcement could have put her over the edge." He shook his head. "But it's all hearsay and speculation."

As I clutched my bag with the sketches, Nick turned in his seat. "Ladybug, be careful." The unnecessary endearment, likely for Werner's benefit, was not quite a request for a pissing contest, but it was certainly an "I know something you don't."

Werner gave me a look.

I shrugged, denying the implication. "Speaking of hearsay and speculation, why did you arrest Deborah?"

"I resent that."

He could resent it all he wanted, but I had a better case against Amber than he could possibly have against Deborah.

Werner put away his notes.

"I have reason to believe that Jasmine Updike was

blackmailing Mrs. Vancortland into letting her live with them, into acting like she, Mrs. Vancortland, liked Jasmine better than Sherry, and ultimately into helping Jasmine become her son's bride."

"Blackmail," I said. "Good motive. I didn't see that one coming." One for the Wiener.

Werner's expression said he thought he'd topped me. "Mrs. Vancortland also has a prescription for the antianxiety drugs that were found in Jasmine's system."

I read his body language and decided to call his bluff. "How many people at Sherry and Justin's engagement party have prescriptions for the same antianxiety drug?"

"Damn it, Madeira. If it's a thorn, you're going to find it. And if I'm not bleeding from it, you're going to push on it until I do."

"Ouch. Too many, I take it?"

"Seventeen, including the doctor who prescribed it for most of them."

No point in shoving the thorn deeper. "So what did Jasmine have on Deborah?"

"We found a *copy* of a document that could be construed as incriminating—we're still investigating—taped to the back of a painting in Jasmine's room at Vancortland house."

"*Could* be incriminating?" I repeated.

Werner leaned back in his seat. "We also found an unsigned, 'I know what you did last summer' kind of note. It outlines the way Jasmine was being fawned over by Deborah, but it doesn't have either of their names on it. It might be enough, though, to use as a trigger," Werner said, almost to himself.

Nick had explained triggers to me on the plane. I thought of my sketches. "So what does Deborah have to say about your . . . evidence of sorts?"

"Mrs. Vancortland isn't talking. She lawyered up and made bail. Oh, and you'll be happy to know that we found a tourist who e-mailed us snapshots of your sister and Vancortland in the boathouse. My experts say they're genuine and not computer enhanced. I made some wallet-sized. You want one?"

I pushed on his arm. "For a cop, you're a rat."

He sighed. "I apologize. Out of nowhere, I seem to get these throwback urges to be vengeful and obnoxious. Let's stick to the facts and be adults about this. My evidence is better than your evidence."

"If I don't agree, you'll take your toys and go home?"

Nick cleared his throat and Werner said nothing.

Ignoring Nick's warning, I took out my sketches, put them in order, and showed them to Werner.

Without a word, he looked them over with the discerning eye of a detective, and while he did, I told him the story of each.

Werner shook his head. "How could Jasmine know about Deborah getting Pearl Morales out of Cort's life?"

"From her mother?" I suggested. "Mildred was Deborah's nurse shortly after she married Cort."

Werner grunted as if he'd known that. I showed him that sketch but he barely looked at it.

"The town gossips say that Deborah was pregnant when she and Cort married, but Justin is too young to be that child."

Another grunt, as Werner flipped through the sketches for the third time as we crossed the state line into Connecticut. He turned to me. "Did you get these from the Morales family? Were they Pearl's?"

Nick unbuckled his seat belt and turned all the way around to watch me try to escape the web I'd spun myself into, his seat-belt reminder beeping a warning.

I kept myself from exchanging glances with him. "Lytton, what matters is that I have this information, not where it comes from."

"Not true. Depending on your source, these could be used as evidence. Are they evidence?"

"They're not," I said. "They're as good as your vague and unsigned documents against Deborah, pretty much worthless."

Lytton turned into an interrogator before my eyes, slapping one handful of sketches against the other. A bit of subtle intimidation. "Madeira, who drew these sketches?"

I decided to heed Nick's warning. "I hardly know the person who sketched those pictures. Some sort of psychic who would lose credibility if I gave you a name."

True? Of course, true.

"I've hurt enough people in my life," I added, making a point Werner could appreciate.

He rubbed the back of his neck. He wasn't going to push me further. "Billings?" he said to his driver. "You didn't hear this conversation. If you did, you've got a desk job."

"Hear what, Sergeant?"

I crossed my arms and schooled my features to hide my relief.

"Madeira, I think the pepper spray episode might have been the high point of our relationship."

"What relationship?"

Nick coughed.

Werner shook his head. "So, there's no way to prove either of our theories."

"There might be," I said. "I have an idea. It's a long shot, but it's an idea."

Twenty-nine

Don't spend time beating on a wall, hoping to transform it
into a door.
                                            —COCO CHANEL

"Let's go," I told my father and sister as I hung up the
phone the following morning. "Against all odds, Werner
has agreed to my idea, or a version of it, anyway. Dad, I'll
call Nick while you drive."

My dad and Sherry were quiet on the drive to the Cortland House. Nervous anticipation made us all somber.
Luckily, the trip was short and soon we were pulling up in
front of the gaudy mansion. Just behind us, Werner drove
up in a squad car with Amber in handcuffs in the back.
She'd been arrested for kidnapping Sherry, of course, but
evidently, no one had seen fit to bail her out.

When a second cruiser arrived with a woman carrying
a toddler, Werner uncuffed Amber, and she ran toward the
child, who opened her arms and called her "Momma".

Nick's car was making its way up the drive.

Werner came to meet me. "That's the little girl's nanny,"
he explained. "I didn't want to get Children's Services in-
volved if your information is correct and Vancortland is

the toddler's grandfather. If so, it's a given, he'll get custody until after Ms. Delgado serves time for kidnapping your sister."

Evidently, Werner still believed that Deborah had murdered Jasmine. And the more I watched Amber, the more I tended to agree with him.

Nick joined us as Amber, holding her daughter, looked up at Cortland House, raised her chin, and walked to the front door as if she belonged there, which she did.

I could see Cort in her. Tall, graceful, his classic bone structure. A born aristocrat. I saw her mother in her, too, and kicked myself for not noticing the resemblance sooner. The pearlescent skin, dark hair, those dark, gorgeous features. Beauty incarnate. No wonder she and Cort had been sizing each other up at Sherry and Justin's engagement party.

Cort had probably wondered who she reminded him of, but I was betting that Amber knew she was looking at her father, possibly for the first time.

I felt bad for her. Deborah would be a formidable opponent, if this scheme ran anywhere near my original idea.

Werner introduced us to a psychologist, a white-haired gentleman. "Ms. Delgado's in another world," he said. "No emotion. No admission of guilt. No admission of any kind except that her mother had taken the name Delgado to pretend that she wasn't an unwed mother."

He regarded me and nodded toward Werner. "The detective here mentioned that you, Miss Cutler, think she might have seen your sister's engagement announcement. That could have triggered a mental relapse, given her theoretical background. At any rate, I'd like to observe her as she confronts her mother's past."

"And I'd like to catch the killer," Werner said, eyeing Amber at the front door. "Let's get this done."

Cort, Justin, Deborah, and their lawyer waited for us in the foyer.

"This is highly irregular," the lawyer said.

"Shut up, William," Cort said, watching Amber with confused interest, or staggering recognition. "Pay attention. If we need you, we'll let you know."

"No, Cort," Deborah said. "This isn't a good—"

"Deborah . . ." Cort warned.

She raised her chin but said nothing.

"Detective Werner, can you make the introductions?" Cort asked, not taking his gaze from Amber's, or her child's.

Werner introduced us all around, names only, without titles or relationships. Amber's name meant nothing to Cort. That was apparent.

He took control. "Come in then," he said. "I had the small drawing room prepared. Plain. Comfortable. Nice view."

There, Werner encouraged everyone to sit, though he remained standing. "I have information that I'd like Miss Delgado and Mrs. Vancortland to interpret."

Deborah rose. "I have no connection to this girl and I don't see the point of—"

Werner snapped his fingers and two uniformed officers flanked Deborah before she could say another word. "This is a murder investigation, Mrs. Vancortland," Werner reminded her, "a murder for which you've been arrested."

She sat down and turned to her lawyer.

"Don't look at William, Deborah," Cort said. "Look at me and cooperate."

I wished I was anywhere but here. My heart never sped so fast. Well, maybe when I found Jasmine's body, and at the police station when they took Sherry for questioning. What if the visions *were* figments of my certifiable imagination? Could they cause more harm than good? Fiona said I had a psychic gift, and I trusted her, but I didn't trust my so-called gift. I wondered if I ever would.

Nick covered my hand and squeezed, sensing my nervousness, I suppose. We'd always been in tune. That's why we sparked off each other.

"I feel like I'm in an Agatha Christie novel," I whispered, "with all the suspects gathered in the living room."

Nick leaned closer. "Except that in this version nobody has any evidence. Who's Werner? Hercule Poirot?"

"He must be. I'm not old enough to be Miss Marple, and it doesn't look like they're serving tea."

The look Werner shot us put period to our silly speculation. I was nervous, or I never would have given in to it. This was our only shot.

Werner's men brought in a corkboard easel on which a couple of my drawings were pinned: the one with my first vision of Pearl in the gown, and the one where Deborah sent Pearl packing for good.

Cort sat forward as he examined them.

Deborah looked away and covertly covered one trembling hand with the other.

Amber had style, though she had dressed in a plain black tube dress today, her pearl earrings a complement to the dark hair waving away from her ears, almost to showcase the earrings.

My heart stilled. Her *swan* pearl earrings. Pearl's earrings.

Cort's gaze shifted from the picture of Pearl in her wedding dress, to Amber, and back.

Werner's gaze encompassed everyone in the room. "I'd like Miss Delgado and Mrs. Vancortland, in turn, to each have an opportunity to speak. After they've both addressed the pictures, if they'd like to debate the implications, so be it. Miss Delgado, will you begin?"

Amber stood, cool, collected, in control, and gave her daughter, well-worn board book in hand, to her nanny. Good. The child was well occupied.

Deborah controlled her slight tremble as she scratched the polish off her perfect manicure, her gaze darting about the room, a sign that her mind ran in every direction.

Was she searching for an escape?

Amber pointed to the first sketch. "This is my mother, Pearl Morales Delgado. She worked here. She fell in love here and became engaged to the master's son. This house is where I was conceived. Before her wedding, in this picture, my mother was told to go away from here."

Deborah opened her mouth and Werner raised a hand to stop her.

Amber eyed Deborah with a look that could kill, but she didn't speak until she had all our attention once more. "My mother was sent away by the woman the master married. You, Mrs. Vancortland."

Deborah couldn't know that Amber's words might exonerate her from a murder charge. It wouldn't work if she did, and whatever the outcome, the cost to her could be life-altering.

"My mother," Amber said. "She lived the last years of her life calling herself the throwaway bride. She mourned for her wedding gown, her wedding day, but more than anything, she mourned the loss of her bridegroom, the love of her life. She had no interest in getting up from childbed, so my aunt came to live with us and care for us. When I was seven, my mother died calling my father's name. 'Cort.' Always, 'Cort.'"

I squeezed Nick's hand and swallowed my emotions. I didn't know who looked more thunderstruck, Cort, Justin, or Deborah, though Deborah certainly looked the most frightened.

Amber's daughter began asking for her mother, so Amber took her from the nanny, approached Cort, and handed him the child. "Here, Papa, your granddaughter. Her name is Vanessa. Vanessa Vancortland Delgado. I gave her the name that she would never bear otherwise. You will hold her while I explain the pictures?"

Cort nodded, barely, and Vanessa became quietly intrigued by him.

Amber seemed to stand outside herself, while Cort held the child so he could see her face. He touched a tiny hand to his lips, his granddaughter's, while tears slid down his cheeks and covered those small fingers. "What have I done?" he said to himself, though everyone heard.

At the easel like a robot, any passion long drained from her, Amber examined the sketch of my first vision. "This is well done, but whoever depicted the room forgot the Majolica jardinière on its matching stand. The colors run together, blues, yellows, greens, so bright and alive. I remember how much I loved it."

She remembered?

I sat straighter. Had she taken on her mother's persona?

"In this picture, I'm trying on my wedding gown, hiding my work-worn hands, though I needn't have bothered. I worked beside the seamstress fitting me. The people of Cort's class, they hated me, though not as much as the people of my own class, but I put up with all of it to be with him."

Amber studied another picture. "And this," Amber said, "is where Deborah—" She stood straight, her stance aggressive as she turned and skewered Deborah with her gaze. "You notice I do not call you Mrs. Vancortland, because you are *not* better than me, except perhaps at lies, deceit, and greed."

Deborah raised her chin, but she couldn't hide her trembling hands any more than Pearl had been able to hide her callused ones so many years ago.

"I remember everything about this day," Amber said. "You told me to take off your gown. Cort would marry you because you were expecting his child. You put much effort into catching him that way. Before I left, the old lady you paid for the brew to put in Cort's drink at the country club came to me. She felt bad that she'd played a role in my loss, and she told me everything. But I had more class than to try and trap a husband with a child."

She gave Deborah a nod, almost of respect but not quite. "Congratulations. You knew the right words. You said Cort could take you to the country club but he could never take me. That was mean and bitter, but shrewd. That's what broke me, that I *wasn't* good enough for the man I loved. I can tell you this now; you don't look good enough for him, either."

Amber studied the faces around her. "Which is the child I lost Cort to?"

"I miscarried," Deborah said, her face mottled. "I couldn't help that."

Werner got up, took Amber's arm, and led her to a chair beside her father and daughter. Then he called for something more to be brought in by the officers. Another easel. This one with the drawing of Mildred Updike nursing Deborah, and a signed document of some sort, though it was impossible to read from here.

Werner cleared his throat. "Do you have a quarrel with anything Miss Delgado said about the first drawings, Mrs. Vancortland?"

"Of course I do. Her accusations are ridiculous, all of them."

Big mistake, I thought.

"Of course," Werner echoed, acerbically, indicating the second easel. "Can you explain these sketches?"

Deborah went and pointed to the picture of the nurse. "This is the nurse who took care of me when I miscarried and this is a certificate of dead birth to prove it."

"To prove it," Werner repeated. "Most people don't care to see proof. Would you like to elaborate?"

"No," Deborah said. "I think it's self-explanatory, and the memory is still painful." Deborah sat and held a regal pose.

"Fine, then, if you won't elaborate, I will. Mildred Saunders is your old chum from Miss Finley's Finishing School. And this *proof* is signed by her, for which she may lose her nursing license. She's under investigation as we speak. This document is a fake, but you know that. An official certificate of death would have been signed by a coroner or the attending physician. No hospital within a fifty-mile radius has a record of your miscarriage that summer, by the way."

"I miscarried at home."

"That's not what you told me." Cort stood, holding the sleepy little girl against his shoulder. "You said you'd been rushed to the hospital. I've felt guilty for that business trip for thirty years."

Werner went and looked down at Deborah, who suddenly appeared quite small. "*Were* you pregnant at the time of your marriage, Mrs. Vancortland?"

Deborah's mouth worked like a fish out of water.

"Your friend Mildred, who helped you fake your miscarriage, was Jasmine Updike's mother. The fake miscarriage; that's what Jasmine Updike used to blackmail you. Is that why you strangled her, Mrs. Vancortland?"

Deborah looked at Cort, but he ignored her as he returned to rocking the sleeping child, his gaze only for Vanessa, his hand clutching Amber's at her child's back.

I felt bad for Deborah but I felt worse for Amber, who'd been riddled with emotional pain since childhood.

But which of them killed Jasmine? We still didn't know.

"I didn't kill Jasmine," Deborah said. "I'm all the rotten things you're all thinking, I guess—"

She guessed?

In her pregnant pause—a rather large slap of poetic justice—she waited for someone to refute her statement.

No one did.

Quizzing the silent faces around her, she sighed. "I *don't* deserve you, Cort, nor you, Justin. But I'm not a murderer."

"In a way," Cort said, looking at her. "You killed the woman I loved. In another way, I helped you. I should have taken *Pearl* to the country club that night. I had just enough doubt in me to let you talk me out of it. I'll never forgive myself."

Cort looked up at Justin. "I love you, son. No regrets there." He cupped Amber's cheek. "I wish I could have raised you both. Will you let me make it up to you, Amber?"

"There is no going back," she said. "Our time has passed."

"Think about it," Cort said, with raw emotion. "You and your daughter can come and live with me."

Deborah squeaked, but Justin squeezed his mother's shoulder and she shut up.

Cort barely spared Deborah a glance.

Werner nodded to the psychiatrist, who came forward. "Miss Morales," he said, addressing Amber as if she were Pearl. "Did you strangle Jasmine Updike?"

"No, I did not," Amber said, holding her head in the exact way I'd seen Pearl hold hers. "I never heard of anyone named Jasmine Updike."

That might have been true the night of the murder. In fact, Amber might have kept to herself to the point that she didn't realize she'd killed the wrong woman. Only when Sherry had arrived on her doorstep had she realized the true identity of the next Vancortland bride. After a night of questioning about Jasmine Updike's death, though, she had certainly heard of her by now.

Amber had, I thought, but maybe not Pearl.

"Did you strangle the Vancortland bride?" Werner asked her.

"No, I did not."

I stepped forward with a thought that had only come to me as I donned my mother's treasured pearl earrings this morning. "Pearl, did you use olive oil to polish the pearls Cort gave you?"

Amber smiled. "How did you know?"

Everyone but the psychiatrist stilled.

Amber beamed. "Aren't they beautiful?" She touched her throat. "But where are they?" She thought for a minute. "Oh, I used them to turn Deborah Vancortland into a throwaway bride like me. I've been waiting to do that for years." She smiled.

Werner waved his hand to halt the vocal reactions. "You didn't use only the pearls, Ms. Morales."

Amber looked Deborah's way. "I knew the pearls wouldn't be strong enough alone, so I braided them with several of the pretty twines I use to tie my pastry boxes." She shook her head as if rethinking her words.

"Wait. No, that can't be right." Amber, or Pearl, licked her lips, and reconsidered. "I used *my mother's* bridal pearls with *my* twine to strangle the woman who ruined my, no, *my mother's* life."

She turned on Deborah and narrowed her eyes. "Why aren't you dead like my mother?" She leapt at Deborah before Werner, or anyone, could anticipate her.

That fast, her hands were around Deborah's throat, her thumbs pressing so hard, I backed into Nick's chest, his arms coming around me.

Justin got to them first.

"Amber!" He pulled her hands from his mother's throat. "You're my sister. I'll help you." He captured Amber's hands and crushed them against his chest as he held her, while Werner's men escorted Deborah to the far corner of the room.

Amber struggled from Justin's hold and reached for his throat.

Sherry screamed.

Amber stopped, her hands in midair. "I have a brother?" She turned to Cort, her daughter asleep in his arms. "Papa, help me." Amber Delgado covered her face with her hands and wept.

The knot in my throat hurt too much to contain.

Cort got up and gave the sleeping Vanessa to Sherry. "Take care of your niece until we get back, will you, sweetie?"

Sherry nodded and kissed the sleeping child while Justin comforted his sister. When Cort reached them, Amber sobbed once and threw herself into her father's arms. "I'm so sorry. I . . . always hoped to make you proud, not shame you."

Cort consoled her. "I'm glad you're my daughter. We'll get through this. We're family."

Werner put Amber's arms behind her back to handcuff her.

"Is that necessary?" Cort asked.

The psychologist nodded. "She could harm herself, as well as anyone, right now."

"It's best," Werner said. "We know what we heard. I'm guessing she wasn't herself at the time of the murder, either."

"I'm coming with her," Cort said. "We'll get you the best criminal lawyer money can buy."

Deborah's head came up. She, too, caught the irony. He hadn't hired the best lawyer money could buy for her.

Justin kissed Sherry's brow. "I'm going with them. I'll be back as soon as I can. There's a nursery upstairs; I'll have a crib brought down. Keep her with you. She'll want her mother. Use my room. I need to know you'll be waiting for me when I get home."

Sherry nodded.

Cort spared Deborah a glance. "It's been over for a long time. I accept equal responsibility for the past. You won't want for anything."

Deborah came out of her fog. "What?"

Two officers escorted Amber from the drawing room in cuffs, followed by her father and brother.

"Renee," Cort said to Deborah's maid. "Pack your mistress's bags, enough for tonight at least, and find her a hotel. She'll let you know where. We'll forward the rest of her things, later. She's moving out."

Deborah screamed, though she hadn't reacted to her past sins or their deadly consequences. She hadn't reacted to Amber's hands on her throat or her part in Amber's illness. Not even when her son put his life in danger to save hers did she say a word.

Nothing scared that woman more than the thought of losing her lifestyle.

Thirty

The creative universe begins with its essentiality, and, whatever path the imagination takes, ends with its purity.

—GIORGIO ARMANI

On a bright Sunday morning in early September, Dolly Sweet attended my sister's wedding at Cortland House wearing her Katharine Hepburn gown.

Oy!

I raised my thoughts to the universe. *Please* don't let Dolly leave to join Dante during Sherry's wedding. Or her reception.

Sherry deserved a perfect wedding day, especially after the month that led up to it.

When the family adventurer walked in, my panic subsided. I ran and caught my sister Brandy in my arms. "I can't believe you made it!"

"Me, either." She squeezed me tight for a minute. "At one point, I offered to fly the plane to get here faster."

"Did they let you?" Middle sister or not, Brandy Cutler could be pretty damned persuasive. Just ask anybody whose life she'd touched in the Peace Corps. And, yes, she could fly a plane.

"No, but the pilot was intrigued by my offer. We have a date tomorrow night."

I laughed and stepped back so I could get a better look at her in Mom's strapless jonquil-print sundress. "You look super."

My eyes filled and so did Brandy's for a minute. "I remember her wearing this outfit with platform wedges, sunny Bakelite jewelry, purse and all." Thanks for leaving it on my bed. If I'd had to decide what to wear, I might have given in to jet lag and missed the whole thing." Brandy fiddled with the clasp on her purse. "I owe you an apology, Mad. I thought you were crazy when you kept Mom's clothes. I was wrong."

"But you still think I'm crazy for pandering to moneyed fashion plates."

She bit her lip for half a second. "True . . . but for Sherry's sake," Brandy whispered, "I won't mention that I could feed a starving continent for a year on the cost of her wedding." Her voice rose with every word. "And don't get me started on this twenty-four-karat gold bordello."

Cort coughed behind her. "You have a problem with my bordello, Miss Cutler?" He winked.

Brandy colored but she raised her chin and accepted Cort's offered arm. He led her toward the dressing room where Sherry waited to take center stage. They stopped on the way, however, and I knew by the body language, the way Brandy spoke and Cort listened, that she'd gone into fund-raising mode. Poor Cort.

I respected my sister's passion for her work, and maybe after she saw Sherry in her wedding gown, Brandy would respect mine. I was sorry she had missed the rehearsal dinner, but she'd made the wedding, and that was what counted.

Last night, as a maid of honor gift, Sherry and Justin had given me the glass slipper inkwell I loved, the one on a filigreed brass stand.

When Brandy emerged from Sherry's dressing room a short while later, Cort met her, handed her a check, and escorted her to the Cutler family seating area. I guess Brandy had more than one reason to celebrate today.

Cort took the mike up front and suggested people take their seats.

When Sherry emerged, cameras went off from every corner. I'd gotten my friends from New York to do a cover spread in a bridal magazine. The Vancortland gown would be the launch design for Vintage Magic. The article would announce my grand opening on Halloween.

Fast, I know, like all my decisions. But with luck and more fast thinking, I could pull it off.

After all, I could fix anything.

Right now, my carriage house—Dante waiting inside—still looked like a shack, but the architectural design rocked, and I'd pick a construction crew within the week. I had a lot of work to do, but I was ready to jump in, proud in my Pradas.

Most important, Sherry was happy. Justin, too. His parents had been miserable; their split was a relief, even to their son.

Justin and Sherry had moved into the mansion to help Cort raise Vanessa until Amber came home, which she would . . . in time. Her new family visited her regularly at the high-security psychiatric wing of the hospital.

We'd been assured that Amber's plea of insanity should stick. Not only were her psychiatric records available, but the loss of her fiancé in Iraq—a surprise to us all—had put her sanity on a very slippery slope. She'd found herself suddenly an unwed mother raising a daughter alone . . . like her own mother had done.

The Vancortland engagement announcement had been the last straw.

While Sherry posed for some pre-wedding photos on

the grand staircase, Eve and I watched Deborah come around the side of the house on the arm of a mature, buff member of the country-club set.

Dripping diamonds, she forced her way into the first row on the groom's side. Yes, she came through the yard, instead of the house, but she couldn't be self-effacing if her life depended on it.

Cort might have been shocked when she asked him to move down, but he didn't show it. He stood, ever the gentleman, but he stubbornly retained his aisle seat *and* the one next to it for his granddaughter.

These days, he looked . . . content . . . driving around Mystick Falls with an occupied toddler seat in the back of his Mercedes. DNA tests had proved that, yes, Amber was his daughter and Vanessa his granddaughter, so he got custody. I'd never seen a man beam as much as he did when he got the word.

He often took Vanessa to the hospital to have lunch with her mother, so the little girl who spent most of her time with her aunt Sherry wouldn't forget which was which.

The groom's side might be sparse, but the bride's side overflowed with Cutlers and friends. First row: Brandy, Alex, his wife, Tricia, with baby Kelsey, being passed from relative to relative. The aisle seat remained empty, waiting for my dad.

Eve and her parents sat behind them with Fiona and the Sweets. The rest of our Mystick Falls neighbors and our downtown Mystic friends filled the bride's side.

Nick, the best man—Justin's and mine—escorted Justin to his spot at the gazebo.

I waved, and Nick raised his chin, his piercing dark eyes filled with promise.

I shivered and turned my attention to Sherry as the orchestra began to play the wedding march. I smoothed my sister's train, and remembered how she'd swirled with the flare of the first dress I'd made her. She might have been three at the time.

Our stubborn little blonde with the infectious laugh had turned into a swan.

Oh, how I wished my mother could see this bride in whom I held so much pride.

I turned to my handsome father and dusted the lapels of his tux, before I took my place in front of them.

When it was time to begin, I patted Vanessa's tiny peau-de-soie bottom. The two-and-a-half-year-old began her trek down the silk carpet, across the flowing back lawn toward the gazebo near the river, scattering red rose petals, slowly, carefully, making sure to drop no more than one petal at a time.

When she dropped two, she picked one of them up.

A chuckle ran through the guests, and I'm sure a hundred more people fell in love with her.

I'd made her a mini bridal gown and pouch purse with the fabric from the train of the Vancortland gown. Vanessa adored purses and who was I to argue?

A crown of white rosebuds nested in her dark curls. Her tiny pair of kitten-heeled shoes were a bit too big, but she'd mastered the walk. During fittings she'd kept stepping into our spikes and walking away, so we found her a pair of her own, sort of.

The little girl playing dress up simply added to the imperfectly perfect . . . the wedding of Sherry and Justin's dreams.

When she reached Cort, Vanessa raised her arms. "Pa-pop. All done."

I preceded my sister down the aisle wearing another of my mother's dresses, a full-length Grecian halter gown of flowered red chiffon, though you could barely see the flowers, they were so muted. I wore the red Louboutin pumps with the heels that left a rosette imprint and carried white roses.

With her Vintage Magic gown, Sherry wore embroidered satin shoes by Philippe Model and carried red roses.

Paces ahead, I still heard Deborah's gasp as Sherry walked by.

As I approached the gazebo, alive with roses of every color, I saw . . . a vision . . . that raced my heart.

My mother stood beside the minister. Young, beautiful, and alive, if only for a minute, her heavenly blue chiffon gown and cinnamon hair flowing in the breeze off the water.

A quick glance toward Aunt Fiona, smiling through her tears, confirmed it.

Wanting Mom to get the full view of Sherry, her baby, as a bride, I turned to the side of the gazebo a bit sooner than I'd planned and gave my sister center stage.

Mom smiled wide, nodded in approval, blew each of her loved ones a kiss, and then she was gone.

A Tip for the Vintage Handbag Lover

THREE BAGS FOR THE PRICE OF ONE

Look for this vintage find at yard sales, antique stores, thrift shops, or at a secondhand shop like the Cottage in Amesbury, Massachusetts—which is where my daughter found hers.

It's described in a book called *Handbags*, by Judith Miller, as "A three-way convertible bag with detachable black cover from the fifties."

The outside is a high-quality brown simulated crocodile, which is reversible to black velvet, an outer layer whose rings slip off the magnetized knobs at the top sides. Beneath that, you'll find a high-quality black fine-corded satin-covered bag.

We've found it without the outer layer, as well, so hold out for the full package.

It's shaped like a large clasp purse, has a gilt metal frame, and a Lucite handle.

The bottom is square and curves slightly to the top. It's 9 inches wide, 7¼ inches tall, and 2½ inches deep.

The label is on the inside pocket. Ours is faded. We can only make out the word "Paris." At least we think it says Paris. Happy hunting!

**To see pictures of Annette's purses,
go to www.annetteblair.com.**

Make Your Own Evening Clutch

A FOLD-OVER PURSE

Instructions for a fold-over purse:

Draw a rectangle about a foot long and about nine inches wide on paper, to use as a pattern. Choose a heavy stiff or quilted fabric for the body, or add interfacing to give the fabric body. Follow the directions on the interfacing package if you choose to face it. Using your paper pattern, cut two pieces of outside fabric, right sides together/face-to-face.

Using the same pattern, cut out two pieces of lining fabric right sides together.

Pin a piece of outside fabric to the liner fabric right sides together along the nine-inch straight edge. Sew only that edge together, using the standard five-eighths setting on your sewing machine.

Open the two pieces of fabric and iron the seams open—in a butterfly effect, one wing of lining, one of outside fabric.

Repeat the procedure for the second side.

Now match the lining fabric together and the outside fabric together.

Pin.

Starting about four inches down from the straight-edge seam on the liner fabric side, sew all the way around using the standard five-eighths setting on your sewing machine. Be sure to stop sewing about two inches before you started so there is an opening to turn the fabric right side out.

Trim the corners but leave the long edge of the seam to help give form to the purse.

Turn the entire thing right side out and slip stitch closed the opening in the lining. Now push the lining fabric inside the outside fabric to form the inside of the purse. It makes a long pocket with a finished straight opening at the top.

Fold the pocket about one-third of the way down to create a self-flap. Iron the crease once you have it where you want it. This will give you a fold-over clutch purse.

Embellish it however you want. Our sample piece is black with an acrylic rosette painted to the left of the flap. Possibilities are beads, ribbon rosettes, sequins, or fringe.

You can also get creative with the shape of the bottom and top to vary the design. Enjoy!

**To see pictures of Annette's purses,
go to www.annetteblair.com.**

Magic or destiny, Annette Blair's bewitching romantic comedies became her first national bestsellers. Now she's entered a world of bewitching mysteries and designer vintage, a journey sure to be Vintage Magic. You can contact her through her website at www.annetteblair.com.

M5G0508